Blowin' My Mind Like a Summer Breeze

Benjamin Roesch

Winnipeg, Canada

Developmental editor: Margaret Larson
Proofreader: Francisco Feliciano

Published July 2022 by Deep Hearts YA, an imprint of Deep Desires Press and Story Perfect Inc.

Deep Hearts YA
PO Box 51053 Tyndall Park
Winnipeg, Manitoba R2X 3B0
Canada

Visit deepheartsya.com for more great reads.

For Red
And for my students.

Blowin' My Mind
Like a Summer Breeze

Side One:
A Week on Lake Michigan
July, 1995

Track Zero
I Am So Not Ready

Hotel ice chips are melting down my knuckles. Juliet's warm breath is on my neck. Our eyes meet in the bathroom mirror. Our lips wear the same shade of purple.

"Harder," she says.

I jam the ice chips harder against my flesh, wondering if I'm doing it right, then feel them beginning to slip. I can't feel my nose anymore. My fingertips are tingling.

How do I slow my heart down?

"Are you remembering how to punch yet?" she says, pushing her black hair away from her face.

"Almost," I say.

"Good," she says. "Right in the balls."

I laugh in the uncomfortable way I do.

The music from the bedroom is so loud I can feel it rattling my chest. Wailing guitars and vocals drenched in reverb. I can't decide if I want her to turn it down—or turn it up. Either way, her music is starting to grow on me.

Juliet has yet another swig of her grape soda. I do the same, determined to keep up, wincing as I swallow. How much vodka did she put in here?

"Will it hurt?" I ask.

She says something in response, but I'm so dazzled by the

snap and glow of her lighter flame as she plays it across the stud's sharp metal point that I don't hear.

"That's enough ice," Juliet says, then draws the tiniest X on my left nostril with a blue pen, an action I can barely feel from the numbness, then hands me the freshly sterilized stud.

"Ready?" she asks.

I take another sip. I am so not ready.

"I think so," I say.

"Push really fast and really hard," she says.

"Fast and hard," I say, as if this advice is supposed to make me feel better.

I try to hold the metal point still above my nostril, then press it against the X on my skin, yanking my hand back in terror the moment I feel it. It's not pain. Not yet. Just a horrible pressure.

"I don't think I can do it," I say. I hate myself for being so afraid.

Juliet takes my shaking hand and looks into my eyes, and, it feels like, all the way down into my soul where nobody has ever been before.

"I'm right here," she says.

Push the rewind button. Right there. Stop.

Track One
Pirouetting to Nowhere

I quit.

Two words. Two stupid little words. Subject + verb = I get a whole new life.

So why are they so hard to say?

The backstage green room of The Groovy Rhino, the past its prime nightclub in downtown St. Louis where The Cobb Family Band is playing tonight, has stained carpets and lazily graffitied walls. Back in the seventies, my parents played palaces, places like Carnegie Hall in New York City and The Ryman Auditorium in Nashville, but I don't really remember the good old days. Instead, I'm stuck in the unimpressive present.

The remnants of our dinner lay scattered on a geriatric folding table: Domino's Pizza, wilted bag salad, and a jug of Sprite. My family already went out, which leaves me here alone, staring into a dirty mirror and trying to summon the courage to say two stupid little words. *I quit.*

"Rainey?"

I jump at the sound of my mom's voice. Our eyes meet in the mirror, until I look away.

"It's time," she says. "Let's go." I haven't seen the size of the crowd yet, but I can tell by her impatient tone that it's small. Again. The last four shows we've sold a total of twelve CDs.

"Okay," I say. She turns to go. "Wait, Mom?"

"What?"

I quit. I quit the band. I don't want to do this anymore. I'm sorry your life didn't work out the way you wanted, but it's not my fault. I want a different life.

"Rainey? The house lights are already down, so if you have something you wan—"

"When we get home," I blurt out, too nervous to even form a coherent thought, let alone say the two words I'd intended.

"When we get home—what?"

"At the end of tour. When we get home. I want to take a break. From this. The band, I mean."

"What are you talking about?"

I want to say more, but my words get tangled in my brain like hair in a drainpipe.

"I can't talk about this right now," she says, and then she's gone.

"That went well," I tell the girl in the mirror.

I hurry out to the stage and sit down behind the piano, which at sound check earlier I discovered is way out of tune, has three—*three*!—broken keys, and a seriously janky bench that feels like it's about to drop me on my ass at any second.

The Cobb Family Band plays a patented blend of R&B with a country flare, and a bit of straight blues on the side. The first few songs are a blur, and I have trouble disappearing into the music. Usually, the second my fingers touch the piano keys, I forget about the fact that I'm a girl with no friends who's never set foot inside a school. That the long and winding career of Luce and Tracy Cobb, my famous parents, is on life support, and I'm forced to sit bedside and watch it slowly die.

My mom barely looks at me the entire set, and when she does, her eyes burn with confusion and disappointment. I'm relieved the last song is an old blues standard instead of one of my parents' hits. I tickle out the opening chords I know so well, then feel the drums and bass slide in behind me. I close my eyes. Fill my lungs. Then sing the tale of a woman scorned.

As the audience claps, I open my eyes, no longer a woman scorned with revenge in her heart, but a thirsty girl with sore fingers. My mom and brother go backstage, but my dad comes over and asks if I'm okay. He can always tell when something's not right.

"C'mon, Rain Man," he says, "spill it."

"I'm fine," I say. "I'm just going to stay out here and get something to drink."

"Willful teenager," he says.

"Grumpy old man," I say, then drift alone through the sparse crowd, studying the floor.

I smile meekly at Estelle, the punk bartender with the blue hair and the biker chick tattoo. Her eyes go to the stage, then back to me. I can feel her wondering how old I am.

She fills my glass with Coke from the spray gun and glides a lime wedge around the rim, nodding her head to trendy grunge on the house speakers. "Killer set," she says. "I knew your parents were awesome, my mom used to play their records, but your voice is insane."

"Thanks." I suck down a gulp, enjoying the burst of lime before the bubbly sweetness.

A guy in a Cardinals cap steps up. Estelle pours him a golden beer in a tall mug, and he drops his change into a jar on which a picture of Mr. T warns *I PITY THE FOOL THAT DON'T TIP!* Trendy grunge fades and a U2 song starts.

My brother, Walden, plops down on the stool next to me at the bar. The black X on his left hand matches mine. We sometimes joke we're in a secret gang called Black X.

"What happened with you and Mom?" he asks.

"What do you mean?"

He eats some peanuts from a bowl on the bar.

"Mom hasn't said a word since the set ended," he says, "and you're here by yourself."

"It was nothing," I say.

In a Day-Glo mural behind the bar, a rhino in a pink tutu dances beneath a glimmering disco ball, eyes blissfully shut. U2 becomes the Ramones becomes trendy hip hop.

"Do you ever think about what it would be like to be a totally different person?" I ask.

Walden sips his Coke. "Not really," he says. "Do you?"

I shrug. I'm closer with Walden than anyone in the world, but even he doesn't know how bad I want to quit the band. The houselights dim. My dad plugs in his white Telecaster. My mom picks up her bass, then tap-tap-taps the microphone.

"Be careful what you wish for," Walden says, "because with these crowds, we're all going to end up working at Sears. C'mon, time to rock and roll."

When I was a little girl and first starting to realize who my parents were, I'd stand on the side of the stage and watch them play. I'd feel the audiences loving them and dream of the day when I could be out there too. I thought I was the luckiest girl in the world.

Estelle comes back over, wiping the bar with a white rag.

"Do you like being a bartender?" I ask.

"It's okay," she says. "I get to meet a lot of cool people."

I smile. "Were there other things you wanted to do?" I ask. "Before?"

"Um, yeah, a million other things."

Walden slaps his snare drum, a cue that I need to hurry up. "Gotta go," I say.

I sit down behind the piano and look at my mom, who doesn't look back.

My dad calls out the first song and my hands kick into my parents' only top ten hit, "Tell the Truth," my fingers banging the keys, my foot keeping time. I start singing, harmonizing with Dad's lead. The audience presses forward. I watch them watching me.

Behind the bar, the dancing rhino is still stuck on the wall, pirouetting to nowhere.

Track Two
A Charcoal Sky Dotted with Occasional Stars

A few hours later, somewhere between St. Louis and our next gig in Louisville, I'm lying in my saggy bunk in the back of the RV reading *Jane Eyre*, trying to block out Walden's snoring. That's when Howard the Duck, which is what I call our Ford Econoline Mallard RV—clever, I know—trembles hard enough to shake me in my bed. I open the curtains and squint out into the endless prairie night for signs of mischief, wondering what happened. Then I feel it. We're slowing down.

Walden awakens with a snort. "What happened?"

"You snored so loud the world broke apart and we all died," I say. "This is heaven."

Our two bunks are 39 inches apart, about the length of a guitar, closer than any girl should have to sleep to her own brother, especially one who snores and recently developed an unfortunate cologne habit.

"Another breakdown," I say.

"You suck, Howard," he says. "This band seriously needs a new mode of transportation."

Every year before our summer tour, my parents go RV shopping and Walden and I perch by the window, salivating over the thought of a gleaming new Airstream with beds that don't sag and a working microwave. But every year without fail,

Howard the Duck limps back up the driveway and my parents are fighting.

I go out with my dad to have a look, holding the heavy Maglite while he pops the hood and inspects Howard's coiled metal guts.

"What do you think?" he asks, lighting a cigarette and scratching his graying beard.

"Battery?" I say, heat coming off the engine like a dying fire.

"Yeah, probably," Dad says.

I used to love helping Dad fix the RV. He taught me how to change tires and oil, how to replace a spark plug and jump a battery. We'd laugh at how dirty our hands always got. It made me feel so close to him, like we spoke a secret language no one else understood. It never even occurred to me what it actually meant was that our RV broke down all the time and we couldn't afford a new one.

"What now?" I ask, remembering how we already used the backup battery weeks ago.

Dad holds up his thumb and points it toward the road.

"Shit," I say.

"Yep," he says. "Shit."

Dad and I perch ourselves by the side of the highway and stick our thumbs out. I look over at Howard where my mom sits in the darkness of the passenger seat, watching us, biting her nails to nubs. During load out behind The Groovy Rhino, we had an awkward moment where she pulled me aside and said, "I didn't mean to snap at you earlier. It's just not a good time, okay? You're only fifteen, Rainey. And we couldn't do this without you."

"Okay," I told her, too scared to say more, not realizing I was walking into a trap set to keep me right where Luce and Tracy Cobb really needed me—behind a piano.

With every set of headlights that approaches, I stick my

thumb out further, hoping it will catch some of the light. But every car flies right by us and up the length of I-64.

I stretch out my road-battered body. Throbbing piano hands. Aching back from hauling amplifiers. Strained singing voice. By the end of every tour, I'm as creaky as an old lady.

A heavy sigh slips out of me.

"Uh oh," Dad says, "it's the 'I wish I was born into a different family' sound."

"There's no sound for that," I say.

"Sure, there is," he says. "It sounds like this." He imitates me, placing his palm dramatically on his forehead. He's trying to lighten things up, but I'm not in the mood.

"Dad, stop," I say. "I don't wish that. I'm just ready to go home."

"I know, Rain Man," he says. "Look at it this way. You'll never run out of stories to tell, even if you live for a hundred years."

Stories. Like the time I watched Stevie Nicks brush her smooth golden locks with a pearl handled hairbrush like it was a holy ritual. "Take your time," she told me. "Until it's soft as silk."

Stories are what I have instead of friends. My bizarre birthright.

But what good are stories if you don't have anyone to tell them to?

"So, what would you do?" he asks. "If you took a break from the band?"

I snap my head toward him. "She *told* you?"

"Don't be mad. I pried it out of her."

I shrug. "I don't know. Nothing. It's stupid." All the energy has drained out of me.

Just when we're ready to give up, a pick-up screeches onto

the shoulder. A guy with a ZZ Top beard pops out and says, "Y'all look like you're in a tight spot."

As he clamps cables to batteries, ZZ Top keeps looking at my dad as if trying to remember the name of an old friend. I know what's coming. After Howard's battery is happily humming, he says, "Hey, buddy, aren't you Luce Cobb? As in Luce and Tracy Cobb? That's her in the camper, isn't it?" He points at my mom. "I used to love your music when I was younger, man. But hell, I didn't even know you guys were still playing. You on tour? In this old rig?"

Without missing a beat, my dad says, "No, but we get that all the time. We must really look like them. Thanks for the help."

It's a quarter to four when we get going. Two sweaty hours by the side of the highway, and our only reward is more highway. I'm so tired of being on four wheels I could scream.

I get a travel wipe out of my duffel bag and scrub my face until it stings, and the wipe is caked with brown. I put on some deodorant but can still smell engine fumes and sweat on my T-shirt. I'd kill for a shower, for a bed that doesn't squeak with every bump in the road.

I gaze out the window at a charcoal sky dotted with occasional stars. I breathe. I settle. My mind wanders. Somewhere, a girl in her bed, sound asleep. She's dreaming. Tomorrow she'll go to her part-time summer job at the local pharmacy. She's polite with the customers, friendly with her boss. Every paycheck goes into her college fund. After work, she changes into a cute dress, then meets her best friend for pizza at their favorite spot. They share a pepperoni with extra cheese and talk about how crazy it is that their lives are going by so fast. They giggle at inside jokes, pretend not to look at a table of boys across the restaurant. They go outside and hug goodnight and look up at a charcoal sky dotted with occasional stars, having no idea there's another girl out there, a girl who plays a hundred and thirty shows a year and lives out of a duffel bag. A girl with a million stories and no one to tell them to.

The highway hums, and I hum softly back, up a third, so that we're harmonizing.

I'm waiting for something. I just wish I knew what it was.

Track Three
A Girl with Black Hair Walks By

Press the fast forward button. Right there. Stop.

Three shows later. Three cities later. Louisville. Indianapolis. Chicago. By in a blur of piano chords beneath my fingers and applause from anonymous crowds. In a montage of solitaire and rest areas and Chicken McNuggets. Rinse, wash, repeat.

It's noon on Saturday when we drive through the gates of Cascade Family Resort, which sits high and mighty on a hill overlooking the glimmering shores of Lake Michigan. This is it. The last stop. We've been on the road since early June, thirty shows in the rearview, and now we're ending our summer tour here with a week-long gig. Then the long ride home and a few weeks off.

Beneath Cascade Family Resort, there's a smaller sign that reads: *Where families go to be families again.*

We unload our gear through the back door of Evergreen Ballroom where we're playing all week. In the ballroom's front windows, yellow and red posters with our picture on them announce The Cobb Family Band featuring "the legendary" Luce and Tracy Cobb. *Two sets! Only $5 for resort guests! $15 for general public. Be there!*

Our first show here isn't until Monday. And after playing

nearly every night for the past six weeks straight, two days off without having to touch a piano or sing a note sounds like a dream. Even better, Walden and I have our own rooms for the week. I can't wait to be in a quiet room, all by myself, blissfully alone.

Bleary eyed, worn to the bone with road fatigue, we take a walk around.

To me, the Cascade Family Resort looks like some place out of a summer camp movie. Fresh cut lawns. White lifeguard towers with tanned boys twirling whistles on strings. Relaxed-looking people in sunglasses doing relaxed-looking people things. Groups of giggling teenagers playing volleyball. Shirtless guys and girls in tiny bikinis.

Unfortunately, the bubble on the individual room thing bursts pretty fast. There was a mix-up. Walden and I are sharing after all. Fabulous. On my tombstone they're going to write: *Here Lies Rainey Cobb, She Died from an Extreme Lack of Privacy.*

"We thought both kids were girls, and that they'd want to room together," the receptionist explained, sounding apologetic. "We were sure Walden was a girl's name. Wal-den. It sounds girlish, doesn't it?"

"Well, it's not a girl's name, as you can see," said Mom, gesturing to my six-foot-tall brother. "There's really no available rooms?"

"Sorry, but no. It's the busy season."

Mom gave us one of her patented Tracy Cobb tough love looks, the one that roughly translated to *suck it up, nobody said any of this was going to be easy.*

Ten minutes later, Walden surveys our shared room with a shake of his head.

"Just once I'd like to have a room all to myself," he says.

"Oh, and I wouldn't? Your cologne is reaching radioactive levels."

"Chicks dig cologne, Rainey. It's a proven fact."

"What chicks?"

"Just...chicks. Not to mention a man needs space to think so he can contemplate the nature of existence and his place in the world."

"How would you know?" I ask.

There are jets in the bathtub, which seems promising. Otherwise, it's a copy of a copy of every other hotel room.

Walden plops down on the bed closer to the window, takes his drawing pad and Walkman out of his backpack, then slips his fuzzy orange headphones over his ears. The second I hear Bob Dylan's stupid voice for the millionth time this summer, I grab my backpack and find my way down to the beach to have a look around and do my homework.

There I am nestled in a seat of sugary white sand, stuck on an algebra problem with a lot of Xs and Ys, when a girl with black hair walks by using one of those claw grabber things to put beach trash into a white bucket. She's wearing baggy camo cargo shorts, a black T-shirt, massive aviator sunglasses, and a black trucker hat with a skull on it. Add in her nose ring and purple lipstick, and she looks like a movie villain or a member of the X-Men.

When she stops right in front of me, I realize I've been staring at her for a while.

"A little light reading?" she says.

With my algebra textbook open in my lap, notebook and pencil in hand, I look like I'm ready to show the Pythagorean Theorem who's boss.

Before I can respond, she's already walking away, weaving through sunbathers and boom boxes and freshly made sandcastles. Instead of leaving the beach, though, she puts her bucket and claw thing up near the rocks far from shore, strips off her shorts and T-shirt to reveal a black one-piece bathing suit, straps on a pair of goggles that appear from I don't even know where, then bounds into the water and starts slicing through Lake Michigan like she's suddenly grown fins. I've never seen anybody swim so fast or gracefully.

After doing laps back and forth, she climbs onto the dock and dives off in a perfect arc, barely raising a splash. Then, coiled at the dock's edge, she launches herself as fast as she can into the water, over and over, like simulating the start of a race.

When she comes back onto the beach, I do that thing where you try to watch someone without them knowing it, looking down but actually staring at them out of the corner of your eye. She's impossible not to look at. Even the way she gets dressed has swagger, as if life is a performance and she doesn't care who's watching. Still, I'm disappointed when she slips a cigarette into her mouth and starts patting her pockets. She walks over to me.

"You got a light?"

"Uh. No."

But then she finds her lighter, a silver Zippo like the one my dad has, and lights up.

"You want one?"

"No, thank you. Smoking's really bad for you." It just slips out. But smoking really is bad for you! My grandpa died of emphysema. And sometimes my dad has these coughing fits so bad it sounds like his insides are being cut apart by a chainsaw. I can't get him to quit, so I've promised myself I'll never start.

A long beat goes by where neither of us says anything. Seeming unfazed by my comment, she takes a big puff. I take a deep breath. The sun pings off her Aviators. It's probably no more than a few seconds, but that moment pulls apart like silly putty and keeps going and going. Almost like she's decided not to speak again until I do. My heart is pounding. Why am I so nervous? Some words slip out.

"Do you work here?" I gesture over toward her trash bucket.

"Kind of. I live here. My parents own this place. They make me do odd jobs in the summer. Trash duty. Maid service. Making omelets in the Sunday buffet. They say it builds character, but I don't think it's working."

"Are you in training or something? Your swimming, I mean."

"Yeah," she says. "I want to get a scholarship in a couple years. Anything to get me out of having to run this place. You're one of the Cobb kids, aren't you?"

How does she know that?

"My mom said you and your brother are homeschooled. Who else would be doing homework on the beach in July? She said if I ran into you, I should try to make you feel welcome. How am I doing?"

"Good. I guess."

"You got a name?"

This girl is so confident. Like she's not afraid of anything.

"Rainey."

"That's a cool name."

"Really?" No one has ever described my name as cool. Not once. Not ever.

"I've never met anyone named Rainey before. Have you? Besides you, I mean?"

"No."

"See. That makes it cool. You're one of a kind."

I notice the way her wet bathing suit has made a dark imprint of itself on her dry T-shirt.

For some reason I tell her that I'm named after Ma Rainey, one of my mom's favorite blues singers, which I've never really told anyone, because honestly, who gives a crap? I even add that Ma Rainey's real name was Gertrude, so it could have been worse.

"I'm named after a Shakespeare character," she says.

"Which one?"

"Juliet," she says, "of the house of..."

"Capulet," I say.

"You like Shakespeare?"

"Yeah. But not *Romeo and Juliet.*"

"Why?"

"It's kind of immature," I say. "I'm just not sure love is worth killing yourself over."

She laughs. "Have you ever been in love?"

She sits down only a few inches away and we sort of fall into a conversation, spending the next half hour talking like this. While she talks, her fingers make aimless trails through the warm, soft sand. I find myself focusing really hard on everything she's saying. The voices around us, all the laughing kids and instructing mothers, seem to fade away.

Sometimes conversation feels like a test, but talking to Juliet is easy. Like a test I've been studying for my whole life. She asks about my smoking comment, and I tell her about my grandfather and the coughing fits my dad has.

"That sucks," she says.

She gushes about music and all the bands she loves. Smashing Pumpkins, Nine Inch Nails, Bjork, The Breeders. Her favorite band is Nirvana, but when I tell her that the only Nirvana song I've ever really heard is that one they always play on the radio, Juliet looks at me like I just claimed the Earth is flat.

"This madness cannot stand!" she says in a booming God voice that dissolves both of us into hysterics. I'm not even sure what's so funny but I can't stop laughing.

"What are you doing right now?" she asks.

"Um," I say, "algebra."

"Screw that. Come listen to some music. I have every Nirvana album in my room. I'll pop your Nirvana cherry. Sorry, that was gross. But you know what I mean."

I have no idea what she means.

She reaches out and actually takes my hand in hers. I shake people's hands every day—firm grip, two pumps—but this feels different. Tender and purposeful. Her hand is dappled with tiny grains of sand that lightly scrape against my skin. Her fingernails are slick with shiny black polish.

Our eyes meet.

"Are you ready?"

"I guess so," I say, having no idea what I'm supposed to be ready for.

Only that I'm prepared to follow Juliet anywhere.

Track Four
Like Lightning That Doesn't Stop

Confession #1: I'm kind of a snob when it comes to music. But it's not really my fault. I blame my parents, who have surrounded me my whole life with music whose greatness has already passed the ultimate test. Time.

Confession #2: Because of the logic explained in Confession #1, I don't really like Nirvana. Sorry.

I'm sitting on the edge of Juliet's bed while she subjects me to their "masterpiece," *Nevermind,* with the sonic fury of her massive stereo. This is the album that's such a big deal? With so much distortion, how can you appreciate the melodies or understand the lyrics? I'm holding the CD case in my hand, and yep, that's a naked baby. In a pool. With a dollar bill attached to a fishhook in front of him.

"Can you turn it down a little bit?"

Jesus, I sound like my mother.

"You're a musician!" she shouts over the noise. "How is it you've never heard the best album of the last ten years?"

I know it's her enthusiasm talking, but there's something a little weird about how teenagers are so obsessed with what's happening right now, as if it's automatically better than what came before. It's a pretty reductive view of art. Especially since all new music is influenced by the music that came before it. How many people under eighteen even know who Bessie Smith is? Or Fats Waller? Or Erik Satie? Or even Black Sabbath, who obviously influenced Nirvana? You're telling me those musicians are less exciting just because most people who have big screen TVs and wear Reeboks don't know who they are? Pardon me, but that's bullshit.

Okay, now I really sound like my mother.

What I do love without question, though, is Juliet's bedroom. Scratch that. Her suite. The Overlander Suite. As in, her freaking bedroom is actually a hotel suite that has its own name. The room I share with my brother at home is half the size of this. Maybe less. But Juliet has her own small kitchen. Her own living room, bedroom, and bathroom. She has her own toilet! Her own posters of musicians and athletes. Her own trophy case packed with shiny medals and gleaming trophies of golden figures frozen into swimming poses. Her own bookshelf stuffed with paperbacks and battered, heavily read copies of *Spin* magazine. I notice none of her books have used stickers on them like most of mine do. The bookshelf is within reach of the bed, and I lean forward and slide a book called *The Color Purple* off the shelf.

"You should read that," Juliet says. "It's so good. But kind of intense. There's girl sex."

"Really?"

"Really."

Most of all, I can't fathom having this much personal space to disappear into. It feels like an unimaginable luxury I'll never get to enjoy. Juliet's three sisters all have their own suites as well, and the oldest, Ardelia, only uses hers when she comes home from med school. It just sits there empty most of the time. Juliet's older sister Cordelia, who's seventeen, lives next door, and her next oldest sister Ophelia, who's nineteen and decided to skip college to help run the family business, lives in the suite next to that.

"My mother wrote her master's thesis on Shakespeare," Juliet explained when I asked about her sisters' names. "That is, before she married a guy whose family owned a hotel. I think she wanted to be a writer when she was younger, but she never talks about it."

Juliet gets me a grape soda from her small fridge and, feeling thirsty from the sun, I suck down half the can in a single swig. Licking my lips clean, I drum my fingertips against the can's aluminum belly.

I start to feel funny being in Juliet's room, like I'm somewhere I'm not supposed to be. It felt so exciting racing across the bright green grass with Juliet, dodging guests and golf carts and dogs on leashes, laughing at our own excitement, then stepping through the door of the Overlander Suite, watching her pull a CD from a massive tower and slide it into the stereo. But as the music plays and the minutes pass, the reality sets in that my parents and Walden have no idea where I am. That I met Juliet not even an hour ago. I'm sure it's totally normal for teenagers to hang out in each other's bedrooms and waste entire afternoons together doing nothing, but my life isn't like that. And with clothes and underwear all over the floor, it's the first time I've ever seen a girl's bras that aren't mine or my mom's.

I slip into the bathroom to calm down. My palms are sweating. Nirvana rages on.

The bathroom smells like flowers on steroids, the female opposite of Walden's cologne. Make-up tubes and containers are scattered messily across the counter. There's a deodorant stick. A hairbrush bursting with swirling strands of Juliet's black locks. Some stray tampons. A hairdryer. Black hair dye. Some bottles of lotion, one of which, Bath and Body Works Freesia, turns out to be the smelly culprit. Some pictures taped to the left-hand corner of the mirror in an L-shaped gallery of Juliet's life. Juliet and her perfect family all wearing matching polo shirts. Palm trees on a beach at sunset. Juliet with her swim team. Juliet beside a wrinkled, smiling, old woman wearing a Mickey Mouse sweatshirt. Juliet with her arm around a pale boy with curly hair and bright blue eyes.

Her black bathing suit is draped over the shower curtain. I reach out and touch it, rubbing the stretchy elastic material, still damp from the cool water. A shudder runs through me, knowing it was against her skin.

Coming out of the bathroom, a song catches my ear. A soft beginning, like an afterthought. A lightly distorted electric guitar playing arpeggiated chords. D to F# minor to G.

"What song is this?" I ask.

"Lithium," Juliet says. "My favorite. This is the song I would take to the moon."

This doesn't make much sense, and yet, I know exactly what she means.

I sit back down, and we listen to "Lithium" all the way through without talking. It's good. Actually, it's really good. The first song I've liked. The distortion I could still live without, but underneath all that, it's a Beatles song at heart. And the way Kurt Cobain keeps repeating himself at the end feels like someone's most desperate inner thoughts that come tumbling out.

Confession #3: Maybe I jumped the gun a little bit on Confession #2. Not sure what that means for Confession #1. Will report back later.

"Can we listen to that one again?" I ask.

"Are you kidding? I could listen to it all day."

While the song plays again, Juliet lays down, then pats the bed beside her, which I guess means I'm supposed to lay down too. So, I do. I glance at Juliet out of the corner of my eye.

With her eyes closed in listening bliss, her face is full of deep secrets and elaborate stories waiting to be told. People are always asking me what's wrong or if I'm okay. People tell me I should smile more. I'll bet no one has ever said any of those things to Juliet. She wears dark purple lipstick and has a nose ring like it's no big deal. I picture what my mom's face would do if I showed up with a nose ring.

When "Lithium" ends, Juliet asks if she can see my "domicile."

"Sure, I guess," I say.

But when I lead her to the room I'm sharing with Walden, she laughs and says that she meant our "tour bus." We're already here, though, and Walden is sitting on his bed watching a movie on TV. He doesn't have a shirt on, which I would normally barely notice because half the time he doesn't have a shirt on, but somehow, a shirtless guy in my room feels scandalous with Juliet standing there.

"This is my brother Walden. This is Juliet. Her parents own the resort." I realize that he must be confused by the fact that I walked off alone two hours ago and came back with someone, so I add, "We just met on the beach. Or whatever. A little while ago."

"Oh. Cool. Hi," Walden says.

"You're the drummer, right?"

"Yeah."

"Cool. I love drums," Juliet says.

Is she flirting? Walden's sucking in his belly and puffing out his chest, but he's so skinny the effect is ridiculous. He does push-ups and sit ups all the time, but like my dad, he's tall, skinny, dramatically unmuscular, and somehow never gains a pound no matter how many burgers and fries he devours.

"Yeah anyway, we were just leaving," I say, grabbing my keys off the dresser and setting down my backpack, which now holds Juliet's loaned copy of *The Color Purple*.

"Your brother is kind of cute," she says as we walk to the parking lot.

"Gross."

"I don't mean for me," she says, nudging my arm. "He's not exactly my type. But I think my sister Cordelia would like him. They're both seventeen. Does he have a girlfriend?"

"No."

She rubs her hands together. "Matchmaker time."

What is Juliet's type, I wonder? Come to think of it, what's my type? Do I have a type? I know I'm supposed to be guy crazy by now with my hormones raging beyond all control, but I'm not. I look at boys, but not much happens. Maybe if they weren't so gross.

I almost ask about the blue-eyed boy in the picture in Juliet's bathroom. If he's her boyfriend. But something inside of me doesn't want to know.

Howard the Duck, which is pretty much the opposite of a tour bus, looks even more pathetic than I remember. Parked at the far end of the guest parking lot, his rusty undercarriage splattered with mud, he takes up almost five spaces across, like something someone abandoned. I'd rather crawl in a hole than take Juliet inside.

I show her the beds, the bathroom, the kitchenette, leaving the door open to air out Howard's funky, lived-in smell, an odd brew of dirty clothes, bacon, cigarettes, and hairspray. It's a pretty short tour. There's a milk crusted cereal bowl in the sink. A peanut butter smudge on the counter. It feels ridiculous that we actually live in here. To judge by Juliet's face, though, we might as well be touring the Palace of Versailles. She plops down in one of the captain's chairs and twirls around with her feet splayed out like a little kid.

"This is the coolest thing ever. You guys really live in here?"

"Most of the time. Me and Walden sleep in the bunks in the back, me on the left, Walden on the right. My parents sleep up there." I gesture to the queen bunk in a compartment above the front seats. "Every four or five days, we stay in a hotel. Otherwise, this is home. Until we get home."

"Which is where?"

"Fairview. It's in Vermont."

"Ver-mont," Juliet repeats, like it's a word she's never heard before. "What's the farthest away you've ever been in this?"

"Mostly we tour the Northeast and the Midwest, but last summer my parents got invited to play at a festival in San Francisco, so we drove all the way out there and did some dates on the way back."

"California! I'd kill to go to California. Tell me about life on the road."

Her curiosity is a little unnerving, the way she's so interested in my life. But it also feels nice, like when the sun peeks out from behind the clouds and warms your face on a chilly day.

"You're looking at it. Lots of driving. Lots of crappy sleep. Lots of reading and solitaire. Lots of smelling my brother's farts and cologne. We play every night and then drive to the next place and do it all over again. It's pretty boring."

"You're kidding, right?" she says, and I can tell she really means it. She almost sounds offended, and her eyes tighten together. "Rainey, you live the least boring life of anyone I've ever met."

"It's not that great."

"You travel all over the country playing music. Crowds cheer for you. Not to mention your parents are famous! You probably sign autographs, don't you?"

"Sometimes."

"See!"

I shrug. I know I should feel proud and flattered by all this, but all I can think about is how much I'd rather have The Overlander Suite for my bedroom and be on a swim team with other kids my age so I could tape their pictures to my mirror. I think about telling my mom how I wanted to take a break from the band. About how she brushed me off like a fly on her shoulder. About how weak and terrified I am.

Sometimes it feels like music chose me and not the other way around. The story's simple but unchangeable. My parents were touring musicians who didn't want to be away from their kids, so they brought us on the road and homeschooled us. We spent all our time in dressing rooms and at after parties, surrounded by adults, not another kid in sight. When Walden and I got good enough, we took over as the band and my parents re-branded themselves The Cobb Family Band. The end. I love music more than anything, but sometimes I feel like a character in a fairy tale who doesn't realize she was born in a prison until she tries to go outside for the first time and the guards stop her at the door.

"Well," Juliet says, kicking off and spinning around and around and around. "I think your life is really cool."

That night, after having dinner in the lodge and watching an orange sunset on the beach with my family, I stay up late reading *The Color Purple* and immediately get sucked into the story. Thankfully, the noisy air conditioner mostly drowns out Walden's snoring.

The book is told in the form of letters, which I've never seen a book do before. The letters are being written to God by the main character, Celie. Within the first ten pages, she's already gotten pregnant when her own father rapes her and then ships her off to be a housewife for some jerk named Mr _______, who treats her like dirt. The saddest scene so far is when Celie goes into town with Mr ______ and she sees a little girl who she instantly knows is her own daughter, the one that came from incest who was given away. But, of course, Celie can't say anything. She has to sit there and watch. It's like she has no voice of her own. It's like no one loves her. Reading *The Color Purple*, it's hard to feel too sorry for yourself because almost any life seems better than Celie's.

I try to go to sleep, but I can't get my mind to power down, so I take out my journal and my lucky pen. The one my grandfather used to write letters home while he was in the South Pacific during World War II. It's made of heavy polished silver, smooth and solid in my hand. My grandpa died before I was born, and I like the feeling of holding something that he held, that he used the same way I do.

I'm a list maker. It's my thing, I guess. Making lists helps distract my restless, spastic brain. I start writing. Enjoying the easy, smooth rhythm my pen makes as it glides across the heavy paper.

First, I make a list of the *Best Books I've Read This Year (East of Eden, Dubliners, The Handmaid's Tale…)*. Then *Things I Hate About My Body (*belly, pimples, small feet, cow lick…), followed by a list of *All Time Best Female Blues Singers (*Bessie Smith, Ma Rainey, Bonnie Raitt…), then of *Things That Are Red Besides My Hair (*blood, cinnamon gum, roses…).

I keep thinking about what Juliet said about my life, the buzz of her enthusiasm still echoing inside of me. It's not easy for me to see myself through someone else's eyes, but I try.

I just met Juliet earlier today, but it feels like I've known her for so much longer. I didn't know meeting someone could feel like that. Like lightning that doesn't stop. I think about the way her wet bathing suit felt between my fingers.

Things I Like About Juliet

1. She has a nose ring.
2. She also kind of works for her family.
3. She swims like a dolphin.
4. She's funny.
5. She's ambitious, but not in an annoying way.
6. She ACTUALLY thinks my name is cool.
7. She might know even more about music than I do.
8. She's named after a Shakespeare heroine.
9. She's probably the coolest person I've ever met.

Because a list of nine feels incomplete, I try to think of something else to add. When I do, I make sure Walden's still asleep, then put my pen to the paper.

10. She's pretty.

But *pretty* doesn't look quite right on the page, doesn't do her justice. So, I cross it out and write what feels closer to the truth.

She's beautiful. That's the truth.

Track Five
Off to the Races

Ten o'clock Sunday morning, our first of two rehearsals today, and Dad's already making excuses. Not a good start. His target at the moment is the shoddy sound system in Evergreen Ballroom where we're rehearsing for our first show tomorrow night.

I'm at the upright piano stage left, my hair up in a ponytail because it's so hot in here. At least all the piano keys work. Walden's behind his drum kit. Mom and Dad are up front, Dad on guitar, Mom on bass. Then, standing in a line beside Mom, is the St. Regis Horn Section, three handsome guys who showed up a few minutes ago from Detroit, all in suits and sunglasses, all looking really slick. Though my mom looks nice, as always, in black jeans and a white blouse with her long red hair spilled around her shoulders, my dad, as usual, looks a bit, let's call it ruffled. I wish he'd burn that wrinkled flannel and buy himself some new Levi's. The horn players are all freshly shaved, musky and clean smelling.

When I hand them the horn parts I wrote, they look at me, then at each other.

"I heard you were young, but c'mon, man," the trumpet player says, giggling.

"Ignore Damon," says the saxophone player, shooting the trumpet player a look. "My little brother was born with his foot in his mouth. I'm Simon. And you must be Rainey." He offers me his hand and I shake it. "They all said the same thing about Stevie Wonder when he first came on the scene. Just keep doing what you do."

"Charts look damn good, though," the trumpet player, Damon, says, flipping pages. "You really wrote these?"

I shrug, feeling my cheeks flush with pride.

"You've already met Damon," Simon says, "and that's Chad, the black sheep of the family." The trombone player laughs at this, I think because he's white and Damon and Simon are both black, then waves and says, "Yo yo yo."

Similar to the shows we've been doing all summer, our five shows here are each two sets. What's different this week is that set one is going to be stripped down, Dad and Mom playing as a duo like when they first started out. Mom thinks that seeing Luce and Tracy in the classic format that made them famous will pull on the audience's nostalgia strings and send them to the merchandise table. I hope she's right. Set two, though, is going to be a burner, an electric set packed with Cobb hits and soul and R&B classics like "Knock on Wood" and "Get Ready." Before tour started, Mom got this idea to add a horn section for the residency and asked me to write horn parts for the songs she chose. I'm not a horn player, but I can hear harmony really well. I've been working on them off and on all summer, listening to lots of Stax and Motown to get inspired. I'm nervous but excited to hear the horn players bring my charts to life.

Dad kneels down and repositions his monitor, then fiddles with the tone knobs on his Fender tube amp. He's right. The sound in here sucks. Buzzing monitors. Old microphones. A boxy room with flat walls that don't lift and carry the music.

But the real problem isn't that Cascade Family Resort clearly needs a sound system upgrade. It's that Dad's obviously nervous and acting weird. Skittish, distracted, temperamental.

When I was younger, maybe nine or ten, which is around when it started being an issue, stage fright used to be something he could control. Something we could even joke about. He'd get antsy in the days before we left for tour. Then about an hour before each show he'd start pacing the dressing room. Chain smoking Camels. Re-tuning his Telecaster a million times. My mom sat me down one day and said, "You know why he gets like this right?"

"No."

"It's because he's scared."

"Scared? Of what?"

"Of playing. Of the crowd. Of making mistakes. Of feeling exposed."

"But Dad's been playing music his whole life. How can you get scared of doing something you're so good at?"

"I don't know. It doesn't make any sense to me either. But it's nothing that you've done, okay? Or me. Or your brother. It's something Dad's going through."

My dad throws up every night 10-15 minutes before we go on stage. I'm not kidding. If he seems extra nervous, my mom will ask him if he remembered to "take out the trash," which is code for him finding the nearest bathroom and sticking his finger down his throat. Some nights he's his old, relaxed self. Lazy Luce Cobb they used to call him because he was so laid back. Other nights he sweats through his shirt before the show even starts, and my mom has to practically drag him on stage.

Lately, Dad's stage fright feels more and more like a volcano. And all volcanoes erupt eventually.

Rehearsal starts with "Tell the Truth," my parents' best-known song. The one everybody knows because it's still a fixture on light rock radio, slipped in there somewhere between "Lay Down Sally" and "Listen to the Music." But Dad keeps stopping us halfway through, turning dials on his amp, tapping the microphone, saying "Check one two, test test." As if he's trying to find the reason it doesn't sound right. He walks over to the edge of the stage and looks out into the empty house. I look at the horn players, who look at each other. The looks on their faces say something like, *We showed up expecting to play with Luce Cobb, and we get this guy instead?*

"Sorry," Mom says, sounding stressed, tying her hair in a bun and rolling up her sleeves, "we haven't played with horns in a couple years. We'll get there."

After talking to the sound guy, who's not a sound guy at all but a handy man at the resort, she and I both now know what the horn players don't. That not even a third of the tickets for our opening night show have been sold yet, meaning it could be a very small crowd. Small crowds have been haunting us all tour, and we still have boxes and boxes of CDs and T-shirts left.

"Hey, it's cool," Simon says. "But we got a lot of songs to get through."

"Luce?" Mom says, but Dad stands there frozen like a statue. "Luce?"

There's more to the story, though. Mostly it has to do with money and never having enough of it.

Mom's pretty unflappable, but sometimes when she gets really frustrated with Dad, or when the crowds are lousy on back-to-back nights, I'll catch her saying things like, "I don't know what went wrong. This was supposed to be easier by now."

Back in the late 70s, Mom and Dad were on the cover of *Rolling Stone,* "Tell the Truth" made the top ten, and they played all over the world. They opened for The Eagles and Neil Young and headlined their own shows across the country. But there's only a little bit of room at the top in music, and when New Wave took over in the 80s, their country soul got pushed to the side. Every year, the crowds got a little bit smaller. Don't even say the words Duran Duran in front of my dad. He'll get really mad.

In other words, it's really important that we play great tomorrow night to generate some buzz for the rest of the week.

Cautiously, I get up from the piano and walk over to my dad, like he's an animal I'm trying not to spook. My mom says I have a calming effect on him. And I guess that's true. He looks down at me with fear in his eyes. Underneath the shagginess, Dad's still really handsome with freckles and auburn hair that curls at the tips. I think he has the world's kindest face.

"I thought ballrooms were supposed to have chandeliers and gold walls," I say. "This looks like a place old people play bingo."

He chuckles. "How'd you get so smart, huh?"

"I get it from my dad."

"Sounds like a hell of a guy."

"He has his moments."

"I'll bet."

I nod back over at the band.

"Should we try it again from the top? We get one good one under our belt and then we'll be off to the races."

It's the expression he always uses. Like, if we finish a good show, he'll say, "Man, we were off to the races tonight!" If anyone else said it, it would sound stupid, but Dad makes it sound funny and sweet. Like you're part of something important.

"Sure," he says. He winks at me, then turns and rips out a blues line on his guitar that bursts like a thunder crack in the empty ballroom. The St. Regis Horns nod in approval, and for a moment, it feels like everything is going to be all right. Dad counts us in.

"One, two, three, four..."
And we're off to the races.

Track Six
A Cloud I Get to Climb On

Even though Juliet mentioned making omelets in the Sunday brunch buffet, when my family and I go to Hobner Lodge to eat between rehearsals, I can hardly believe it when she's actually standing there in a chef's hat and an apron.

"Look at all this character being built before your very eyes," Juliet says, spreading her arms wide. She's positioned between the self-serve waffle maker and the hand-carved ham station. I can smell stewed strawberries and maple glaze. "It's better than picking up trash, though. And I'm getting really good. You want an omelet?"

"Um…okay," I say.

Juliet clicks on the single burner portable stove in front of her, then rolls a hunk of butter around a hot, non-stick skillet, the butter foaming at the edges like churning surf. Chunks of diced ham, green pepper, and red onion join the party, then a ladle of liquid egg. Using her rubber spatula, Juliet moves egg away from the edges.

"What are you doing today? Wanna hang out?"

"Sure," I say, loving that we already seem to have a routine. "I have rehearsal again at two. But I can after that."

"Ooh, can I come?"

"To rehearsal?"

"Yeah. I want a sneak peek."

Juliet puts an aggressive mound of cheese on half the omelet and folds the other half on top of it.

"Check this out," Juliet says, and with a quick push-pull motion flips the omelet so that it lands perfectly on its back.

"That was amazing," I say.

I peek at my family seated near the picture window. My dad's drinking coffee and watching hummingbirds battle for space at a massive feeder filled with candy red liquid. Walden has his nose in Stephen King's *The Stand*—again. Of course, my mom, who never misses anything, is studying us intently, looking away only when I catch her.

Juliet brings her sister Cordelia to our second rehearsal, and they sit out there watching us from chairs in the fifth row, an audience of two. Where Juliet is on the short side with black hair and a tiny waist, Cordelia is taller with light brown, almost blondish hair, broad shoulders, and curves. I remember the bottle of black hair dye I saw in Juliet's bathroom and wonder what her real hair color is. Cordelia is dictionary-definition pretty, with a beaming smile and big round eyes, but not as interesting looking as Juliet, whose eyes are narrower and more mysterious. The sisters giggle and whisper while we play and it's hard not to notice the way Juliet's face lights up when I start singing.

Luckily, our afternoon rehearsal is way smoother than this morning as we run through the electric set again. Maybe it's having people listening, or the four cups of coffee he drank at brunch, but Dad seems to have shaken off his nerves. And the St. Regis Horns are so good it's almost scary. During "Knock on Wood," they trade solos back and forth on their horns, flying over their instruments with effortless ease.

And with Juliet watching, my confidence in my own performance grows. You'd think that since I felt nervous being in Juliet's bedroom yesterday, I'd feel even more nervous having her watch me sing, but I don't. Not at all. I like it. I know that's weird.

A stage is about the only place in my life I *don't* feel nervous. In regular life, I'm nervous all the time. I always feel like I'm going to say the wrong thing. I obsess over how I look and sound and what people are thinking about me. But music is a cloud I get to climb on and rise above all that petty crap. When my fingers touch the piano keys or I start singing, another me takes the wheel and I feel totally relaxed.

After rehearsal, Juliet introduces me to Cordelia.

"You're the most amazing singer I've ever heard," Cordelia gushes. "I can't believe how deep and sultry your voice is."

How do you respond to that? A simple thanks is the only thing I've come up with so far.

"Thanks," I say.

I introduce them to my family. My dad, cigarette already in hand, says a quick hello and then sneaks off for a smoke. He's not much for small talk. But my mom stops and gets super chummy. I told her about Juliet after brunch and she thinks it's nice that I made a friend. They both act a little star struck around my mom, which I'm pretty used to. My mom is not only famous, she's famously beautiful with shiny red hair and megawatt green eyes. My features are similar, I guess, and everyone tells us we look so much alike, but I don't see it. To me, I look like my mom's younger, less attractive stunt double.

Walden comes over and says hi in his awkward way, his hands in his back pockets, his feet moving around while he talks, his posture curved like a question mark. He has his drumsticks pinned under his arm, which I know is just for show because he usually never holds them like that. My brother tries so hard to be cool, but it's not in him. There's a cool gene out there and we Cobb kids didn't get it. Still, when Cordelia tells Walden what an awesome drummer he is, he stands up a little taller and I'm glad for him.

Cordelia leaves to go meet a friend and Walden and my mom go back to the hotel, after which Juliet and I walk out into the golden sunshine.

"I have a top-secret mission for you," she says, sliding on her aviators, "should you choose to accept it."

This sounds exciting, until I learn what the top-secret mission is. You see, she's out of cigarettes. Such a tragedy. And the only way she can get more is to buy them from the cigarette machine over at the golf course pro shop. Problem is they cost $3.75—in quarters—and the only way to get that many quarters is to raid the change stash in her father's office in Hobner Lodge. The plan goes something like this: I'm supposed to "distract" her dad while she steals the change. After that, I'm supposed to create some sort of further distraction so Juliet can slip fifteen quarters into the machine without getting busted. Easy.

"The trick is to act natural," Juliet says as we walk around the main desk in Hobner Lodge and down a long hallway full of offices with people talking on phones and typing on computers. "Then he won't suspect anything."

"Oh great."

Juliet walks me into the corner office where a man with a mustache is writing on a legal pad.

"Hello, my dearest father," she says, leaning down to kiss him on the cheek before introducing me.

"It's so nice to meet you," he says, aggressively pumping my hand while he shakes it. He has a deep tan and a big beer gut, but his clothes look expensive and there's a gold ring on the pinky of his right hand. "I've wanted to come over and say hello to you all, but it's such a busy time of year around here. I'm glad that you and Jules have become such fast friends, though. I hope she's been making you feel welcome in our little slice of paradise."

"Oh yeah, she's been a great tour guide," I say.

"And look at that Jules, a young lady of fifteen without a nose ring, isn't that refreshing?"

Out of the corner of my eye, I can see that this comment stings Juliet because she wriggles up her lips in a fake smile but doesn't say anything back.

"Well, we're sure looking forward to hearing you all perform tomorrow night," her dad continues. "And all week. I don't mean to gush, but I've loved your parents' music for longer than I can remember. Now please don't go repeating this to my wife, but I used to have the biggest crush on your mom. What a beauty. And aren't you just the spitting image."

Sorry to say it, but Juliet's dad is kind of a creep.

"Daddy," Juliet says, "Rainey heard what a big fan you are and wanted to play something for you on the lobby piano. I told her how hardly anyone ever plays it."

I turn to Juliet with my mouth wide open. Did she say what I think she said?

"Did she? Well, isn't that sweet. I'd be honored."

"Why don't you show her where it is?"

"Oh my God," he says. "This is incredible. I have to find your mother. Sue!"

Which is how five minutes later, I'm finishing a rendition of "I'm Going to Sit Right Down and Write Myself a Letter," the first song that flies into my head, to a small crowd of guests who have gathered around an out-of-tune piano in the lobby. Juliet's there when I finish the song, too, and after the crowd claps and we run outside, she shows me her pockets, which are bulging impressively with quarters.

"You jerk, why didn't you tell me you were going to do that!"

"I was improvising. It just came to me. Sorry. I couldn't think of anything else. Do you hate me? It worked, though, didn't it? And everyone loved you. Of course, they did. You're amazing."

Riding the current of her infectious energy, and, let's face it, the fact that she called me amazing, I go along with the next improvised part of Juliet's plan, which involves me faking a sprained ankle to distract golfers from going inside for a minute.

By the time we're in her favorite smoking spot in the woods, a little hidden glen by a small creek surrounded by birch trees and bright green ferns, I feel such a buzz from having gotten away with it all that I'm not even mad.

"So, do your parents not like your nose ring? Is that why your dad said that?"

"My mom doesn't really care that much, but my dad *hates* it. He freaked. But the thing is, I think he only hates it because of how it might make him look. You know? Like my choices are more about him than they are about me. Does that make any sense? He even told me that it might hurt my chances of getting a swimming scholarship. He's obsessed with making people happy, which I guess comes with running a hotel and having to smile and meet people all the time, but he never stops to think about what I want. He never even asked why I did it in the first place, he just jumped right into his assumptions about the kind of people who have nose rings and all that stereotypical bullshit." Then Juliet puts on the biggest, guiltiest grin. "Wait until he finds out I have tattoos."

"You have tattoos? Where?"

Juliet's wearing black, low-top Chuck Taylors with no socks, and she takes off the left one and shows me the bottom of her foot, which is home to a wandering constellation of tiny, perfectly imperfect stars, all outlined in black ink. I count six.

"This one's the newest," she says, pointing to the biggest one, which is right in the middle of her heel. "I'm getting better."

"You did them *yourself*?"

"How else am I going to get them? You have to be eighteen to get a tattoo. I numb the shit out of my foot with ice, have a little liquid courage, and go for it."

"You're crazy," I say.

"As if there's any other way to be?"

She opens up her fresh pack of Winston's, drops the plastic wrapper on the ground, and then lights one with her Zippo. I fight the urge to pick up the wrapper.

"Why do you smoke?"

She thinks about it for a second. "It's fun. I don't know. It relaxes me. I know it's bad for me, but it's not like I'm going to do it forever. I'm not an idiot. I don't want to get cancer. But a few cigarettes while I'm fifteen isn't going to kill me no matter what the after-school specials say. What, you've never had a puff?"

"Never," I say, but she frowns as if she doesn't believe me.

"Aren't you a little bit curious?" She holds her cigarette out to me. "C'mon. Try it." And for some reason, I can't deny it, I am a little bit curious. There's something magnetic in her eyes that I'm drawn toward. I reach out, but just before she's about to hand it to me, Juliet pulls the cigarette back and frowns at me, shaking her head.

"That was a test," she says, "and you failed miserably."

She actually sounds kind of mad. I'm so confused.

"You don't smoke for a really good reason. It killed your grandpa and it's hurting your dad. You're prepared to abandon all your beliefs because I smoke?"

I shrug.

"People are jerks, Rainey. And they'll try to get you to do all kinds of things you don't want to do. Believe me, I've learned that the hard way. You have to be stronger than that."

"But what if I actually want to?"

"Well, that's different. But the thing is, I don't think you do want to. Maybe you want to try other things you haven't done before. But I don't think smoking is one of them."

And you know what? She's right. I don't want to smoke. Not ever. In fact, I hate myself for the one moment of weakness I just had. I feel so grateful I want to hug her, or ask if I can hug her, but that would be weird because hugging is supposed to happen naturally, isn't it?

"You're funny," she says.

"Funny how?"

The trees around us cut the sunshine into bars and make these long, angular shadows which fall like stripes across Juliet, making her look cool and mysterious.

"Well," she says, blowing a series of smoke rings, "in some ways, you're like this old lady stuck in a teenager's body. You sing like you're some diva from another century, and you travel around and don't even go to regular school, so you have all this wisdom and strength from your experiences. But, in other ways, you're like a little kid who's still learning how to walk."

"Oh, gee thanks."

She walks over and touches me softly on the arm.

"No," she says. "I don't mean it in a bad way. Sorry, maybe that came out wrong. It's just. I've never met anyone like you before."

We look at each other for a long time without speaking, and my whole body buzzes. There's this energy inside me that builds up like water behind a dam. It almost hurts. Juliet doesn't look away, and neither do I. That is, not until her cigarette burns her fingers.

"Oww, shit!" she screams, jumping up and down, sucking on her burnt finger, and I can't help but laugh.

"Told you smoking was bad for you," I say.

"Smart ass."

That night I stay up late reading again.

In *The Color Purple,* Celie and Mr ______ are sitting at a table in Harpo's juke joint listening to Shug Avery sing. She sings "A Good Man is Hard to Find" by Bessie Smith, which is a song I love. And while she's watching her sing, Celie realizes all these things she feels about Shug. Romantic things, I guess. It makes her heart hurt to look at Shug because she knows, or at least she's afraid, Shug doesn't feel those same things about her. Shug feels them about Mr ______. It's so confusing for Celie. Celie also feels horrible about herself because Shug looks beautiful in a shiny red dress and pearls, and all Celie has to wear are the frumpy old outfits Mr ______ buys her because he's a cheap bastard and he doesn't respect her. But then the last song Shug sings is one she calls "Miss Celie's Song" and it's the first time in Celie's life that someone's done something nice for her. It's the first time she feels special. Alice Walker sure knows how to squeeze your heart.

Before I turn off the light, I make another new list in my journal.

Things I Learned About Myself Today

1. I'm not half bad at faking an ankle sprain.
2. Apparently, I sing like a diva from another century.
3. I'm like an old woman trapped in a teenager's body, but also like a little baby.
4. I gave in to peer pressure faster than I ever thought I would.

5. I wanted to kiss Juliet in the woods today. That was the feeling I felt.

I think about number five for a long time before I fall asleep.

Track Seven
The Song Juliet Would Take to the Moon

I've got a sour feeling in the pit of my stomach.

It's Monday night, only minutes away from the start of our first show. Walden and I are standing backstage in Evergreen Ballroom while Juliet's dad introduces my parents to the crowd. I'm stuffed into a knee-length black dress with thin straps. Not my favorite look, but Mom insisted I look "pretty" for opening night. When I point out that Dad and Walden aren't dressed up, she gives me that look again. The tough love one that says *suck it up, no one said this was going to be easy.*

If I ever have kids, I hereby pledge I'm never giving them that look.

It's not just that the crowd is thin, only half-full, if that. It's Dad. Something's not right. He keeps wiping his hands on his jeans, as if trying to get the sweat off. Mom turns and says something to him that I can't hear. He nods. Then wipes his hands on his jeans. His nerves are back. Big time.

"Did Dad take out the trash already?" I ask Walden. We're standing about ten feet behind them.

"Yep. I heard him in there a few minutes ago when I was taking a leak."

"Gross, Walden."

"Hey, you asked. Why?"

"I don't know. He seems off."

"What else is new? He's always off."

"Give him a break."

Walden isn't as sympathetic to Dad's stage fright as I am. Of course, he assumes it's more about weakness than fear. Like Dad should be able to arm wrestle his feelings into submission. I'll admit that I'm confused by it too. Sometimes it feels about as logical as if suddenly Larry Bird is afraid to play basketball with people in the crowd. But somehow, I also know it's not that simple.

"Now, of course our legendary featured act needs no introduction," Juliet's dad tells the crowd, "but I can't help myself because this is truly a landmark moment in the history of our little resort, a moment that would make Granddad Morrison very proud. I know he's looking down on all of us right now." He pauses and looks up at the ceiling for dramatic effect. My dad wipes his palms again. I want to walk up and touch his shoulder, to help in some way. But I'm afraid I'll make it worse.

"I'll never forget the first time I heard Luce and Tracy Cobb," Juliet's dad continues, then tells some never-ending story about a summer night in high school dancing under a full moon with the girl of his dreams. "I probably shouldn't say this in front of our daughters, but girls, lemme just say that if it wasn't for Luce and Tracy, y'all might not be here right now."

"Jesus, how corny can you get?" Walden says.

"Now after this incredible show is over, I want you to go out and spread the word far and wide so we pack this place the rest of the week. Would you please give a warm Cascade Family Resort welcome to the one and only, Luce and Tracy Cobb!!"

Dad follows Mom on stage. They plug in their guitars. Mom has her big Gibson Super Jumbo acoustic, Dad his white 57' Telecaster. Spaced about five feet apart, two stools sit center stage, each bathed in golden spotlight swirling with tiny dust motes. Out there in the darkness, scattered eyes watch them with anticipation.

My mom, radiant in a tight black skirt and a gold sequin top with a deep V-neck, greets the crowd, thanking them for coming, saying how excited they are to be here. The usual. The crowd claps warmly in response, but it's even emptier out there than we feared, and the applause doesn't add up to much. Even worse, everyone's sprinkled around. A half-full crowd doesn't look so bad if they're all scrunched together in a big block, at least there's a sense of unity, but when they're spread out, it looks more random, like people have wandered in off the street.

In spite of the crowd, though, Mom and Dad start out well. Mom digs deep into her vocal range, singing sweet and soulful the way only she can. Dad's harmonies blend just right and his guitar playing is smooth. He's really going for it. And by the time they're into the fourth song, a cover of "Landslide," I breathe a sigh of relief because everything is going to be okay.

Dad's halfway through his guitar solo on "Landslide" when out of nowhere he stops playing, leaving Mom's orphaned finger picking echoing out into Evergreen Ballroom like a lost bird. Totally naked and alone. At first, I think maybe Dad's amplifier has cut out or there's a problem with the sound, but then I see his arms at his side. He's not playing anymore. Why isn't he playing?

One of the rules of live music is that you never stop playing in the middle of a song. Ever. You can't. No matter how bad a mistake you might make, you have to keep going.

Walden and I exchange looks of absolute horror.

"He broke a string," Walden says, pointing, and he's right. A little silver coil dangles and dances from my dad's guitar neck. But a broken string is nothing. It happens all the time. Dad always just plays through it and then grabs a back-up guitar for the next song.

But instead, he stands up from his stool and starts walking off stage. Sweat dripping down his face, he hustles past me and Walden without a word, looking like a ghost, and then pushes out into the hallway. My heart feels like it's about to leap out of my chest and splat on the floor. This has to be a dream. But it's not. It's very real.

My poor mom is out there by herself. She briefly turns toward us, still playing, and though she's obviously trying to look calm for the audience's sake—*everything's normal, folks, nothing to see here!!*—there's panic behind her eyes. I give a helpless shrug. She winds into the song's ending, stretching it out, repeating that last line over and over, way more times than she normally would, singing *Yeah, I'm getting older too. I'm getting older too.*

I run out into the hallway. Dad's on the floor in a defeated squat, his back flattened against the wall behind him, his guitar in his lap and his hands hiding his face.

"Dad," I say, approaching him like I'm walking up to a car accident where I don't know if anyone's hurt. "Are you okay?"

He looks up at me. Tears drip down his face and then lose themselves in his shaggy beard. Gazing down, he ponders his right hand, which is lightly shaking, then makes that hand into a fist and slams it into the concrete wall behind him.

"God I'm such a loser," he says.

Footsteps behind me, and I turn to see Simon and Damon from the St. Regis Horns standing there, looking totally confused and more than a little worried. They're probably wondering what the hell they've gotten themselves into.

"What's up? What happened?" Simon asks. "He okay? He sick or something?"

I wave them away. "Give us a second."

I squat down beside my dad. I force the calm into my voice.

"Dad. Dad, you have to go back on. Mom's out there by herself. You can't just leave her out there alone."

"I can't."

"Dad you have to."

"I just—can you go on for me, Rainey?"

When Dad uses my real name instead of Rain Man, something is very wrong.

"Please," he says. "I'll fix it for tomorrow night, I promise. Please. Help me. I'm so sorry."

I've never seen anyone look so scared in my life, and the fact that it's my dad rattles me down into my bones. But there's no time to make any meaning out of this mess right now.

"Stay with him, okay?" I tell Simon and Damon, then walk back into Evergreen Ballroom. My mom is already into the next song, an original from the early days called "No More Whiskey, No More Tears."

When she finishes, she jokes to the crowd, "Bet y'all didn't know how good I sounded by myself, huh?" I suck in the deepest breath possible and walk on stage. Warmth and brightness from the lights washes over me. A few people in the audience clap when they see me, and I wave and force a big smile onto my face, as if this is exactly what we had planned all along. Juliet and her whole family are sitting about halfway back. Seeing me, my mom's eyes narrow more in confusion than relief.

Leaning down, I whisper "Careless Love" into her ear, naming one of our favorite songs to play together. "Follow me." She nods in response.

I walk over to the piano, take another breath, and lean into a blues in G, following my fingers, which always know what to do. Mom starts teasing out 7th chords on her Gibson and, before you know it, we're off to the races.

Ninety minutes later, the show is over and somehow, we're all still alive to see it. Amazingly, the world didn't end. The audience is even still there. Mom and I finished the first set as a duo, and then Dad managed to pull it together for the electric set. The audience, which started out a little unsure, rises for a standing ovation as we take our bow, seven across, and walk off stage. As we stand in the wings before the encore, my mom looks dead on her feet, like she just survived a war. The crowd keeps getting louder and louder, like they want us to play all night.

"Should we do 'Ain't No Mountain High Enough' like we talked about?" Simon asks.

Mom shakes her head, then says, "Why don't you go out, Rainey?"

"Me? By myself?"

"You stole the show, girl. They loved you. Seems only right that you take it home." She turns to the horn players. "You guys mind?"

"Hell no," Simon says. "She deserves it."

"Go get 'em, Rainey," Chad says.

Damon high fives me.

And then somehow I'm back onstage, only I'm by myself this time, walking toward the piano, with no idea what I'm about to play. I've never done an encore by myself before. I've hardly ever been on stage by myself. I sit down and adjust the bench. The room has grown whisper quiet. Someone coughs. Someone sneezes. I see Juliet out there in the crowd, and when she smiles and throws up a secret little fingertip wave, that's when it hits me.

I quickly re-visit the chord sequence in my head, D to F# minor to G, double check the words in my memory bank. Then work my way into a moody, bluesy version of "Lithium," the song Juliet would take to the moon.

Track Eight
A Big Fat Line Through Number Four

"I think that was the worst fight they've ever had," I say to Juliet.

"Sorry," she says.

My parents' raised voices from behind the dressing room door keep echoing in my head, not so much the words themselves, which were hard to make out, but how mad they sounded at each other. Words soured by hatred and disgust.

Juliet and I are sitting on the beach in the exact same spot where we met two days ago. Lake Michigan is whooshing down there in the dark, the black rolling water endlessly coming and going. According to my Timex digital, it's thirty-seven minutes after midnight.

I'm not supposed to be here, by the way. For the first time in my life, I snuck out. I guess that officially makes me a rebel. Better late than never.

After signing autographs and greeting fans in the lobby, including Juliet, who gave me a huge hug and whispered, "Meet me at the beach in a half hour," my family walked backstage. There was fire in Mom's eyes, and I wasn't surprised when she told me and Walden to wait in the hallway while she ushered Dad into the dressing room and closed the door behind them. They screamed at each other for fifteen minutes, then both emerged, silent and stone-faced.

"Let's go," my mom said.

After the short walk back to our rooms—my parents' room is only two doors down from mine—I asked if I could hang out with Juliet, which my mom immediately shot down. "It's already after midnight," she said. "I don't want you out running around this late. It's been a long night, and we have to do it all again tomorrow. Get some sleep."

"Okay," I said.

But I couldn't stand the thought of Juliet down there waiting for me. So, after twice swearing Walden to secrecy, I tip toed past my parents' room, ducking beneath the peep hole just in case, then ran down to the beach where I found Juliet laying in the sand by herself in jean shorts and a gray hooded sweatshirt, smoking, studying the stars. Before she even knew I was there, I looked up at a pulsing blanket of light. How is it that a sky full of stars always takes your breath away no matter how many times you look at it? Makes you want to grab someone and say, "Look!"

I didn't mean to start talking about my parents' fight. I didn't want to be a downer. But the memory just tumbled out. It was all I could think about. Not the standing ovation I got after playing "Lithium." Not the buzz from the fans. Just my parents screaming at each other behind a closed door and this horrible feeling that my family was going to break apart.

After I get it all out of my system, we're quiet for a while, then, out of nowhere, Juliet starts crying very softly, which is a strange turn of events indeed.

"What's wrong?" I ask.

"Nothing."

"You can tell me."

"Watching you tonight, watching all those people watching you," Juliet says, "was amazing, but it made me feel like such a loser."

"What do you mean?"

"Forget it, it's stupid." She wipes away tears.

I wait. It's a trick my dad taught me. If you want someone else to say more, you have to say *less*.

"Being the youngest one in my family, no one ever notices me. It's like no matter what I do, or how many trophies I win, they look right through me like I'm not even there." She talks about feeling outshined by her older sisters, who she believes are all more beautiful and more accomplished than she'll ever be. "Ardelia is already halfway to being a brain surgeon. Ophelia skipped college to run the resort, so she might as well walk on water. And Cordelia gets straight As and is in all these clubs and stuff. And she's so pretty it's stupid."

"You're pretty," I say.

She looks over at me.

"You think so?"

"Well...yeah," I say. I know I should feel more afraid to say these words, but I don't. Maybe it's the stars, or the eternal pulse of the water, or the way her eyes swallow and reflect the moonlight. I don't add that I gave her an upgrade from pretty to beautiful in my journal, though.

"Thanks," she says, and knocks her shoulder into mine.

I start to wonder if her relationship with her family is the reason Juliet has a nose ring. Or why she smokes. Or why she gives herself tattoos. Maybe it's her way of trying to stand out, to get them to notice her.

"Sorry," she says, wiping away her tears, "I hate people who cry."

"It's okay," I say. "So do I."

She pushes her mostly burned cigarette into the sand and slides her black hair behind her ear, but the gentle wind pushes it right back out.

"I thought it was pretty cool that I was probably the only one there tonight who knew why you played 'Lithium,'" she says.

"Um, you were definitely the only one."

"You changed it so much I hardly recognized it. You made it sound like an old blues song or something."

"Yeah, this slowed down version popped into my head."

"Did you go to the mall and buy the CD? You could have borrowed mine, you know."

"No. I didn't even know I was going to play it until after I sat down at the piano. I thought we were going to do a full band encore, but then my mom had this idea for me to go out alone, so I did. It was actually seeing you in the crowd that gave me the idea."

As the words come out, I realize how weird they sound, but I can't get them back in my mouth. Can't unsay them. Predictably, Juliet looks at me like I've started speaking in Dutch.

"But you must have heard it again after the other day?"

"Um. No. I mean, I don't think I did."

"Not even on the radio or something?"

"No."

"Are you sure?"

I shrug. She waits, putting the pieces together.

"You mean you only heard it those two times in my room? How did you know all the words? And all the music and stuff?"

I don't want to explain any of this, but what choice do I have?

"I can just sort of remember things," I say, trying to sound as casual as possible.

"Like whole songs after hearing them only twice?"

"I guess."

"Do you have like—a photographic memory?"

"I don't know. Maybe." I hate that expression, and yet, it feels pretty true for how my brain works.

"That's so cool."

"It's really not. I kind of hate it, to be honest. My brain feels so overstuffed sometimes."

"I'd love to be able to remember stuff like that. I'd never have to study for tests again."

"It's not really like that," I say. "And believe me, it's not as great as it sounds."

"Prove it," she says.

"When I was seven, my parents picked up on it and they used to bring me out at parties to entertain their friends like I was a dog who could do flips. They'd put on records and play me songs I'd never heard, then have me play them back perfectly on the piano while everyone watched. I used to like it because I thought they were all looking at me with all this love. Now I can see they thought I was a freak."

"Okay, that kind of sucks," she says.

"It's okay."

"Guess we're both freaks, huh?" she says.

"Guess so."

She turns toward me, and she looks so beautiful in the moonlight it hurts to look at her. My body buzzes and I get that feeling again. That pressure inside. We both lean forward until our faces are almost touching. Our lips hover without coming together, pause, as if trying to decide, and then finally, touch. It's only for a second, but still, they touch. And when they do it feels like a part of me slips out of my body and starts dancing in the breeze above our heads.

All the way back to my room, I feel dreamy and light as a

feather—until I find my mom sitting in the hallway reading a book. Talk about spoiling the moment.

"Rainey, it's two-thirty in the morning!" she says, standing up. "Where have you been?"

She's bleary eyed from lack of sleep and looks scared.

"Just down at the beach. It wasn't a big deal."

"I think I'll be the judge of what's a big deal or not, young lady. I came to your room to thank you again for tonight, but you weren't there. Walden said he didn't know where you'd gone. I seem to remember saying no to you almost two hours ago. What were you doing?"

"Nothing. Hanging out with Juliet."

"Well, I think I'll be having a little talk with her mother tomorrow. I can't imagine she'd approve of this either."

"No, Mom! Please don't. Seriously. You don't have to do that. I'm sorry. Really. It's just, I'd already told her I would meet her, and I felt bad not going." Then a little lie slips into my head, and then right out of my mouth. "Her boyfriend broke up with her. She needed someone to talk to."

The lie works. Mom calms down, and though she looks disappointed, says I should go right to bed, and she'll see me in the morning. For some reason, I throw my arms around her and tell her I love her.

"I love you too, honey," she says, then sniffs the air and says I smell like cigarettes.

"Dad," I say, unable to stop another lie from tumbling out. What's happening to me?

Mom nods, then says, "Rainey, I mean it, thanks for tonight."

I slip into my pitch-black room, Walden snoring in the dark, almost in time with the hum and pulse of the air conditioner. Acting fast, I grab my journal and scurry into the bathroom.

While I pee, I flip back fifteen or twenty pages until I find what I'm looking for, a list I made earlier this summer entitled *Things I've Never Done Before.* I'd forgotten about it until tonight.

1. Gone to school
2. Had friends
3. Played Nintendo
4. Kissed someone
5. Gone to a party
6. Fallen in love
7. Gotten my heart broken (see #6)
8. Stood up to my mom
9. Done anything rebellious
10. Felt truly satisfied with my place in the world

I remember feeling really depressed after I wrote it. But now, smiling to myself, I put a big fat line through number four.

Then I turn to a fresh page, and write at the top *Things I Did for the First Time When I was Fifteen*

I take a deep breath. I write.

1. Kissed someone.

I pull the journal forward and hold it against my chest where my heart is still pounding.

Track Nine
The Talking Piece

A gray Tuesday morning, already our fourth day at Cascade Family Resort, starts with school. Yay.

The Cobb Family Band is arranged around a picnic table under a huge weeping willow, not far from the building our rooms are in. It's cloudy and a little chilly this morning, so I'm bundled up in a sweatshirt with the hood drawn up over my ears. My coffee has lots of cream and sugar in it, wisps of steam rising and curling into the morning air, my palms growing warm against the paper cup.

I used to love being home schooled when I was younger. The freedom of it. The intimacy. We didn't keep a regular schedule. My parents always told us how lucky we were and, of course, we bought it. Believing that kids who went to regular school must hate being stuffed into crowded classrooms where no one could really pay any attention to them, where they weren't invited to really speak their minds as we were. Where they were always stuck in one place, unlike us, roaming vagabonds always in motion.

But now that I should be in high school, it all feels different, and I wonder if I've been wrong all along. If either my parents were lying to me, or they just didn't know any better. And hearing Juliet talk about her swim team and her favorite classes and teachers makes me wonder more than ever what it would be like to go to school with other kids every day. To eat lunch in a cafeteria. To go to dances and school plays. To have teachers who aren't my parents. It's not that my parents aren't good teachers. They're really good actually. Dad teaches social studies, history, debate, and current events. Mom teaches math, science, literature, and English. They love ideas and learning, and we have deep discussions and they're both so smart. It's not them. It's that, well, I've always wondered about the parts of life I might be missing by being on the road all the time. And ever since I met Juliet, I can't stop thinking about them. They run on repeat in my mind like a highlight reel. Maybe all the things I'm missing would disappoint me. Maybe they would suck big time. But how can I know for sure unless I actually experience them?

Discussing our current book, *Jane Eyre,* after reading *The Color Purple,* is a major let down. And the fact that I have plans with Juliet this afternoon makes the minutes crawl by.

After school, we have our weekly family meeting. Family meeting has two parts, announcements and share. Announcements are pretty self-explanatory. For share, we pass around a piece of lime green sea glass as a talking piece that Dad found in the waters of the Caribbean Sea when he and Mom played in Jamaica a million years ago. I love holding its rough smoothness between my fingers.

When each of us has our turn with the talking piece, we share roses and thorns.

Mom starts. She says her roses are that she got to lay out in the sun and go swimming. And that the first show turned out okay despite a "rocky" start. I know she's holding back a lot here, but I'm glad she doesn't say more. Dad deserves some major flack for last night, but I'm not in the mood, and if they start fighting again, I might lose it. Her thorn is that she says she didn't sleep very well and feels a little groggy this morning. At this, she raises her eyebrows and cocks her head to the side in a knowing way, but she doesn't give me away. Just passes me the talking piece.

"Roses are that I like being here," I say. "I made a friend which is pretty different since I don't have any. It's nice to sleep in a decent bed for once. No offense to Howard. Another is that I'm reading a book I really like called *The Color Purple.*"

"Since when are you reading *The Color Purple*?" my mom asks.

"Tracy," Dad says. There's a strict no talking policy when someone else has the talking piece. Apparently, it's a Quaker thing.

"I liked the show last night," I say. "It was fun doing the duo set, and playing with the horns. And doing the encore on my own was cool."

I start to pass the talking piece to Walden.

"No thorns?" he says.

I shrug. "I don't know. I'm kind of tired of being on the road. And being home schooled."

"Since when don't you like school?" my mom says.

"We do algebra in the middle of the summer. It's weird."

"For consistency. Year-round school is far better for retention. All the research says so."

"Tracy," my dad says again. "How can you expect her to speak honestly if you comment on everything she says?"

"Sorry," my mom says.

"That's okay," I say. "I'm done."

Now holding the talking piece, Walden takes a deep breath. I can tell he's thinking hard about what he wants to say. "Roses are that this place is cool. I can't believe people take vacations like this. Uh, another rose is that I met a girl. Cordelia. She's really nice." My parents exchange a coy glance at this. "My thorn is that, uh, I was so mad last night when you walked off stage, Dad." His voice is shaking slightly, and I can tell the words are hard to get out. But he keeps going. "I feel like you really let Mom down. Like you let us all down."

He passes the talking piece to my dad, who looks like he got the wind knocked out of him. Dad nods to himself to buy some time before speaking.

"I, uh," my dad starts. "A rose is the breakfast buffet here. You all know how I treat pancakes like a religion. These ones are really good. No Vermont maple syrup, but hey, beggars can't be choosers. I also enjoyed Rainey's encore last night. That was an…interesting song choice." Dad pauses and sets down the talking piece. He takes his cigarettes out of his pocket and flicks one from the pack. He doesn't light it, though, just slips it behind his ear. "My thorn is," he begins, but instead of saying any more, he says, "excuse me," then gets up and walks away.

"Way to go, you jerk," I say to Walden, smacking him on the arm.

"Sorry," Walden says. "But what's the point of saying our meetings are supposed to be honest if we can't actually be honest? And it's true. He did let us down."

"It's not his fault."

"Oh really? Then whose fault is it? Fleetwood Mac's?"

"Guys," Mom says. "Let's not do this."

"What if he does it again tonight?" Walden asks.

"He won't," Mom says, but she doesn't sound convincing.

Track Ten
Blowin' My Mind Like a Summer Breeze

"Catch," Juliet says and tosses a cassette tape into my lap. It's an hour after school, and we're sitting on the couch in the Overlander Suite, munching Nutter Butters, drinking grape soda, and watching MTV. "It's a mix. I stayed up almost all night making it after I got back from the beach. It's going to change your life, okay, so get ready."

Mix tapes are one of my favorite things in the world. I often make them for myself to bring on the road, and sometimes make them as presents for my family. But no one's ever made me a mix before. One made just for my ears to hear.

The cover is a picture of a palm-tree studded beach, some of the palm trees standing straight up, others leaning down toward the sand as if to pick something up. The picture looks so familiar, and then it hits me. It's one of the pictures from the mirror in Juliet's bathroom, cut to fit and then folded perfectly into the shape of a tape case. Carefully, I pull out the cassette, cradling it like a scared object. *Blowin' My Mind...* reads the label for side A, *Like a Summer Breeze* finishes the label for side B, a beautiful phrase split in half.

Blowin' My Mind Like a Summer Breeze. I'm not quite sure what that means, but I like the sound of it. Like a song lyric.

On the inside cover, the songs for each 45-min side are

written out in black pen, arrows pointing from the song name to the artist.

A DATE / TIME NOISE REDUCTION ☐ON ☐OFF	B DATE / TIME NOISE REDUCTION ☐ON ☐OFF
Army of Me -> Bjork	• Just A Girl -> No Doubt
Seether -> Veruca Salt	• People Everyday -> Arrested Development
Fade Into You -> Mazzy Star	• Cannonball -> The Breeders
Loser -> Beck	• On Your Shore -> Enya
You Outta Know -> Alanis Morrissette	• So Whatcha' Want -> Beastie Boys
Feel The Pain -> Dinosaur Jr	• Silent All These Years -> Tori Amos
Dreams -> The Cranberries	• Will Work For Food -> The Halo Benders
Lithium -> Nirvana	• Fuck and Run -> Liz Phair
Where Is My Mind -> The Pixies	• Joyride -> Built to Spill
Deeper Than Beauty -> Sloan	• 1979 -> Smashing Pumpkins
Nothing Compares To U -> Sinead O'Connor	• Glory Box -> Portishead

I say the names in my head, most of which I've never heard before. Bjork, Mazzy Star, The Breeders, Sloan, Liz Phair, The Halo Benders, Beck, Portishead. I like the images they create in my mind, the unheard melodies they promise.

"Thanks," I say, but that one word feels so inadequate compared to what I feel.

I was pretty nervous about seeing Juliet today, afraid it might be weird, or she wouldn't like me anymore. But it's not weird. It's easy. Neither one of us has mentioned the kiss, though.

"You want to listen to it?"

"Yeah."

She slips the mix into her stereo, and we lie side by side on the carpeted floor while it plays, holding hands, our fingers intertwined like tree roots. It's unlike anything I've ever heard before. Moods and sounds dancing around and shifting without warning, yet all somehow fitting perfectly together like the pieces of a puzzle.

Mixes are magical because they're one of a kind, never to be repeated the same way again, which is kind of the point. The art of mix making is that you're choosing songs in the hopes that the person you're making it for will love them as much as you do, but then putting those songs into the exact perfect sequence to create the most love in that person. You want them to fall in love and be swept away by *those* songs in *that* order. You're trying to capture their heart.

I guess when it comes down to it, mixes are love.

The last song fades and the tape clicks off. Juliet and I have barely spoken for 90 minutes. My lips feel dry. We're still holding hands, and I can smell Juliet's Freesia scented lotion in my hair.

"Well?" she says.

"Wow," I say.

"I told you. So good, right?"

"So good."

"Do you ever have that feeling," she asks, sitting up, eyes opening in excitement, "where you listen to music so hard and so carefully you almost become the music?"

"Um, all the time. I thought I was the only weirdo who thought that."

"And then there were two," she says.

I immediately want to hear it again, but Juliet wants to go swimming.

"Swimming?" I ask, as if it's not something people normally do.

"Yeah, c'mon, it'll be fun," she says. "The lake is so warm right now. I'll see if Cordelia wants to come too and we'll meet you and Walden down at the beach. Cord and I have to do some landscaping work later for my dad, but there's time."

"Okay," I say, feeling unsure about squeezing into my bathing suit, and not wanting to break the spell of the past two hours.

Reluctantly, I trudge back to my room to change into my dreaded navy blue one-piece. My nemesis. Somehow, I knew I couldn't avoid it forever.

After I slip it on, I stand there looking at myself in the bathroom mirror, trying to trick myself into not hating what I see. Why are humans, especially girls, pre-programmed to hate how we look? It's crazy when you think about it. Not to mention sadistic. I heard this thing once about the power of positivity. The idea is that if you force positive thoughts onto something negative, you can gradually change negativity to positivity. I make a list in my mind.

Things I LIKE about my appearance

1. I'm 5-7. Tall, but not too tall.
2. I don't have that many pimples.
3. I get freckles across my nose and cheeks in the sunshine that I kind of like.
4. I have brownish-red hair, the exact same color as my mom's.
5. I have really long fingers that are good for piano playing.
6. I have a nice smile.
7. I'm not too hairy.

There, that wasn't so bad.

At first, Walden, who's watching a Tom Cruise movie on TV, says he doesn't feel like coming to the beach, but when I tell him that Cordelia will be there, he jumps into action, digging his wrinkled swimming trunks out of a drawer.

We stroll between buildings and across grassy courtyards toward the beach. The sun is high and bright, and the morning chill is long gone. I like how after four days, I can already get around Cascade Family Resort without really thinking about where I'm going. My feet just guide me. A left at the Coke machine takes you to the beach, a right takes you to the horseshoe pits. The tall green fence means you're near the putting green.

Walden is a few inches taller than me, which means, as usual, his stride keeps him just ahead of me. When we were little, I always used to force myself to speed up so that I could keep up with him. I wanted to be right next to my brother at all times. Today, I walk at my own pace, content to be out of sync.

"What *was* that song you played for the encore last night?" Walden asks, unrolling his white hotel towel and slinging it over his shoulders. Last month, he bought a set of army dog tags at a second-hand store somewhere in upstate New York, and they jangle lightly as he walks.

It's probably stupid, but I don't want to tell Walden about "Lithium" or Nirvana because I'm afraid he'll be a jerk about it. Like me, Walden is a proud musical snob, even more so, and I'm afraid he'll think I'm betraying the cause.

"Just some song I heard."

"Where?"

"I don't know. The radio or something. Wherever people hear music."

"Who's it by?"

"I forget."

"Please. Says the girl who literally can't forget things."

"I heard it and liked it, so I played it. What are you, the music police?"

I realize I sound more annoyed than I mean to.

"Okay, relax. Jeez. It was kind of weird, so I was curious. I just don't know why you'd play some random song that nobody even knows," he says. "That's not even in our repertoire."

"People know it," I say. "Just not you."

"Touché," he says and lightly whips me with his towel.

I give him a playful push.

The four of us swim out to the dock and lay in the sparkly sun. Juliet and Cordelia are both wearing bikinis, and I feel a little old lady-ish in my blue one-piece, but I don't think I'd ever have the guts to put my pudgy belly on display to the whole world. The sun dries our bodies while we squint into the yellow heat, then we jump back into the cool lake, then dry off again. The pattern feels wonderfully primal, like something alligators would do.

Cordelia, who used to take gymnastics, can hold a handstand for almost a full minute, even with Walden jostling the dock to try to knock her over. She and Walden giggle a lot, and at one point they hold hands for a few seconds.

Juliet tries to teach me how to dive, which results in a spectacular series of painful belly flops, but I have fun anyway, not feeling as self-conscious as I normally do. Juliet's a surprisingly good teacher. Specific, encouraging, forgiving.

"You'll get it," she says. "My swim coach taught me that jumping headfirst isn't a natural sensation, even if it's into water. We naturally want to protect ourselves. You just have to get used to the feeling."

Sitting on the dock, swimming and laughing and not thinking about anything, not the next city or the next show or Dad's stage fright or Mom's stress or the meaning of my life, feels like the most normal thing I've ever done. Now, if I could only put this moment into a bottle and hold onto it forever so I could pull it out when I wish my life was different.

At one point, Cordelia and Walden have a contest to see who can hold their breath the longest. Juliet and I are already sitting kind of close to each other near the dock's edge, but while they're underwater, Juliet scoots even closer to me, our bare legs touching, and puts her head on my shoulder for a few seconds. Lays it right there like the most natural thing in the world.

"What are you going to play for me tonight?" she asks.

Then we steal another kiss.

Track Eleven
Something is Broken Inside

Around three o'clock, I get back to my room, feeling buzzed from the sun, my skin splotchy with assorted pink continents. We're due at the ballroom for sound check at six-thirty before the show at eight. Walden says he's taking a nap and falls face first onto his bed.

"Ow," he says, his face muffled by his pillow.

My brother can be pretty funny sometimes.

I want to listen to my mix again, but I certainly can't do it here, so I throw on my running gear. Sneakers, shorts, sports bra, T-shirt. Hair in a ponytail. Red Sox hat. I grab my Walkman, stretch a little, and set out. Only, when I open my door, my dad is standing right there. He has his hand raised to knock, and we startle each other, and both jump back laughing.

"Just the person I wanted to see. Got a minute, Rain Man?"

"Sure," I say.

"Step into my office," he says, and nods for me to follow him.

When we were little, Walden and I used to quietly compete for our dad's attention. With Mom, well, she was always available. Always there. And you could get as much attention as you craved. But Dad's always been a bit of a mystery.

Here's what I mean. I remember one day when I was eight

or nine, Mom sent me outside to call Dad in for dinner. I walked out into the back yard and Dad was perched on an upside-down bucket, sanding a piece of wood with fine grade sandpaper, whistling to himself. When I got a little closer, I could see that the wood had been carved into the shape of a beautiful bird and he was delicately sanding and shaping the wings. It was incredible. Perfect, even. Something you would see in an art gallery. But he acted like it was no big deal. "You want it?" he said and gave it to me right then and there. I still have it on my dresser at home. A hummingbird in flight. What I mean is that I went the first half of my life not knowing my dad could carve beautiful birds out of wood.

Anyway, we each had our ways to steal some solo time with Dad. Walden's was going to Lake Monster baseball games in Burlington and eating hot dogs. Mine was going fishing. There's a pond a short walk from our house in Fairview, and we'd dig some worms from the garden, pack a lunch, and set out with a backpack, our rods, and a small tackle box. Anyone could use the beat-up old canoe always parked at the shore's edge, and we'd row out into the middle of the pond and drop our lines into the greenish water.

Sometimes we'd sit in silence and stare out at the day. Sometimes Dad would bring a book of Walt Whitman poems and read out loud. Sometimes we'd talk about things. Sometimes we'd do ear training. One of us would hum a pitch and the other would have to name the note and try to harmonize a third above or below. I have perfect pitch, so I'd usually win. Sometimes we'd catch a bunch of fish and occasionally bring a couple home for dinner. Sometimes there was barely a nibble. But it didn't matter what we did or if we caught anything or not. I felt so content sitting there with him knowing it was only the two of us. That Dad wasn't paying attention to anyone, or anything, but me.

I don't remember when we stopped going to the pond.

Dad and I walk to the same picnic table that we had school at that morning. He sits, but I stay standing.

"I have a favor to ask you, but you can't tell anyone."

"Okay," I say. Where is this going?

"You have to promise you won't tell your mom or your brother. This has to stay between me and you, Rain Man."

"I promise."

Dad lights a cigarette and blows some smoke over his shoulder where it drifts and slowly dissipates in the afternoon breeze. Crooking his arm against his mouth, he lets out a rattled series of ugly coughs. He's wearing the same tattered jeans and flannel as always, his sleeves rolled up to the elbow. Like he often does lately, he seems a little nervous, a little unsure of himself. Like an awkward, insecure teenage boy has taken over my father's body.

"I can't play the duo sets this week," he says.

"Okay," I say, trying to project calm.

Dad scratches his face and takes another pull on his cigarette.

"God, your mother would wring my neck if she knew we were having this conversation."

"Dad. It's okay. I can handle it."

"I know you can, but you shouldn't have to."

"It's really okay."

"Something is broken inside of me, Rain Man. There's a wire loose in there somewhere that makes me feel like I'm going crazy. Even when I was younger, I knew it was in there, just sort of waiting for me. I'm going to fix it. I promise. But I can't fix it this week, so we have to find a way to get through it. Sit down, will you, you're making me nervous."

I sit down across from him.

"We can't let the ship go down on our watch, you know what I mean?"

"I think so."

He finishes his cigarette, then folds a piece of Juicy Fruit into his mouth.

"You know how important this residency is," he says.

I nod.

"I know your mom never wants to talk to you kids about money, but I'm going to do it anyway. You're old enough to know how the world works and how much is at stake when we go on the road. It's a funky arrangement, but the way this week is set up is that we're only going to make our full fee if the crowds are better than half full every night. Last night, it was just under half. But if we don't sell more tickets, this week could actually end up costing us money. And I don't need to tell you this tour hasn't exactly been a lucrative endeavor. In our contract with the resort, though, it also says that if we have at least two sell outs, we'll not only make our full fee, we'll make a hefty bonus as well. And we need that bonus, Rain Man. We need to get Howard a new battery. And buy you guys some new clothes. And..." but he trails off, as if he knows he's said more than he wanted to.

I wait.

"I can play the electric sets. And if we build up a head of steam and blow the roof off the place the next couple of nights, I'll bet we generate some buzz and get those sell outs and this will all be fine. A few weeks from now we'll be back home laughing about all this crazy nonsense. Now, I tried to tell your mom that I can't do the duo sets and suggested that you take over. Hell, you were off to the races last night."

I smile.

"The problem is, Mom won't go for it. She's so damn stubborn. As if I need to tell you that. She doesn't want to put you in that position. Frankly, neither do I. But I don't know what else to do. I'm afraid if I have to go out there like that again that…hell, I don't even know what will happen. But last night." He runs his hands through his hair and looks off into the distance, before looking back. "I've never felt like that before, and I don't ever want to feel like that again. The whole world was on my back and I couldn't take the weight of it. Like I was being crushed. And if you hadn't saved our bacon, well, I don't know."

"I'll do it," I say. "I'll play. But how? I mean, if Mom doesn't want me to."

"I have a plan."

Track Twelve
Flowers Blooming as You Walk By

With Dad's words still bouncing around in my head, I slip on my headphones and make my way over to a jogging path that, according to the map, snakes up and around through the woods and comes out over by Hobner Lodge. I'm more one of those fast-walk joggers, but still, it feels good to move and I have the path all to myself. The shadowy dirt trail. The tree roots and the chipmunks. The hard packed soil and the pointy ferns. They're all mine, and the mix is my soundtrack. Before long, I'm caught up in the songs, the singers, their words, all riding the steady pulse of my breath.

Blowin' My Mind Like a Summer Breeze sounds different the second time through. Juliet's mix isn't a smooth stretch of highway you coast down mindlessly. It's a windy, thrilling ride, going one minute from Enya's ethereal bliss to The Beastie Boys' lyrical pyrotechnics. It feels like stumbling on the coolest, weirdest radio station ever. And it's all just for me.

Honestly, "Where is My Mind" by the Pixies kind of freaks me out. A movie I'm not sure I want to watch. Other songs, though, make happy lightning in my stomach. The opening song, Bjork's "Army of Me" is like an anthem for an all-female nation that doesn't even exist yet. There's "Fade into You" by Mazzy

Star, which I think is the most beautiful song I've ever heard. That is, until I hear "On Your Shore" by Enya on Side B, which has to be the most beautiful song I've ever heard. That is, until, impossibly, it's topped two songs later by "Silent All These Years" by Tori Amos, which I'm ready to put on the Mt. Rushmore of great songs.

As I hop over roots and run over the firm dirt path, the woods smelling like wild herbs and mushrooms, I think about how people have always loved music, even before they called it music. Cavemen clapped and sang and smacked sticks together. They listened to the birds and imitated what they heard. They discovered that if they beat on stretched animal skins it made a pleasing sound. I like to think it was because it helped them express something they felt inside that they couldn't express any other way. Music was a solution to a problem that we're still trying to solve. How to feel less alone in the world.

"Great Balls of Fire" was the first song I fell in love with. I don't remember when or where I first heard it, but there was something about the energy of it that sent me spinning. I was hooked. I saw a video of Jerry Lee Lewis banging on the piano with his hair flying all over the place and I went right to the piano in my living room and put my leg up on the keys and started banging away like I was Jerry Lee.

Some songs you fall in love with because you love the melody. Some because of how they're shaped and put together. Some because of the words. Or they're just fun to play.

The first song I fall in love with on Juliet's mix is "Dreams" by The Cranberries because it feels like walking down the sidewalk on a summer day with the sun on your face and flowers blooming as you walk by. Like a person scribbling secret things in her journal.

Other parts of the mix? I'm no prude, but the cussing—well, it's kind of shocking in a way I didn't notice as much the first time.

Several songs come right out and say fuck, and it's hard not to imagine what my mom would say about that. Probably something about how Cole Porter and Dolly Parton never use profanity when they need the perfect word. But I find myself wondering, what if fuck represents a conscious artistic choice, not the easy way out? I don't think Liz Phair was taking the easy way out in "Fuck and Run." I think fuck was the only word that could express what she meant. A key perfectly notched to slide into that particular spot.

Some of the songs are going to take a few more listens. "Loser" by Beck is a wild pinball machine of a song that won't sit still long enough for me to see it clearly, and Portishead's "Glory Box," the side B closer, is a haunted, black and white dream.

But by the time I've gone through the whole thing again, and I'm dripping sweat and my legs are burning and I've done the jogging path three times, there's no doubt that music-wise, I'm not in Kansas anymore. I'm not sure I ever want to go home again.

Confession #4: It turns out there's actually some really decent music being made in the 90's. I don't know how I'm going to break the news to Walden.

I slip my headphones off and walk back through the grounds of Cascade Family Resort. I pass a game of horseshoes, a couple fighting in hushed tones, two boys juggling a soccer ball. I round the corner by the Coke machine, and nearly slam right into Juliet and Cordelia, who are coming the other way. Juliet is pushing a wheelbarrow stuffed with clumps of gangly weeds and a small shovel. Cordelia has a garden hose over her shoulder and a spade in her hand. We look at each other, all of us disgusting and sweaty, and burst into simultaneous laughter.

"Are you listening to what I think you're listening to?" Juliet asks, motioning at my Walkman. I nod.

"Yes!" she says, then turns to Cordelia. "I made Rainey pretty much the best mix ever."

I start walking with them, and though I don't mean to, when they ask me what's going on, I start talking about parts of the conversation I had with my dad.

"That's really intense," Cordelia says. "I wondered why he left the stage last night, but it all seemed normal when you came out to play."

"Yeah, no, it was not normal," I say, knowing I'm probably giving a little too much behind the scenes access. "It's fine. I'm going to play the first set with my mom, but I wish we could sell a few more tickets for tonight. I think it would help my parents relax a little bit."

We arrive at a small garden shed with a rusty metal roof where Cordelia and Juliet put away their tools and dump the weeds into a trash can. The shed smells of manure and gasoline. On a high shelf above a window, a small platoon of painted garden gnomes stands in a tidy line.

"Hey, how much money does everybody have?" Juliet asks.

"Why?"

"I have an idea."

A half hour later, we're all showered and riding into downtown New Buffalo in Cordelia's ancient white VW Jetta, which she affectionally calls the Ice Queen. Duct tape barely holds seat wounds closed, the clock is busted, and the change jar is a riot of rusty pennies. But her pride in having her own car is obvious.

Juliet is riding shotgun and I'm splayed out in the back seat. In my hands is one of the posters we snagged from Evergreen Ballroom advertising our shows this week. I'm a year younger in the band picture (Mom and Dad sitting on a couch, me and Walden standing behind them), and I can't believe how much different I already look than the skinnier, less defined, bangs-wearing girl staring up at me. A rap group called Wu Tang Clan is blaring from the crappy stereo, bass practically shaking the entire car, perfectly in sync with the recklessness of the moment.

Cordelia drives us to a copy shop, and from our pooled resources, we're able to make three hundred copies of the poster and buy a huge roll of packing tape. From there, we carpet bomb New Buffalo, taping a poster to every telephone pole and sign board, slipping one under the windshield wipers of every parked car. We go through the McDonald's drive thru and buy vanilla milk shakes and greasy tubs of French Fries, then drive up the Lake Michigan coast with the windows down and our hair flying everywhere and do the same thing in the next town over until all three hundred posters have been released into the world.

"There," Juliet says after taping the last poster to the brick wall outside a record store and then loudly slurping the final half-inch of her milkshake. "Now we sit back and let the power of advertising work its magic."

"Didn't your parents advertise?"

She shrugs. "I only work here."

Over Juliet's shoulder, the beginnings of a purplish sunset are gathering in the softly darkening sky, which is right about the time that, having left my Timex digital back in my room, I remember that clocks exist.

"Hey, what time is it?"

"A little after seven," Cordelia says, checking her watch.

"Oh shit," I say. "Oh shit, oh shit. We have to go."

"What?" Juliet says, without a trace of irony, "are you late for something?"

My mom is not happy. After I yank on my dress, which is horribly wrinkled because I forgot to hang it up after the show last night, and sprint through the backdoor of Evergreen Ballroom, she corners me and subjects me to the full wattage of the death stare, another of her patented looks. This one translates to: *you only have five seconds left to live; do you have any last words?* All things considered, I'd prefer the *nobody said life was going to be easy* stare.

"The show starts in *fifteen* minutes, Rainey," she hisses more than says. "Where the hell have you been?"

"Sorry, I lost track of time."

"Were you with Juliet again?"

I nod. "And her older sister. But it wasn't their fault. Really. It was my fault."

I want to tell her what we were doing. About the posters. That we were trying to help. That it was Juliet's idea. But I'm too stunned and ashamed to speak so I just stand there and take it.

"Sneaking out last night. Late tonight. I'm stressed enough without this extra crap, Rainey. And I can't find your father anywhere. He was here a minute ago and now he's wandered off God knows where. Jesus!"

It's right about then that I realize Dad's master plan isn't so masterful. It's pretty stupid actually. The way he explained it to me earlier, if he disappeared shortly before showtime, he wouldn't be able to play because he wouldn't be there. Then I could calmly offer to play and slide into his place for the duo set. Easy. But we weren't counting on a number of important factors. First, Mom's stress level. Which, as she paces around frantically asking if anyone has seen my dad, then sends Walden and the St. Regis

Horns off on a search party, is cranked up to atomic levels. Second, me being late and turning up the tension between me and Mom right before showtime.

Dad and I have really managed to screw things up.

Track Thirteen
Stupid

I sleep late Wednesday morning and wake up feeling so sad it's like there's a weight on my chest. I can still smell the beach in my hair. Taste Juliet's cigarettes and cherry Chapstick on my lips.

I lie there for a while looking up at the way the dark cracks in the white ceiling wander and spider over each other, trying not to cry, feeling almost sick to my stomach with sadness. Walden's bed is empty. Good. I love my brother but he's *always* there. The week is already halfway over, which means we'll be leaving soon. Only a few days ago, I couldn't wait for this tour to be over. I was resisting every new stretch of highway we drove down, every Wal Mart parking lot I woke up in. Every chicken nugget I ate. But now? Now I don't want to go home. I like it here. I miss our dog, Django, and the treehouse in our back yard in Vermont where I like to hang out. But I don't want to leave Juliet or her big bedroom or her sonic revelations. I feel like myself here. Maybe for the first time ever.

And the thought of having to leave that feeling behind empties me out and scares me. I'm afraid I'll never get it back.

I pick up *The Color Purple*. Celie has just discovered that her long lost sister Nettie is not only alive, but she's been writing letters to Celie all these years that Mr ________ has been hiding. I'm happy for poor Celie, but I don't feel like reading.

I get out my Walkman, then shake Juliet's mix from the sock I've been hiding it in. I know if Walden or my parents find it, it will be a whole big thing, so it's better to keep *Blowin' My Mind Like a Summer Breeze* out of sight. Crawling back under the covers, I rewind to the beginning of side A, and push play.

Bjork's voice feels a little harsh for the moment, and it turns out, I don't really feel like listening to music either, so I slip my headphones off and stare at the ceiling some more.

Remembering that there's jets in the tub and some complimentary bubble bath, I decide to take a soak. Baths always make me feel better, and since I never get to take them on the road, I might as well take advantage of it while I still can. I flip on the fan to keep the mirror from fogging up, then crank on the hot water and squirt some of the bubble bath into the spray, which creates these massive fluffy piles of white suds that smell like apricots. It's hard to feel grumpy in the bath, and I lay there for a long time and let my mind drift.

Though highly imperfect and beyond clumsy, last night's plan did, in fact, accomplish its intended goal. No one could find Dad, of course. I still don't know where he went during his short disappearance. And so even though she still had nuclear fire in her eyes from how late I showed up, Mom had no choice but to ask me to play the duo set. We played our butts off, too, and I could tell the crowd liked us up there together. Mom has a sticky musical memory like mine, crammed to bursting but very reliable, and since there wasn't time to write out a set list, we took turns choosing songs, me at the piano and Mom on her Gibson Super Jumbo. One of us would start playing and the other would follow right along and the set had a spontaneous, relaxed feel about it, almost like a conversation. My favorite moment was when I got it in my head that we should play this old jazz standard called "St. James Infirmary," so I ran backstage and grabbed Simon, Damon, and Chad from the St. Regis Horns who came on stage and belted out some jazzy solos the audience loved.

During set break, right on cue, Dad wandered in with his tail between his legs and beer on his breath. But he pulled it together for the electric set, just like he said he'd be able to, and we were off to the races for real. We played "I'll Take You There" by The Staples Singers for an encore, but the crowd was cheering so loud after we came off that, like last night, Mom sent me out alone to finish out the show again. I thought about that moment in the sparkly sunshine when Juliet put her head on my shoulder and asked me *what are you going to play me tonight?* so I played "Dreams" by The Cranberries. I transposed it down a full step to fit my vocal range better, and though I can't yodel or make my voice quaver and float like the singer from The Cranberries, I can do other things with my voice. Moans, howls, whoops, and groans. So, I did that. I moaned. I howled. I whooped. I think I may have even groaned. Sometimes when I play, I turn into that girl from *The Exorcist*.

Even better, the crowd was bigger than Monday night. Still not full. But almost three-quarters. I don't know if our last-minute poster drop helped at all, but it felt like the word was getting out. Now, we just needed a sellout.

After the show, Juliet and her entire family came backstage.

"We just wanted to say a quick hello and introduce our beautiful daughters," Juliet's dad said.

It was strange to see Juliet with her sisters, all of them in pastel-colored summer dresses, except for Juliet, of course, who had on a black skirt, a white V-neck T-shirt, and a jean jacket covered with band patches.

"Now, we already knew you two were good," Juliet's dad said

to my parents, smiling big, his fat belly fighting the fabric of his too-tight button-down shirt, then pointed at me in a way I dreaded because I knew one of those impossibly big compliments was on the way, "but we didn't know about your secret weapon here."

"You, young lady, you are going to be a star someday," said Juliet's mom, who was tall and toothy and looked more like Cordelia than Juliet. "How old are you?"

"Sixteen," I said.

"Fifteen," my mom corrected.

"Well, either way, it's no small feat to steal the show two nights in a row from Luce and Tracy Cobb."

"Thank you," I mumbled, then snuck a glance at Juliet, who mouthed *I'm sorry*.

"You must be so proud of this little lady," her dad said.

"You have no idea," my dad said and winked at me.

After saying goodnight to my parents and fake yawning a bunch to make it seem like I was all tuckered out, I swore Walden to double secrecy, which cost me five bucks this time, then snuck out again. I met Juliet down at the beach where we laid in the soft, cool sand and kissed until time disappeared.

"You can't ever go home," Juliet said, tracing her finger around the curve of my ear. "You have to stay here. I just met you and I already don't know what I'd do without you."

I come out of the bathroom with a towel wrapped around my torso, still brushing my hair, smelling fruity and feeling a little better about the world, to a horrifying sight. My brother Walden sitting in the desk chair, his long hairy legs kicked up on the edge of his bed, frowning at the tape case he's holding. My earphones are on his head, blaring what I can hear is "Cannonball" by The

Breeders, the third song on Side B of *Blowin' My Mind Like a Summer Breeze.*

"Wow, this is really horrible," Walden says, talk-shouting over the music. Holding the tape case, he reads names aloud at random. "Veruca Salt. The Pixies. Smashing Pumpkins. The Breeders. Portishead. Who the hell are these people?"

I storm over and rip the headphones off his head, "Cannonball" blaring out into the room until I click the stop button.

"I can't believe you!" I yell, clutching my loosening towel with one hand, and cradling my Walkman with the other. "I don't use your stuff without asking."

"You're the one who left it out."

I remember how I left my Walkman on my bed before going into the bathroom. Stupid.

"That's not an invitation to do whatever you want."

"Did you make this?" he says, holding up the tape case.

"No."

"Who then?"

It would be idiotic not to tell him.

"Juliet."

"Ahh," Walden says, smiling and tapping his temple. "Now I get it. That's where the weird encore songs are coming from, aren't they? I heard that one you played two nights ago as I was skipping around on the other side. I knew it sounded familiar. Blowin' my mind like a summer breeze, huh? Are you gay or something?"

"No!"

"I don't care. I'm just asking."

"Well, I'm not, okay."

My heart is racing and I'm so mad at myself for being so

careless. A feeling of absolute panic, like I've dropped something beautiful made of glass and the shards are scattered everywhere.

"I'm surprised Juliet has such weird taste in music. She's so cool. You don't actually like this stuff, do you?"

"I don't know. Sort of. Some of it."

"C'mon Rainey, this is trendy, teenage crap."

"We are teenagers in case you hadn't noticed."

"You know what I mean."

"You haven't even heard any of it."

"Believe me, I heard plenty while you were in there for a year and a half. I skipped around. By the way, can you please put on some clothes? If that towel falls, we're both going to be scarred for life."

I take clothes into the bathroom, dress frantically, then go back out to face my brother.

"There's a song on here called Fuck and Run? Jesus. Rainey, if Mom finds this, you're going to be in so much trouble."

I rip the tape case out of his stupid hand, then, for a moment, almost throw it right in his stupid face.

"You're such a jerk," I say, almost crying.

He stands up and I can see how bad he feels.

"I'm sorry. I didn't know you'd get so mad, okay? I was just curious what you were listening to. Seriously. I wasn't trying to ruin your life or start an international incident."

I storm out of the room, slamming the door behind me, Walden still calling my name.

Track Fourteen
Will It Hurt?

By the time I get to the Overlander Suite, I've mostly calmed down, but my eyes still feel puffy. Juliet, back from working a brunch shift in Hobner Lodge and stinking like scrambled eggs and home fries, looks very un-Juliet-like in khaki pants and a baggy black Polo. If not for her nose ring, she could be working the register at any Burger King in America. She changes into jean shorts and a Nine Inch Nails T-shirt, then gives me a grape soda and some Nutter Butters.

We sit on the couch watching MTV and paint our toenails purple and black in alternating colors. I flip through the current issue of *Spin* with Kim Deal from The Breeders on the cover.

"Are you going to tell me what happened?"

"It's dumb."

But she insists so I tell her the whole embarrassing saga of Walden and the mix. Juliet laughs, as if she can't believe that's what I'm so bummed out about. "Who cares what your stupid brother thinks? You think I care what my sisters think about my music? I mean, who cares what anyone thinks? The whole point of being a teenager is to fall in love with music everyone around you is going to hate. It's a rite of passage. And you know what I say to that?"

"What?"

"Turn it up."

I want to tell her it's different in my family because we're musicians, but I'm not sure if it actually is different or it just feels different.

"I don't want my mom to find out," I say. "She's weird about stuff. Does your mom know your music has lots of swears in it?"

"My mom barely even remembers my name," Juliet says. "And, I think maybe you're being a little paranoid."

"Maybe."

We sit in silence for a few minutes watching a Pearl Jam video and sipping our sodas. I bite a Nutter Butter in half and smooth the peanut butter filling against the roof of my mouth.

"Wanna see something cool?" Juliet asks.

She walks to her dresser and pulls out one of the drawers all the way, and plops it beside me, revealing a wild tangle of disconnected objects. A cherry red lipstick. A Saint Anthony pendent. A JFK fifty-cent piece from 1983. A pair of round-frame eyeglasses. A signed Hank Aaron baseball card in a plastic sleeve. Some cufflinks. A jagged hunk of quartz. A silver money clip with the U.S. Army crest on it. A pair of wooden dice. An orphaned bishop from a chess set.

"Welcome to the Museum of the Lost and Forgotten," she says, explaining that the drawer is filled with items she's found and collected at the resort over the years.

"One of the perks of living here is that people leave a lot of random crap behind. That's where I got this," she says holding up her Zippo lighter. "Last summer. Under the bed in Room 203."

"Do you like living at a hotel?"

"Sometimes. But everyone that comes here leaves eventually. It's pretty, and I love the lake. It's where I fell in love with the water and swimming. But I never get to go anywhere. Not like you do. We never even take vacations because my dad says we live where people take vacations, which is supposed to be good enough. As if a vacation is only about going somewhere and not also about *leaving* somewhere."

I sift through the drawer. A 4H ribbon. A shot glass from The Alamo. A silver earring shaped like a crescent moon. I wonder about the lives of the people who owned the things collected there, if they were sad when they realized their stuff was gone. I pick up the St. Anthony pendant for a closer look. It's a silver medallion on a slim chain, the words *Saint Anthony Pray for Us* around the outside, good ol' Anthony positioned in the middle with a small bouquet of flowers in his hand and a small child perched in his lap.

"My grandmother used to pray to Saint Anthony whenever she lost something and she'd always find it right away," I say, thinking of my mom's mom, who at the end of her life had been bedridden like a child. "Or that's what my mom says anyway. She died when I was four. Of cancer. I don't even remember her first name. Rebecca, I think."

"Wow, you are glum," Juliet says, swigging her soda.

"I think I slept too much last night or something. Is it possible to sleep too much?"

"Um, no. I say let all that shit go. My therapist says a positive attitude begets positivity. Or something. I think that's the right word. Is begets a word?"

"You have a therapist?"

"Yeah. She makes me call her Dr. Susan. Isn't that gross? My mom makes me go. Ever since my boyfriend dumped me and I got really depressed last year."

"You have a—boyfriend?"

"*Had*. Had. Very much had."

I can't help it. I have to ask.

"Is that the boy in the picture? In the bathroom?"

"Yeah. That's him. Good ol' Nathaniel. Plunderer of hearts and wrecker of lives."

Nathaniel.

"But, what about, you know…?"

"What about what?"

What does she mean, *what about what*?

"I'm messing with you," Juliet says, then turns my face toward hers and kisses me right on the lips again.

"I know how to cheer you up," she says.

"How?"

"Whenever I'm in a bad mood, or the world is majorly pissing me off, I always do something reckless and crazy, and it makes me feel better. Like it's a boxing match and I remember I can punch too."

"What do you mean, reckless and crazy?"

Juliet points to her nose ring. Then she lifts up her left foot and shows me her star tattoos again.

"These were acts of inspiration."

Which is how, before I even really know it, I'm numbing my left nostril and hotel ice chips are melting down my knuckles as I watch my nose turn bright red in Juliet's bathroom mirror, my heart ready to pound right through my chest like that creature in *Alien*.

Juliet locks her bedroom door, then puts on the Smashing Pumpkins' *Siamese Dream* album and turns the volume up to wall rattling decibels. She also goes into her closet and produces a plastic bottle of Popov Vodka from the sleeve of a winter coat and says, "I think we're going to need some of this, too," topping off both our grape sodas with the clear liquid. I don't much like the taste at first, but I gulp some down, surrendering to the swirly, floating feeling it gives me almost instantly. Juliet adds more.

"Will it hurt?" I ask.

"A little, but less if you get it really, really numb, so keep going with the ice. That's the key. Let me get my lighter. We need to sterilize the stud so you don't get an infection."

Juliet plays her lighter flame across the stud's sharp metal point, then draws the tiniest X on my left nostril with a blue pen.

"Ready?" she asks.

I take another sip. I am so not ready.

"I think so," I say.

"Just push really fast and really hard," she says.

I hold the sharp metal point above my nostril, then press it against my skin, pulling back in terror the moment I feel the pressure. My hands are shaking. I'm supposed to jab this thing all the way through my nose? It feels insane. Like I'm about to walk across hot coals.

"I don't think I can do it," I say. I'm so afraid of how bad it's going to hurt.

Juliet takes my hand in hers and looks into my eyes, and, it feels like, all the way down into my soul where nobody has ever been before.

"I'm right here. You can do it."

Five minutes later, there's a fake diamond stud in the flesh of my left nostril and I'm standing in Juliet's bathroom contorting my face around, not quite believing what I've just done.

There's a thin circle of blood around the stud and my nose is throbbing and Rudolph red. But I feel triumphant. I feel strong and brash—and invincible. I just pierced my nose. I have a nose ring. I have a nose ring. I have a nose ring.

Juliet tells me it won't bleed for long, and that the red will fade quickly too.

Every time I'm with Juliet, time goes liquid, and we become the only two people on Earth. So, when I look at her clock radio,

I can hardly believe it's already two o'clock. Even worse, since school starts at two today, I'm going to be late. Again. Why does this keep happening? Before this week I was never late for anything.

"I have to go," I say.

"Rehearsal?"

"School."

"God your family is weird."

"And your family isn't?"

"That's a fair point."

"What am I going to say to them? They're going to freak."

"You're going to walk right up to them and sit down like nothing happened. Own it. That's what I always do."

"Own it?"

"Own it."

"Own it."

My family is assembled at our picnic table when I walk up and my dad, who's just taken a big bite of a Granny Smith apple, laughs knowingly when he sees.

"You never cease to amaze me, Rain Man," he says.

Covering my nose with my hands, I whirl around and think for a minute about scurrying off into the bushes.

"What did you do?" my mom asks. "Rainey, turn around. Right. Now."

Lowering my hands, I turn to face the firing squad. The recklessness of my choice comes crashing down on me like an avalanche of stupidity unleashed from the crumbling side of Mount Impulsive. Who am I kidding? I'm not invincible. I can't *own it*. Whatever that even means.

Hating myself, not to mention feeling really lightheaded

from the vodka and piercing my own nose, I mumble "Sorry I'm late," and sit down next to my brother. My spiral bound notebook, pencil, sharpener, and folder are already laid out for me.

I pick splinters from the picnic table while I briefly explain myself. And by explain myself, I mean that I totally chicken out. I say that I'm sorry and that I'll take it out if they want me to. I wonder what Juliet would say if she was sitting here. Probably something brash and cool and smart. I really don't want to care what they think, and I want to stand up for myself, but how exactly do you do that?

"I think Rainey's new friend is having a fast influence," Dad says. "I think Rainey did something impulsive, but mostly harmless. And I vote we leave it at that."

My family has this weird voting system for things.

"Before we've even discussed it?" Mom asks. "I haven't even had time to process what I'm looking at. And I'm personally not very happy about the influence Rainey's new friend is having."

"I'm not voting for that," Walden says, "she didn't ask permission."

"It's her body," Dad says. "She doesn't need permission." He raises his voting arm.

"You're kidding, right?" Walden says.

"No, I'm not kidding," Dad says.

"Luce, she's fifteen years old," Mom says. "Do you really want her walking around with a nose ring? Especially without talking to us about it first?"

"Well, if I'm being totally honest, no, I'm not sure that I do. But I'm trying to look past what I want. If this is how Rainey wants to look, then I respect that. I think we all should. We ask a lot of you kids and you've earned the right to make some of your own decisions."

An uninvited burp releases traces of grape flavored vodka in the back of my throat. Oh no. I pray my breath only smells like the mint gum Juliet gave me before I left, which I'm fiendishly gnawing at, trying to unleash its full minty power. I feel lightheaded and sweaty, like I have the flu or something. Is this what being drunk feels like? I feel guilty for drinking. For piercing my nose. For everything. Why is everything so hard all the time?

A couple of kids speed by on dirt bikes, laughing like maniacs. Occasionally, I can hear the blast of a lifeguard's whistle from the beach.

Surprisingly, a look of reluctant acceptance settles onto my mom's face.

"Just, no tattoos, okay," she says, raising her arm.

"You have tattoos," I say, the words slipping out of me.

"I'm not fifteen. And I don't appreciate that tone, young lady. Walden?"

"No way," Walden says, grinding the metallic pieces of his dog tags together, glaring at me out of the corner of his eye. "If I showed up with a nose ring, or something like that, there's no way in a million years you guys would let me keep it."

"You don't know that for sure," my dad says.

"This is gender bias and a complete double standard. And totally unfair."

"That's two yesses, one no," my dad says.

It's here, of course, that I expect Walden to begin blabbing about my mix tape. About Fuck and Run. About my secret listening life. If he does that, I know I'll really be screwed.

But for some reason, he doesn't. He holds his tongue, and says, "Fine, whatever."

As brothers go, my brother is pretty great sometimes. I want to hug him.

Track Fifteen
The Opposite of Ordinary

I've survived their reaction to the nose ring. Now I have to survive school. Unfortunately, it's debate day.

"Today's dilemma is a good one," my dad says, shaking a Camel loose from his pack of cigarettes and snagging it with his lips. At the same time, he slaps his Zippo to flame with a single quick flick against his jeans and is having his first drag as he slips the Zippo neatly back into his pocket, all in one effortless, ninja motion. It's a trick I've always loved, something you'd see a street performer do.

"And I think with this one," he says, blowing smoke over his shoulder where it trails away in the sunlight, "Rain Man is poised to make a big comeback. Tracy, what's the score?"

"Uh, sorry, hold on," Mom says, reaching into her large canvas teaching bag and taking out a small chalkboard. My and Walden's names are written on either side with hash marks beneath to indicate the current debate score. "Oh jeez. Four to two, Walden."

First person to five wins the round—no real prize, just bragging rights—then we wash the board clean and start over.

"Soon to be five to two," Walden says.

"Shut up," I say, feeling in no mood to debate my brother again, who's a brilliant debater and almost always wins.

"There are one hundred people within a town," Dad says, "who have each contracted the same terminal disease."

"What disease?" Walden asks.

"Itsdoesntmattertosis," Dad says.

"It might matter," Walden says.

"Assume it's something terminal and they're all at the same stage with the disease." Dad takes a final drag of his cigarette, then puts it out on the bottom of his shoe and slips the butt into his pocket. "One day, a scientific breakthrough leads to the creation of a cure, but here's the catch, only fifty doses of the cure can be made. Therefore, fifty people will be saved and live. Fifty will die. The question is, who gets the cure?"

"Why can't they make more doses?" Walden asks.

"It doesn't matter," I say. "It's just a scenario. Like every single other time we do this. Why do you have to know every little detail?"

"I'm just trying to get all the information so I can construct the winning argument," Walden says.

"Assume that this is all the information that's available at this time," Dad says. "Walden, let's see, you'll be arguing in favor of randomness. Rainey, you'll be arguing in favor of a merit-based system."

"What does that mean?" I ask.

"Sorry, you'll have to figure that out. There's a dictionary available. The winner will be the person who makes the most compelling argument, not necessarily the person who is most right. Same as always, you'll have twenty minutes to think and prepare written notes. Opening arguments, rebuttal, questions, closing arguments."

I feel miserable. We've already done algebra and English and it's like somebody has scraped out the inside of my brain, cantaloupe style. There's a cauldron of acid boiling in my stomach.

"Are you okay?" Mom asks. "You don't look so good."

"You're telling me," Walden says.

"That's not what I meant. I mean you look like you don't feel good."

"I'm fine," I say, lying. I am the definition of not fine. I feel hot and clammy at the same time. I feel like I'm going to throw up. This one mosquito won't leave me alone. The wooden bench is unforgivingly hard beneath my body. But there's no getting out of debate, and I force myself to concentrate. You can do this Rainey. C'mon. Merit-based system. I pick up the dictionary and flip its thin pages until I find the word "merit."

Merit, noun. *The quality of being particularly good or worthy, especially so as to deserve praise or reward.*

Huh? A second definition, though, makes more sense. *The state or fact of deserving.*

Okay. So, I guess in this scenario, a merit-based system would be one where the people who get the vaccine are the ones who deserve it the most.

But how do you decide who deserves it the most? How do you decide who deserves to live or die? That, I guess, is my problem to solve. Reaching down and gathering up what's left of my energy, I start making notes.

The winner of the last debate presents the first argument.

"In a sad situation like this," Walden begins, "the only way to achieve true fairness is through a system that gives the cures out at random. We're all equal in our hearts and souls, which means we all deserve an equal chance at life. We could never trust anyone to be fully unbiased when choosing the fates of others, and therefore, the fairest way to decide would be to create some kind of system where the names were chosen by chance, a lottery, maybe, where no one had any control so that there could be no possibility of rigging the outcome in anyone's favor. Of course, it would be difficult to live with the results, especially if you were a person whose name wasn't chosen, or one of their family members. But in this way, at least you could go on knowing they were fair and untainted. It's not perfect, but it's the only way. Furthermore..."

As I listen to Walden, my mind drifts. I feel flushed and fan my face with my notebook. Not only that, my nose itches and throbs from where the nose ring went through. It feels like my nose has been stung by a bee, but I can't see or even touch the sting spot, which is agonizing.

"Rainey?"

"Huh? What?"

"Your turn," Mom says.

I take a deep breath and look down at my notebook. My notes and bullet points swirl, then snap back into focus. Swirl, then snap. C'mon adrenaline, get me through this.

"Though at first it might seem like randomness is the only and best choice," I say, "the system my opponent speaks of has some flaws. Since this situation isn't happening in a vacuum but in a place where societal factors would be involved, like it or not, the powerful would always find a way to rig the system. True randomness, therefore, could never be achieved in a societal structure, even in the best of situations. Even if it was made to look random. Like, who's creating this supposedly random system? Probably someone in a position of power, right? And who's more likely to be in a position of power? Someone with money. It's too much to ask that people in positions of authority could remain truly neutral when they would certainly have family members or maybe close friends who had the disease. True fairness is only a myth."

As I read, I find myself feeling more committed to my ideas. I want to be right. Even more, I want to beat Walden. I look at my parents.

"What would you both do to protect me? Or Walden? You're fair people, but if it was my life or his on the line, if we had the disease and you didn't, I don't believe you'd be able to remain truly neutral—even if you wanted to. I don't believe you'd be content to live with only a random chance at saving our lives, not when you could increase the odds. Your instinct to protect us would overwhelm your desire to be fair to others, and you'd take some sort of action to tip the scales in your favor."

"How? That doesn't even make any sense," Walden says.

"No interrupting," Dad says.

"Additionally, my opponent is preoccupied with fairness, but since when is fairness the most important consideration when people's lives are on the line? Like, who usually ends up going to war? Poor kids. Not rich kids. Dad, what's that CCR song?"

"Fortunate Son?"

"Yeah. Fortunate Son. And fairness isn't as black and white as he would have you believe. Like, who creates the terms of fairness? God? Our leaders? Our parents? They can't be trusted anyway." My dad chuckles at this. "There are also different ways to talk about fairness. For instance, economic and social fairness. In a poor family, if one of the people with the disease is the main money maker in his family, and he doesn't get chosen in the lottery, his family suffers too, and maybe even dies for his bad luck. Whereas, if it's a rich person who doesn't get chosen, his family will probably be fine because they've already got money. In that situation, randomness seems cruel and biased, not necessarily fair.

"And what about a person's age? Should a ten-year-old girl have the same chance of not getting picked as a seventy-year-old woman? That's not fair. The seventy-year-old has already had a long life and doesn't deserve extra years more than the ten-year-old. Who would want to take part in a system that blindly gives a seventy-year-old an equal chance at more life as a ten-year-old? Not me. Therefore, I put forward that access to the cure should be prioritized by age, and then to those families who would be most affected in the case of death."

After the opening arguments, we trade rebuttals, then take questions from the judges (my parents), who try to poke holes in our positions. We're each given ten more minutes to prepare a closing argument, but I've used all my energy, and only manage to scribble a few more words. Walden gives a strong closing. Of course, he does. It's my turn, but I'm spent. I can feel that my shoulders have slumped, and I just want to go back to bed.

"Rain Man?"

"It doesn't matter what I say. You guys are going to say Walden won anyway."

"Wait a minute, not necessarily," Dad says. "You're making some very compelling points. I'm on the fence at the moment. But if you don't give a strong closing, you're going to tip the scales toward your opponent no matter what."

"Fine, whatever," I say. "I kind of don't really care right now."

"How can you not care? You put so much into the argument."

I shrug.

"What's wrong?" Mom asks.

"Nothing."

"It doesn't sound like nothing."

"She's just mad because she's going to lose again," Walden says.

"Shut up," I say, feeling really angry all the sudden. But he's not the problem. Everything is. My whole life. Suddenly, sitting here on a July day having school, debating things that aren't even happening and will never happen, while other kids swim and eat ice cream feels totally absurd. And colossally unfair.

"I don't want to have school like this anymore," I say.

"What do you mean? This is only our second school day in a week," Mom says.

"We've been slacking off all summer."

"No, I mean I want to go to a normal school, with normal teachers and a classroom, and gym class and lunch, like normal kids do."

"Where is this coming from all of the sudden?" she asks. "First that thing you said in Saint Louis, and now this."

"What thing she said in Saint Louis?" Walden asks.

"Nothing," I say. "None of your business."

"I went to so called normal school," Dad says, making air quotes. "You're not missing much, kid."

"But you turned out okay. What's so wrong with regular school? With a regular life? The way we do things is so weird."

"Regular is subjective," Dad says. "It all depends on where you're sitting."

"Rainey," Mom says, and I can feel a patented Tracy Cobb treatise on the meaning of life coming my way—the last thing I'm in the mood for. "We're giving you something far more valuable than a school could ever give you. In a, quote, un-quote, regular classroom, you're one of only twenty students and hardly ever get the kind of challenge or attention needed for you to truly grow. Not to mention we're showing you the world. Or the country at least. And helping you develop a talent you can use your whole life to make yourself and other people happy. And earn a living from, if you choose to."

A living? I think about rusty old Howard the Duck. The way

my bunk shakes with every bump in the road. The way Walden and I still share a bedroom at home. All the boxes of CDs we have left.

"I feel like I'm missing out on a lot of things."

"What? What things?"

"I don't know. Things that kids do."

"Rainey, I know you can't see this yet, but you couldn't be more wrong." Mom pauses, as if she wishes she'd chosen different words. "You're getting the kind of exposure to people and places, to real life, that most kids could only dream of getting. You're going to be ready for the real world in a way they won't ever be."

"I don't even know any other kids. I don't even have friends."

"That's because you're so mature for your age. You're more comfortable around adults. You always have been."

"I don't want to be mature for my age," I say. "I just want to be an ordinary girl!"

"Well, I'm sorry, but you're not," my mom says. "You're *not* just an ordinary girl. Not even close. You're the opposite of ordinary in about every way imaginable. And the fact that you can't see the beauty in that, well…" and here my mom trails off. But then she gathers her thoughts for one more burst. "What I'm trying to say is that ordinary, or what you're describing as ordinary, is fine for other people. But not for us. Not for you."

Track Sixteen
A Bubble Balanced on the Tip of My Finger

I manage to make it back to my room before throwing up, but then all the food I've ever eaten in my life comes flying out of me, like somebody has flipped an ejector switch in my stomach. Stand back, men, she's going to blow! I kneel over the toilet and get sick over and over and over again.

Here's a list of the stupidest things I've ever done:

1. Drink too much vodka.
2. Drink too much vodka.
3. Drink too much vodka.
4. Drink too much vodka.
5. Drink too much vodka.

I'm sure there are others that deserve a place on this list, but that's the only one that matters at the moment. I do, though, cross #9 (done anything rebellious) off my "Nevers" list and add a second item to my list of *Things I Did for the First Time When I was Fifteen.*

1. Kissed someone.
2. Pierced my nose.

Then I lay down on my bed and pass out.

I make it through Wednesday night's show on a wave of desperation-fueled adrenaline, nearly throwing up again during the electric set when the crowd is stomping their feet during "I'll Take You There," imagining grape soda Nutter Butter vodka vomit spraying all over the piano keys and my black dress. This horrible image, somehow, manages to help me choke it down and keep my rhythm steady-ish and my singing on-key-ish. I don't know how Janis Joplin did it.

I can't help but notice, though, that every seat in the house is filled. Finally. We did it. A sellout.

Backstage, as the audience claps for the encore, each clap a whack against my temple, I tell my mom I don't want to go back out, and I'm not even aware of what's played for an encore, or by whom, because my head is in the nearest toilet. I don't think I've ever felt so grateful for indoor plumbing in my life. Hollowed out like a Jack O' Lantern, I'm not even sure what could be left in my system at this point.

"Drink lots and lots of water, so much you can barely stand it," Dad says, pulling me aside. "And take these." He drops six aspirin into my palm. "Take three now, the other three when you wake up in the morning. Live to fight again another day."

"Does Mom know?"

He shrugs. "I think she was a little too distracted to suspect," he says, pointing at my nose ring. "Plus, I think maybe you just ate something funny that upset your stomach, don't you?"

I nod silently, on the verge of tears for about the twenty-seventh time that day, feeling enormous love and gratitude for this strange and wonderful and somewhat broken man who happens to be my father. Then I go back to my room and crawl onto my bed without even getting under the blankets, the pillows so soft, so cool so....

When I wake up, I'm shocked to find it's almost eleven o'clock Thursday morning. There's a note on the nightstand from Walden that reads: *you were snoring so loud I almost murdered you in your sleep*.

Karma's a bitch, I think.

His black Fender Stratocaster lays on his bed like discarded silverware after a meal. Walden may be the family drummer, but his real dream is someday to play guitar as well as James Burton, or George Harrison—or even Luce Cobb.

I get up and pee, chug two glasses of water, choke down the three other aspirin Dad gave me, pee again, then ponder my nose ring in the mirror for a long time, bending my face this way, then that. The swelling has gone down, and my skin isn't so red and irritated anymore. Stalagmite boogers beg to be explored but I force myself to resist. There are times when it's okay to pick your nose, and times when it's definitely not. This is a not time.

Wet tissue in hand, I clean away the thin trace of dried blood that's crusted around the stud. After pulling my hair back, I gently wash my cheeks and forehead with soap and warm water, not having the energy for a full shower yet. Even the thought of the fast-moving water hitting my throbbing head makes me wince.

I slip on my comfy mesh shorts and a Cascade Family Resort T-shirt with a pair of bears paddling a canoe past a stand of majestic pines. I make myself a cup of coffee in the mini pot and add powdered cream and two sugar packets. Then I sit down in the desk chair, prop my feet up on the edge of Walden's bed, and stare softly at nothing for a long time. Minutes meander by. I feel…how do I feel? Somehow both better and worse than I did last night. The urge to throw up has finally left town, but all the sickness that was in my stomach last night has moved north and found available real estate in my head, which pulses and throbs like a screw being twisted into tough wood. I know Juliet topped off our grape sodas with vodka more than once, but how much did we have? I must have lost track.

I click on the TV and flip channels for a while. A golf match. A cooking show. A karate movie. I don't feel like watching TV, though. Click. So, I sit quietly and sip my coffee in the empty room. Eyes closed, breathing slowly, waiting for my headache to turn itself down, which it eventually begins to do, moment by moment, going from a crash to a throb to a dull ache.

I get up and chug some more water and pee yet again, my pee a little less neon yellow and smelly each time. Then, I'm walking out of the bathroom, cinching the drawstring on my shorts, pondering a second cup of coffee when—a song.

It's the strangest thing. Not there one moment, there the next. A vivid painting in my mind, my mother's mouth in motion, my mother's words. Spun around, re-imagined, re-cast.

Drawstring still in hand, I hum a melody low under my breath, not even knowing where it comes from, only that it's there, mumble-singing ever so softly, "I'm not an ordinary girl. You keep your ordinary world. Ordinary is for other people, but not for us."

Not US. No. ME. But not for me.

Moving quickly, but not too quickly, as if I have a bubble balanced on the tip of my finger, I pick up Walden's guitar and sit down on the edge of the bed. Using the white pick threaded through the top three strings, I strum until I find the chords that go with the melody I've been singing. The guitar is slightly out of tune, but who cares? A minor. D minor. G major. I'm not much of a guitar player so my chords are pretty chunky and a little sloppy. But I kind of like it that way.

Over and over, I play those chords, messing with the strum pattern, looking for a transition point, a way I can pivot out of this drone. I find it when my fingers stumble on a B diminished chord, then I go from E minor to F major, then to F minor, which opens a back door to cycle back to A minor and where I started.

Humming the melody on a loop so it won't change shape, or simply drift away into the ether that produced it, stopping only long enough to get my journal out of my backpack, I furiously scribble down the words as they tumble out of my brain, too seized by the moment to even consider messing with the alien musical forces that have taken possession of my body.

I'm not an ordinary girl.

Don't want your ordinary world.

Ordinary is for all the sheeple.

But not for me.

Sheeple? As in sheep people, I guess. I don't quite know where that comes from, but it works.

That's the chorus, then. Good. I scribble down a 1st verse that appears almost fully formed. Images of an endless highway and screaming behind soundproof glass. Of clusters of numb worker bee people scuttling off to offices, of a sliver of color in a black and white world. Then, part of a 2nd verse spills out. A girl on a mountain among the beckoning clouds, drifting above the masses who look up and stare and point as she shrinks and grows, shrinks and grows. What's happening to me? I've tried to write songs before but failed every time. Until right now. I don't know what's different, but I don't care.

Fifteen minutes later, my very first song is done. Well, mostly done. I need to finish the second verse and write a middle eight. But the bubble has popped, and somehow, I know better than to force it. I scrawl ORDINARY GIRL in big capital letters at the top of the page and underline the title twice for emphasis. Boom-boom.

I'm not quite sure what's just happened, but whatever it was, it felt amazing. I wrote a song. Maybe a terrible song. Maybe not. But a song all the same.

Things I Did for the First Time When I was Fifteen.

1. Kissed someone.
2. Pierced my nose.
3. Wrote my first song.

This is getting good.

Songs are mysterious creatures, and I've always wondered where they come from. My mom always says that songs come from hard work. That if you're willing to sit down and do the work, the songs will come. She sees songwriting like building a house. Materials + work + time = song. My dad sees it differently. More philosophically. His feeling is that all songs already exist out there somewhere, butterflies floating around, and that when one floats by, you have to grab onto it, but gently, so that you don't crush it. Butterflies, like songs, he believes, are delicate.

I knock repeatedly on the door of the Overland Suite, excited to share "Ordinary Girl" with Juliet, who absolutely has to be the first one to hear it, before remembering that Juliet told me she has an appointment with her therapist until three every Thursday. I go over to the cafeteria in Hobner Lodge and get a cheeseburger, curly fries, and a Coke, which is about the best thing I've ever tasted. They gave us a stack of free meal tickets when we got here, and I love passing one over and getting whatever I want in exchange. I dip my fries in ketchup and refill my Coke twice while I scarf down my greasy burger. "Ordinary Girl" keeps playing inside my mind, a tiny jukebox with only one song on it. The rest of the arrangement peeks out from the shadows. Drums. Bass. A second guitar. Harmonies. With two peanut butter cookies wrapped in a brown paper napkin, I take my song and my cookies down to the beach.

Past all the sunbathers and volleyball players. Past the squealing toddlers scampering through shallow water in sodden, droopy diapers. Past all the lifeguard towers and snuggling couples and coolers of soda until I find a quiet spot at the far end of the beach. The only other people nearby are a group of teenagers playing the radio on a boom box. I feel blissfully sun-kissed and anonymous.

We live near Lake Champlain in Vermont, and yet, we don't spend much time there. My parents turn into hermits when we're not on the road, recording new music in the studio they built in the back yard, speaking in barely audible grunts for days on end. When we get home from tour, I decide, I'm definitely spending more time at the lake.

Light dances across the surface of Lake Michigan, big as an ocean, stretching out endlessly everywhere it can reach. Now I know why they call them The Great Lakes. Laughter chirps around me. Pleasant but indistinct. Everyone is so happy here. I've never seen so many happy people in one place in my life. Ordinarily, happy people are nauseating, but this week, I'm starting to see happiness in a new light. Being happy is good, I've decided. Not something to roll my eyes at, something to, dare I say, aspire to?

From somewhere, my name is being called. I turn to see Walden plodding through the sand, coming my way. He drops right down and lands beside me like a bag of potatoes.

"I can't wait to get the hell out of this place," he says, hanging his head.

"What happened? Are you okay?"

"Yeah. No."

Remembering the two cookies I brought, I offer one to

Walden. We nibble in sugary silence. I can't remember the last time I've seen my brother so down. Even his chewing seems labored. Of the four members of The Cobb Family Band, Walden is no doubt the steadiest. Maybe that's why he's the drummer. So, when Walden's down, you know we're in trouble.

Though Walden dances around the subject for a few minutes, pretending he's just tired and tour weary, he eventually explains how he saw Cordelia kissing one of the lifeguards earlier.

"Some huge guy with big muscles."

"Did you talk to her?"

"Why, so she could tell me what a loser I am?"

"You're not a loser."

"You know what I mean. What is it with girls? One moment they're all into you, and then the next minute, you don't even exist."

"I don't know," I say. "But I don't think all girls are like that."

"You're just saying that because you are a girl. What are you doing down here anyway?"

"Hanging out."

"How's your stomach?"

"What?"

"Dad said you had food poisoning or something."

"Oh. Yeah. Better. Thanks. What are you doing down here?"

"Looking for you. Dad asked me where you were and none of us knew. We have rehearsal in an hour. Don't be late, okay. Mom keeps asking me about why you're late to everything all of the sudden. She's getting suspicious. It's special teams today."

"Special teams? Really?"

Special teams is a stripped-down style of rehearsal that my mom invented where we focus on vocal harmonies, arrangements, sore thumbs, and new songs. One time she tried to explain why she called it special teams, something about football, but I didn't get it.

"Mom says we need it. She says the harmonies are scrappy. And she wants new songs today, too."

"Why?"

"Because she's Mom and she has to do everything the hard way. You know a million songs, just pick one. By the way, did you play my guitar?"

"A little," I say, panicking, paranoid that I left my journal out. "Is that okay?"

"Yeah," he says. "As long as you're careful." He picks up a handful of sand and hurls it angrily. There's something else wrong.

"Do you think Mom and Dad are going to get a divorce?" he asks.

"What? No."

"I heard them arguing again."

"So? They argue all the time. It doesn't mean anything."

"I think it might this time."

"They're fine," I say, not really sure if I mean it.

"I don't know, they seem really tired of each other. Don't you think?"

I shrug. Isn't that kind of how married people get eventually?

"Sometimes I want them to split up. But I don't really. Does that make any sense? I'm just so tired of Dad's bullshit."

"Don't call it that. He's going to figure it out and get better."

"You really believe that?"

"Wait, what time is it?" I ask, realizing I've forgotten my watch. Again.

Walden checks his. "3:05. Why?"

"Oh my God, I have to go."

"What? Where?"

"Nowhere!" I say and hurry away, then stop and turn back to my brother. "And forget about Cordelia, okay? You're too good for her anyway."

"Thanks, Rainey," he says, and I take off.

"Rehearsal at four!" he calls after me.

"I know!"

"Do *not* be late."

"I won't."

Track Seventeen
Nowhere, That's Where

The first time I stepped into The Overlander Suite, I noticed an acoustic guitar nestled into one of the corners, nearly obscured because it had become a hanging rack for sweatshirts and ballcaps. But after I tune, then use, that guitar to play "Ordinary Girl" for Juliet, I ask her if she'll play me something in return, remembering how she told me she learned a few songs.

I do this partly out of curiosity, and partly to deflect attention from Juliet's gobsmacked reaction to the fact that I only wrote "Ordinary Girl" earlier that day.

"Yeah right," she says. "That would be like Trent Reznor walking up to some idiot in the street, and saying, hey, here's my amazing new song, now you play me something!"

I don't admit that I don't know who Trent Reznor is, but I do insist that she play for me, and eventually, after making me promise five times I won't make fun of her, she gives in. With almost trembling fingers, her black hair curtaining her eyes, she sings a little bit of "Three Little Birds" by Bob Marley in a voice so quiet it's almost a whisper, strumming her guitar with her thumb. Juliet's confidence, which is normally so present when we're together you can almost reach out and grab a handful, disappears when she sings. She's utterly disarmed, vulnerable in a whole new way that makes me like her even more.

"Okay," she says, setting down her guitar, "now that that freak show is over, we have to celebrate. Your first song deserves a first."

"A first what?"

The answer to which is the bottom of Juliet's tattooed foot.

"Oh no," I say, but she's already digging through drawers. An inkwell appears. Then her lighter. Then a pen. "I can't. My mom will murder me. She almost freaked when she saw my nose ring. A tattoo will put her right over the edge."

"That's why you put it in a place where she'll never see it."

"Plus, I have to be at rehearsal in a half hour," I say. "I can't be late again."

Juliet waves at the air. "Plenty of time," she says. She finds a sewing kit and extracts a thick silver needle that she holds up for me to see.

I swallow hard.

"Does it hurt?"

"Yeah, but in a good way."

Juliet sends me down the hall for ice to numb my foot, and when I come back, in a mirror image of yesterday, she's waving her lighter flame across the needle's tip to sterilize it.

As Juliet draws a tiny, perfect star on the heel of my right foot, and then I press the ice hard against my thick flesh, feeling lucky I'm not that ticklish, I wonder: *can something hurt in a good way?*

I guess I'm about to find out.

I walk into Evergreen Ballroom at 4:27 trying to hide my slight limp, afraid that with every step I take I'm going to smear the star tattoo that now lives on the heel of my right foot. But, of course, tattoos don't smear. They last forever. I'm not even sure how many times Juliet dipped the needle in ink and jabbed it into my numb heel, telling me to hold still while I tried to relax, balling up her quilt in my fist and grinding my teeth so hard my jaw screamed. I lost count.

My mom, ever observant, can always be counted on.

"You're limping," she says.

"No, I'm not."

"Yes, you are. What happened?"

"I twisted my ankle."

"When?"

"I can't really remember. I stepped funny or something. Sorry I'm late."

"So are we. But we're getting used to it by now."

"We've been working on harmonies in 'Seven Bridges Road'," Dad says. "Are you warmed up or do you need a minute?"

"I'm fine," I say. "I'm ready."

"Why are you so late?" my mom asks.

"I'm not that late."

"Late is still late, Rainey Cobb."

Thank God I don't have a middle name or I'm sure it would be making an appearance.

"And thirty minutes, by the way, is very late. What were you doing?"

"Does it matter?" Dad says. "She's here now."

"Yes, it matters," Mom says. "I don't understand this sudden lack of professionalism and I'd like an explanation. It's disrespectful to everyone here."

"I'm really, really sorry," I say, then climb up on stage and plop myself in the one empty seat in the circle next to Walden, who's straddling a box drum called a Cajon. Practicing harmonies, I've learned over the years, is all about physical proximity. That's the way the Everly Brothers did it. And it's the way we always do special teams, no matter how we're feeling about each other. Music comes first in the Cobb family, and you have to be able to watch the mouths of the other singers, hear the intake of their breath, anticipate every note.

Normally my perfectionist's brain loves the detailed closeness of this process, but the problem is, I don't want to be here. I'd rather be *anywhere* else doing *anything* else.

We're leaving in two days, and I feel miserable about it. To keep me calm while she tattooed me, Juliet joked that I could stay and live with her family. "Ardelia's room sits there empty most of the time," she said. "With so many people coming and going all the time, I doubt my parents would even notice." Only this doesn't sound like a joke to me, and I've already started concocting an elaborate scheme in my mind that involves me working at the resort, doing odd jobs to earn my keep. Then starting at Juliet's school in the fall.

After we're satisfied with "Seven Bridges Road," we move on to my dad's choice, Robert Johnson's "Come on in My Kitchen." During the second run through, Dad grabs an empty beer bottle from under his chair and uses it as a slide on his guitar. It sounds surprisingly beautiful, proving, once again, that my dad can still make anything sound good on guitar. We work the song a few more times until Dad twirls his index finger in a circle and says, "We got it."

"What did you bring, Rainey?" Mom asks.

"Oh," I say, remembering that I was supposed to bring a new song arrangement to work on. I could probably make something up, but I don't want to. And there's a tiny little part of me that can't wait to see the disappointed look on my mom's face when I tell her I forgot.

"Late *and* unprepared," Mom says, "a double whammy."

"Just do one of your weirdo songs," Walden says.

I swallow. Uh oh.

"What's that supposed to mean?" Dad asks.

"She has this secret mix tape she listens to all the time with all these weird songs on it. There's even a song on there that has fuck in the title."

"A song by whom?" Mom says.

"I don't know," Walden says. "It's called 'Fuck and Run'."

"Well, that's just…I don't even know," Mom says.

"I hate you," I say to Walden. And even though I know I don't mean it, in that moment, I do a little bit.

"Hey," Dad says. "Don't say that."

"It's your own fault," Walden says. "I told you not to be late again. I told you to bring a song. I *told* you."

"It's not like they've never heard that word before, Tracy," Dad says.

"In a song title? What else is on this tape?"

I shrug. "Just songs."

"Go get it please," she says.

"What? Are you serious?"

"Don't I sound serious?"

"But…it's all the way over in my room."

"We'll wait."

Feeling panicked, I look from Mom to Dad to Walden.

"Tracy," Dad says.

"Don't," Mom shoots back.

"But it's mine," I say.

"I just want to see it."

"The songs aren't inappropriate. And that one song is really about other stuff, like how hard it is to get close to people and how even if you're with other people you can still feel empty and alone. She uses bad words to express what she's feeling. It's social commentary."

"Well then I look forward to hearing it," Mom says.

Walden looks panicked now as well.

"You don't need to do that, Mom."

"I certainly do. Please go, Rainey. And come right back. Rehearsal isn't over yet."

Feeling miserable, I hobble over to my room, grab Juliet's mix, and then hobble back to Evergreen Ballroom. There's part of me that almost doesn't come back, but where would I go? Nowhere, that's where. I'm here. I have nowhere to go. Nowhere to hide.

"Blowin' my mind like a summer breeze," Mom reads. "Well, well, well." She says band names aloud at random. "Veruca Salt. No Doubt. The Cranberries. Dinosaur Jr. I've never heard of any of them."

"That's what I said," Walden says.

"There it is. Fuck and Run. Liz Phair. Where did this come from?" But then she nods to herself. "Never mind. I know exactly where it came from. The same place your nose ring and your lateness are coming from. Juliet."

"It's just music," I say. "It's not Nazi propaganda or anything."

"That may be," Mom says, "but I don't think you should spend any more time with that girl."

"What? Why?"

"Because I said so."

"That's so unfair!"

"We'll talk more about it later."

"But—"

"*Later.*"

During the duo set that night, Mom and I barely even look at each other, and I wonder if the audience can somehow feel how mad we are at each other in the way we play. We both love music too much to disrespect it by playing bad because we're mad at one another, but there's none of the warmth or banter of the past couple nights. Not much spontaneity or improv. We play one song, and then the next one. Like it's our job. Which it is.

The electric set has gotten better each night, and tonight it purrs like an engine on a smooth stretch of highway, barely a note out of place. But after a two-song encore, we're all standing in the hallway outside the ballroom, bathed in sweat, shoulders collectively slumped. Four shows in a row has taken its toll. With a lit cigarette in his mouth, my dad is leaning back against the cement wall with his eyes closed. Walden wipes his brow with a small white towel. Mom is just staring, staring. Even the guys in the St. Regis Horns, who almost always have something to say, aren't talking.

"Listen to them," Walden says.

He's already apologized to me, but it's going to take me a long time to forgive him.

The crowd's cheering is riotous, and slowly shifts into something more than shouts and whoops. More than just sound. They're chanting something, clapping as they say it over and over again, a two-syllable pulse.

Some-thing!, some-thing!, some-thing!, some-thing!

Mom is standing across from me. We lock eyes. My name. That's what they're chanting.

"Rai-ney, Rai-ney, Rai-ney, Rai-ney."

Over and over again.

Dad's beside me, and as he squeezes my shoulder, he whispers, "You were born for this, Rain Man."

So, I go back out again. Alone. The more times I do it, the better it feels. I sit down at the piano and say, "Thanks for a great week, everybody," and follow my fingers as they lead me into a slow blues in F. For the third time this week, I choose a song from my mix. A song for Juliet that nobody knows is for her but me, a whisper in the dark. I play "Nothing Compares to You" by Sinead O'Connor.

Sometimes when I'm performing, it's like a dream. Something that's happening to me rather than something I'm actually doing. Like the ME me has stepped outside of my physical body and is drifting around watching while my body plays the music. But not right now. Right now, I wrap my whole self around every word, every syllable. Feel the weight of the piano keys beneath my fingers, the power of my breath in my lungs. I don't ever want to forget this moment.

Track Eighteen
A Word That Rhymes with Dictator

Friday afternoon. Here I am hunched over my brother's guitar, again. Writing another song, again. A pissed off, middle finger of a song this time. It's already my third song in two days, so I guess the songs are writing me at this point. Where are all these songs coming from?

This morning, only four or five hours ago, actually, I wrote a follow up to "Ordinary Girl," a ballad called "Secret Star," in honor of my first tattoo, which still stings, a small tight pain, a fresh bug bite on my foot. The melody was there in my head when I opened my eyes, hovering in front of me like morning mist off a lake.

I've got a secret star,
I'll bet you'd like to know where I keep it.
It's tucked inside a hidden constellation
Where only I can see it.

This new song, though, opus number three, is born out of rage, and aimed at a specific target. Hint: she gave birth to me. It's about being made to grow up too fast and I decide to call it "Peter Pan in Reverse." I don't even care how obvious it is that it's about my mom.

The strum pattern is fast and aggressive, my hair flying around as I play it, and I can already hear thunderous drums coming to life behind it. I hear loud, in-your-face, Nirvana-level distortion.

Right around the time I'm running out of ideas in the third verse, unable to think of a word that rhymes with *dictator*, I lie back on the bed and look up at the speckled white ceiling again. All the same cracks are there. Broken highways and detours to nowhere. I've always heard about heartache and crushes and being love-sick, but those words haven't meant much to me until now, when someone is standing on my chest, and I can't get enough air in my lungs. The one thing in the world I care about in that moment is being with Juliet, and now, thanks to my mom, it's the one thing I can't do.

What a life I lead.

The phone rings so loud I shoot up as if the cops have kicked down the door. Tentatively, I lift the receiver and bring it to my ear.

"Hello?"

"It's public enemy number one," Juliet says.

I'm so excited and breathless I can't speak at first.

"Hello? Rainey?"

"Yeah, sorry, I'm here. How'd you get my number?"

"Don't be too impressed. The phone numbers are the room number and then the pound button. Can you come swimming?"

"I'm, uh, well..."

"I know you're not supposed to hang out with me. My mom already told me what your mom said about what a horrible influence I am. But can you come anyway? My friend Kelly is coming. And my friend Roger too. They go to my school. They're really cool. I mean, what are your parents going to do, put you in jail?"

"When are you going?"

"Just, like, now or whatever."

The line goes quiet for a long beat.

"I can't come to the show tonight," Juliet says.

"What? But it's the last night. We're leaving in the morning."

"I know. But I have to go with my mom to visit my grandma in South Bend tonight. She's really sick and we have to bring her medicine and clean her house and it's a whole big thing. I can't get out of it."

"Oh. Sorry. About your grandma, I mean."

"Thanks. So, are you coming or what?"

"I have rehearsal in thirty minutes. If I'm late again my mom will totally disown me."

"You're pretty boring sometimes, you know that."

This comment hurts so bad I don't know what to say.

"Stay there. I'm coming to you," Juliet says.

"What, no, you..." but the line goes dead.

I fly into the bathroom to brush my teeth. I yank my hair roughly out of its ponytail and drag my fingers through it a few times, then shake the tips. It looks decent enough. I slick on some deodorant and change into a clean T-shirt, then pace until Juliet's knock, after which I pull her inside, my finger crushing my lips telling her to be quiet.

"My parents' room is right down the hall," I whisper, "and if they catch you here, I'll be grounded until I'm thirty."

"Wow, it really stinks like cologne in here," Juliet says, waving at the air.

"Walden's obsessed. It drives me crazy. I watered it down, but it doesn't even help. He bathes in it."

"Oh my god, and he leaves his underwear on the floor?"

Juliet picks up a pair of Walden's boxer shorts and twirls them around by the waistband.

"That's disgusting."

"I always wanted a brother," she says.

Soon we're kissing on my bed, and it's another endless, bottomless kiss. A Hollywood kiss. Her lips gently explore every little part of my neck and my whole body wants to scream. Our hair is everywhere, tall grass tangled up in the wind, and our foreheads keep gently colliding in a way that makes us giggle snort, which makes us laugh even more. Juliet's nose is small, her shoulders bony. My big hands practically cover the entirety of her lower back. I can taste sugary soda and smoke on her mouth.

I keep telling Juliet she should leave, that we're going to get caught, but every time she kisses my words away, and it makes me care about getting caught about as much as I care about the weather in Japan.

But the sound of Walden's key in the door is unmistakable.

Metal on metal. The latch giving. The door swinging open. As if on springs, Juliet launches herself off me so that when Walden steps fully into the room wearing shorts and a tank top with his sunglasses still on, she's lying right beside me in the bed.

Between our touching shoulders, messy hair, and heavy breathing, there's definitely something suspicious going on here. Did my brother just catch me kissing a girl?

"Hey Walden," Juliet says, casual as ever, propping herself up on her elbows. This girl amazes me. You'd think we were sitting here playing cards with how relaxed she sounds.

"Hey," Walden says, taking off his shades and setting his massive Stephen King paperback on the desk. Oh my God. Oh my God. The way he said *hey* was so weird, wasn't it? He knows something is up. I wish I knew what he was thinking. "I thought you two weren't supposed to hang out."

Juliet rolls off the bed and stands up. "Yeah, I know. We're not. But I can't come to the show tonight, so I came to say goodbye to Rainey while I had the chance. I know you're too cool to tell on your sister, though."

There's an awkward pause while Juliet puts on her sweatshirt and slips into her flip-flops. Then she says, "Yeah, so, you know, don't forget to write, you crazy kids."

And with that she's gone. I wonder if I'll ever see her again.

Looking at my brother, I'm not sure what's supposed to happen next. Should I confess and try to explain myself? Jump right into a denial? Wait for Walden to say something? Run out of the room screaming?

The question is, would I care if he knew we'd been kissing? I haven't spent too much time thinking about that. It's confusing. But yeah, I decide, I'd definitely care if he knew.

"She is so weird," Walden says, then walks over to the corner and picks up the canvas bag with all his drumsticks and brushes in it. He stops, opens his mouth, closes his mouth. Then leaves. I don't like when there's tension between me and my brother. But it's his fault. At least that's what I keep telling myself.

Before the show that night, the house manager appears in the dressing room doorway to give us the news. It's a sellout. Our third in a row. That means we get the bonus on top of our full fee. More importantly, it means I don't have to listen to arguments about money all the way back to Vermont.

Simon's beating me at chess. Walden's doing triplets on his drum pad. Mom is messing with the set list. Dad's silently smoking, flipping through an issue of *Newsweek.* Chad and Damon are in the bathroom primping.

"We did it," Dad says, a small hint of pride and triumph in his voice.

"Congrats, you guys," Simon says, casually taking the

remaining knight I was so sure was protected. "This has been an unforgettable gig for us. A true pleasure."

"How did you do that?" I ask.

"You have to pay attention," Simon says.

The one slight relief is that Dad doesn't have to do his Houdini act tonight. Everyone finally seems to understand that I'm doing the duo set, which cuts the tension between my parents a little bit. Mom pulls me aside before the lights go down. I'm still so mad I can barely look at her. She waits until I meet her eyes. I can smell her perfume. See the perfectly laid path of her lipstick.

"I'm sorry if I've hurt you, Rainey," she says. "But one of my jobs in this world is to try to make sure nothing bad happens to you. And sometimes it's a messy business."

I nod.

"I love you, girl."

I nod.

As much as I don't want to admit it, those words feel good to hear.

But that doesn't mean I'm going to say them back.

"C'mon," she says when the lights go down, "time to rock and roll."

After the show, we eat pizza and chat it up with the St. Regis Horns, talking about the week, talking about how we're going to do this again sometime. That's what musicians always say after good gigs. *We gotta do this again.* Nobody wants that good feeling to end so you pretend you can hold onto it.

Before they leave, Simon comes over to me, a stack of papers in his hand. I can see that it's the horn charts I wrote for this week.

"You mind if I keep these?" he asks.

"No," I say, feeling touched, and a little embarrassed. "Sure."

"Keep going, Rainey," he says, "don't stop."

"Okay," I say.

I had this grand plan in my mind about going down to the beach to say goodbye to the lake and feel sorry for myself, but by the time we leave Evergreen Ballroom, it's after one in the morning, and I just want to go to bed. I change into my PJs, wash my face, then read the last few pages of *The Color Purple* to the lullaby of Walden's snoring. Celie and her sister Nettie are reunited at last. It's beautiful. A fitting ending.

Celie has finally found some measure of peace and happiness, but all I can think about after I turn off the light and lie there waiting to fall asleep is how much hell she had to go through to get there.

Track Nineteen
Things I Wonder About

The story is simple but unchangeable.

The residency and our week at Cascade Family Resort was the best week of my life. And now it's over. Seven days. Five shows. Poof.

Here I am packing up my duffel bag in near silence, sipping a cup of coffee with cream and sugar, feeling numb with each T-shirt and pair of socks I slide into my bag. I remind myself how tired I am of the meager assortment of clothes I've been cycling through the past seven weeks, how nice it will be to have my full dresser at my disposal in a few days. It doesn't work.

Walden is doing the same, choking his coffee down black because he thinks it's manly, grimacing with each sip. Guys really are ridiculous.

On the television, a James Bond movie plays on mute. Bond is on skis, dodging bullets.

"Rainey," he says, sitting down on the bed. I turn. His face is full of things he wants to say. Walden looks like Dad, with auburn hair and a round chin. He's been letting his facial hair grow, but doesn't have much to show for it other than a thin layer of scattered whiskers.

"Yeah?"

"I'm really sorry again. I didn't know."

I nod. I want to say more. I know he deserves more. That I played a role in all this too. But I can't find the words.

We look under the beds to make sure we haven't forgotten anything, then we're gone.

As we load up Howard the Duck and the gear trailer, it feels like the whole week, which in some ways seems to have lasted years, has suddenly passed in a blink. Time is really weird. When I first woke up this morning, I spent a long time looking at myself in the mirror, trying to decide if I looked different at all because of all the things that had happened. Does experience show in your face? Other than some new sun freckles, a nose ring, and a secret star tattoo, of course I didn't. I looked like me.

I can't bring myself to leave without seeing Juliet one more time, so, after telling my parents I think I left something in my room, I sneak *The Color Purple* out of my backpack and sprint to The Overlander Suite. Juliet opens the door, looking surprised to see me, and even more surprised that my chest is heaving and I'm out of breath. She's wearing her baggy camo cargo shorts, the ones she was wearing the day I first met her, and a Tori Amos concert T-shirt. It's my first time seeing Tori Amos's face, and shockingly, she looks a little like my mom, when she was younger, I mean. My mom's skin isn't quite as creamy white, and her hair isn't quite as fire engine red. But close. On Juliet's lips is smeared the same shade of purple lipstick as always.

"I forgot to give this back to you," I say, passing over the book.

"You could have kept it," Juliet says, closing the door behind me.

I shrug.

"You guys leaving soon?"

I nod. "Right now."

"I feel like you just got here."

"Me too. I don't want to leave," I say, feeling a flood of tears approaching that I somehow manage to hold off.

"I don't want you to leave."

As goodbyes go, it's certainly not poetry. But maybe that's all there is for us to say.

We hug for a long time, and I breathe in all the delicious smells I somehow know I will associate with Juliet Morrison for the rest of my life—Freesia scented body lotion, grape soda, Nutter Butters. All there in a single whiff. I slip my fingers through Juliet's black hair and move my fingertips through its fuzzy softness, already feeling sad for the loss of it. I never thought I would love the feel of someone else's hair this much.

"I have to go," I say. "My family thinks I'm checking my room for anything I left behind."

"You really need to work on your lying," Juliet says. "Wait. I have an idea. One last thing before you go."

After getting a red magic marker from her desk drawer, Juliet puts her hand on the wall and begins tracing it—right on the wall. By now, I shouldn't be too surprised by anything Juliet does, but I can hardly believe my eyes.

"What are you doing?"

"You'll see."

After she finishes tracing her hand, she takes my hand and traces it right beside hers, our traced thumbs nearly touching. Next to the two hands, she writes, *Juliet and Rainey Were Here.*

I look at our handprints in the middle of her bedroom wall, which seem to perfectly represent Juliet's entire personality. Using her Polaroid camera, she snaps a picture of the traced hands and hands it to me.

"There. Now we'll never forget."

"You're crazy," I say.

"I can't help it," she says, hugging me one last time.

And she can't. In the end, I guess neither of us can help how we are.

We just are.

As we drive back through Cascade Family Resort's front gate, I see the sign again, the one that says *where families go to be families again*. That may work for other families, but as for the Cobbs, it's hard not to feel our family unit has taken a step backward.

The ride home is long and boring. My bunk is still saggy, Walden's snoring still keeps me awake. Howard the Duck's engine still wheezes like he has a cold. But I sort of enjoy the emptiness of the endless drive. It feels good to have nothing to do but ride along. No rehearsal. No show. Just the wheels turning and the endless highway. I help Dad change one of Howard's tires. Help flag down a car to give us a jump when the battery dies.

I make lists in my journal with my grandfather's pen. *The Weirdest Billboards. The Best Beatles Albums. Animals I'm Afraid Of. Favorite Aretha Franklin Songs. Foods That Start with the Letter S.*

Indiana becomes Ohio becomes Pennsylvania becomes New York becomes Vermont. A blurry string of gas stations and rest areas and McDonald's Extra Value Meals.

Things I Wonder About

1. I wonder if Juliet is thinking about me as much as I'm thinking about her.
2. I wonder if the whole past week has been a dream. Or maybe a test.
3. I wonder if I'm living the life I'm meant to live, and how I'll know.
4. I wonder if I'm gay.

5. I wonder if it's important that I know for sure whether or not I'm gay.
6. I wonder what my parents would say if I told them I kissed Juliet—a lot.
7. I wonder if maybe I can go to regular school this year.
8. I wonder if my dad is going to be okay.
9. I wonder if my parents are going to get a divorce.
10. I wonder if my songs are any good.

My whole life is a question waiting to be answered.

Side Two:
The Treehouse Tapes
August 1995–August 1996

Track One
My First Pen Pal

Press the fast forward button. Right there. Stop.

In the weeks after returning home, Dad and I rediscover fishing together. One day, he pulls our rods and the tackle box out of the basement and calls up to me in the treehouse where I'm playing guitar.

"What do you say, Rain Man?" he asks. "Want to help me dig up some worms and head to the pond like the old days?"

One day we're out there on a bright yellow day at the very beginning of August with a sun like an egg yolk when I get a strong bite and reel in a big golden perch. It's one of the biggest fish I've ever caught, almost a foot long, and I can't believe how excited I feel seeing it there dangling from the end of my line.

"I think that's the biggest smile I've seen since we got home," Dad says.

I shrug.

"It's a nice smile, Rain Man. Be nice to see it more often. You look like your mom when you smile."

But when I roll my eyes at this, he holds up his hands as if to say, *sorry, bad choice of words*. Things are still weird between me and Mom. They were getting a little bit better, and then about a week ago Murph came over with a six pack of Bud—Murph has been my mom's best friend since they were young, and my parents' manager since the beginning—and told us that Willie Nelson wanted us to open up a series of theater shows for him in October and November. Mom and Murph considered this the best news ever. But not me. And certainly not Dad. Murph, who's only about five feet tall but has a gruff, deep voice, broke the benefits down like an equation. I've always loved Murph, who's like an aunt to me and Walden, but my heart sank as she talked.

"Bigger crowds equals more exposure," she said. "More exposure equals more CDs and T-shirts sold. More CDs and T-shirts sold equals more money. More money equals more time to keep living your dreams. More time living your dreams equals more happy. Comprende? Am I the only one who gets this?"

Murph can be a little blunt. That's part of what we love about her. She stayed for burgers on the grill and while we ate, the adults got tipsy and spun stories about the good old days. Murph told the one about helping Neil Young find his shoe. Mom the one about driving through a blizzard to make a New Year's gig in Denver and then playing by candlelight when the power went out. Dad about trading licks with Stevie Ray Vaughan in Austin.

At our family meeting that night, after Murph gave us all big hugs and went home, I said that I didn't want to play the Willie shows because I wanted to go to a real school and take a break from the band. It took all the courage I had inside of me not to buckle under the disappointed look on Mom's face. Then my dad said he didn't feel up to playing live again—yet. His stage fright was still too bad.

Things have been pretty tense since then.

That's why Dad has been sleeping on the pull out in the studio, and he and I are both officially on Mom's shit list. Hence, lots of fishing.

The perch is so slippery and slimy in my hands, I can barely stand to touch it. But Dad says that if we're going to catch fish, we have to honor them and treat them with respect. Sometimes Dad is a little out there. I do my best to hold the fish steady while Dad slips the hook free from its mouth.

"Goodbye fish," Dad says.

"Goodbye fish," I say and lower the perch back into the water, holding it gently until it starts moving its tail fin, then I let it go.

Look for the silver lining, a song once said. Here's mine. I have my first pen pal.

Juliet and I write lots of letters back and forth. Her first letter actually beat us to Vermont and was in the stack of mail Mom picked up from the post office. For some reason, that felt magical, seeing it there. Mom looked disapprovingly at the postmark and return address before handing me the letter, which I immediately took to the treehouse and read over and over again like a poem I was memorizing.

Dear Rainey,

Do you know that feeling when you think about a happy memory and for a while it makes you so happy to think about it that you just want to keep thinking about it? But then the longer you think about it, the more you miss it, and then you start to miss it so badly, it kind of makes your stomach hurt?

That's how much I miss having you here.

Where did you go, Rainey Cobb?

As I predicted, things have been boring since you left. Although, I cut a second and a half off my time in the 200m Freestyle, which is my best swimming event. I know a second and a half doesn't sound long, but in swimming, that's a lifetime. My coach thinks if I keep going like this, I have a really good chance of getting a scholarship, maybe even to a Big Ten school like Michigan or Indiana.

She also says if I'm serious about swimming, I have to stop smoking.

I asked her how she knew that I smoked, and she gave me one of those looks only grown-ups know how to give. You know the one I mean.

Boy, do I.

Track Two
Gently Snag the Butterflies

One afternoon I'm in the treehouse strumming a minor chord pattern on my electric guitar, putting the finishing touches on another original song. That makes nine that I've written. As in, seven-eight-nine. Somehow, they keep coming, pouring out of me like a faucet I can't turn off. It makes a nice distraction from thinking about Juliet, which is what I do with the rest of my time.

I wrote three songs while we were at Cascade, starting with "Ordinary Girl," followed by "Secret Star" and then "Peter Pan in Reverse." This one, which I think I'm going to call "A Quiet Place" makes six already since we got home from tour a couple weeks ago. How is that possible? Part of me doesn't trust how quickly they're coming, but another part of me knows that's something I should worry about later. When they stop coming. That my job at the moment is to gently snag the butterflies with my musical net as they float by.

I think it's safe to say I'm more aligned with Dad's philosophy of songwriting.

The guitar I'm writing on is one of my dad's old ones that he said I could have, a cherry red Mexican Telecaster with a white pick guard. I love it so much. It's a little beat up and some of the paint is chipped, but that makes it look sort of tough. My dad told me that nobody trusts a guitar player with a brand-new guitar, and I guess I see what he means.

I've been enjoying playing guitar more lately. I'm still a little clumsy and slow when I change between chords, but I'm getting better, and the fretboard is starting to make more sense to me. A piano is so linear, all laid out in a line. A guitar is multiple pianos braided together. It's more confusing, but there's also more options to play what you want to play. For a long time, I thought there was only one way to play an A chord, and then my dad showed me all these inversions, six different ways to play the same chord all over the fretboard. My head kind of exploded, but things made more sense after that.

Through one of the treehouse windows, I see Dad's shape between the maple and birch trees, chopping wood over by the studio. I worry about Dad. He's more relaxed since we got home from tour. He spends a lot of time in the studio. He reads books and chops wood and plays his guitar. He builds bird houses. But playing live music is how my parents pay the bills, and it would be really bad if my dad couldn't do it anymore. I don't quite know what all that adds up to, but I'm not too naïve to know there's some difficult moments ahead for the Cobb Family Band, financially speaking and otherwise, especially if I'm allowed to go to school. People have this romantic idea about professional musicians and bands like we're all Led Zeppelin and ride around in fancy cars sipping champagne, but that's a lie. Most of the musicians I meet are like us, barely making it, wondering how much longer they can hang on.

One day, I heard my parents arguing, and my mom said, "You're all abandoning me, that's why I'm yelling. So, I guess I should start working at T.J. Maxx!"

Thank God for the treehouse. I think I'd be going nuts

without it. We may have a tiny house, but our back yard somewhat makes up for it.

"All I need," I sing quietly, Dad's wood chopping keeping an unsteady beat, "is a quiet place. A quiet place to call my own. A quiet place that's far from home. A quiet place where we can be alone."

A couple of birds squawk back at me in response.

I recently started thinking about the songs I'm writing as not just individual songs, but as a collection. I think "A Quiet Place" would make a good closing song, or a nice breather sandwiched between two of the angry, fast ones. And I've written some angry ones. Ones that have surprised me as they came out. Ones I think would shock my family if they heard them. Think of them as butterflies with metal wings and fangs. The three songs that came before "A Quiet Place," named "Anger, Part 1," "Anger, Part 2," and "Anger, Part 3," at least until I can come up with better titles, will require heavy distortion and loud drums. And screaming.

Why am I angry enough to write three songs about it? Like a good teenager, my feelings typically outrace my thoughts, and I'm not totally sure yet. I know it's all connected to my family, my mom mostly, and the way I've been raised like a musical species from another planet where no other teenagers have ever been allowed to visit. That it's connected to my week with Juliet and the fact that she's there and I'm here. But the details feel foggy outside of my songs, where I can describe things more abstractly, more with impressions than specifics. With colors instead of lines. My anger songs are Jackson Pollock paintings, which makes them pretty different from "Ordinary Girl," which is more like a landscape or a painting of a bowl of fruit. And anyway, one of the great things about songs is that you can get away with not explaining everything, but still say what you mean.

On the plus side, my parents earned the bonus from our

three sell-outs, and we sold almost two hundred CDs and fifty T-shirts at Cascade. They gave Walden and I $300 each, and with my tour earnings, I bought a CD player and some CDs. What I really wish I had was my mix tape back, but Mom says she's still thinking about it.

I slip *Nevermind* into the CD player, an album that after a rocky first date, I've totally fallen in love with.

Confession #5: I'm still a music snob. But I'm working on it.

Then I lay back on the loveseat and open my journal to a fresh page.

Dear Juliet,

I'm in the treehouse again. I've been spending almost all my time up here lately, hiding from my family.

The treehouse is actually still really sturdy, even though it was built to hold little kids. Plus, my dad put on some extra support beams last week.

What's actually in a treehouse, you might be wondering? The floor is covered with mismatched pieces of old carpet. There's a small table, two folding chairs, a lantern, a bookshelf, plus the small couch that I'm lying on while I write you this letter. Seriously, I still don't know how my dad got a couch up here.

The best thing in the treehouse is the mural on the ceiling. I'm looking up at it now. I don't think I told you about it, but it's one of my favorite things in the whole world. My parents painted it for us when we were kids.

Close your eyes and picture all the different types of forests in the world kind of morphed together into one super forest. There are lots of different kinds of trees all snaking together. A waterfall. Mushrooms on the ground. And tons of creatures that ordinarily would never be in the same forest together. Squirrels and monkeys and butterflies and newts and frogs and foxes. There's a huge black jaguar napping in a tree. A pair of lemurs chasing each other up a trunk. There's even a mother elephant and a baby elephant holding the mom's tail with her trunk. There's pandas and koalas and black bears. A moose.

It sounds ridiculous now, but Walden and I named all the animals when we were kids and we used to make up stories about them. We'd lay on the floor for hours just looking up at the ceiling coming up with stories. Mookie the Macaw. Albert the Ape. Umi the Orangutan. Jeremy the Jaguar. The monkey family, who we named Mort, Mindy, Mellie, and Molly.

I've been writing more songs. I have nine now. They're coming out so fast I don't even know how it's happening. It's weird. I'm thinking of turning them into an album. But I'm not sure how I'll make an album though since...

Mid-sentence, I sit up and set my journal down, then hurry down the rope ladder, which is hard to hurry down, but I try, and run over to my dad, who's sipping a can of Bud in the sun with his axe balanced perfectly against his leg.

"Hey, Rain Man."

"Hey, Dad. Can I borrow some recording stuff?"

"Sure. Like what?"

"Just a microphone. And a guitar cord."

"What are you recording?"

"Nothing."

He laughs gently and wipes sweat from his brow.

"I see your internship with John Cage was influential."

John Cage is this minimalist composer who's famous for a piece of music that's somebody sitting at a piano in silence.

"Nothing *important*, I mean. Just some songs. Kind of demos."

"Songs you wrote?"

"Yeah."

"That's great. I didn't know you were writing songs. Can I hear?"

"Um. Maybe. I kind of want to keep them to myself for now. If that's okay."

"Sure. That's okay. Do you want me to get you set up in the studio?"

I explain my plan, which sort of flew into my head fully formed while I was writing to Juliet, telling Dad I'm planning on using Walden's 4-Track portable recorder and recording in the treehouse.

"So, I need to borrow some extension cords too, I guess."

Dad seems doubtful about many parts of this plan. First, whether Walden will lend out his precious Tascam 4-Track recorder, which he bought with his own money. "You know how he is about stuff like that." Second, whether he has enough extension cords to reach from the nearest power source to the treehouse, a distance of well over a hundred feet. "Though I might." Third, whether I'll even be able to make any decent recordings up there with so much ambient noise. "I hope you like the sound of crickets."

But, to his credit, after he's said his peace, he opens the studio door, and we walk inside.

The studio is actually our old two-car garage, which my dad began turning into a recording studio around the time I was born, and just finished a few years ago. He calls it Paradise Avenue and carved the name into a sign that hangs above the doorway. Behind his back, Mom calls it The Money Pit.

The studio is split into two rooms, a control booth/kitchenette/lounge side, and a recording space side. We're in the control booth side, although with the pull-out sofa open, dishes piled in the sink, and Dad's clothes everywhere, it looks more like a bachelor pad than a working recording studio.

"Sorry, little dirty," Dad mumbles, tucking away Budweiser cans and Domino's pizza boxes.

Through the sound-proof glass, I can see Dad's white 1957 Telecaster on the floor, a banjo and a dobro beside it. A Fender bass is propped in a stand. Even Dad's pedal steel guitar is out. There are cables everywhere, snaking around one another.

"You're recording."

"Little bit."

"What?"

"Nothing important," he says, and winks at me. "Just kidding. I'll give you a sneak peek."

Dad plays me a little bit of what he's been working on, and I'm shocked to hear that it's Christmas music. Jingle Bells. Silent Night. The Christmas Song.

"It's a present I'm making for Mom," he says. My mom has a soft spot for Christmas music. He puts his fingers to his lips. "But you can't tell. It's a surprise."

Dad helps me muscle the gear into the treehouse, then I go into the main house through the sliding back door. I smell coffee and see a grapefruit rind on the counter. Mom's back from her run. Django, our million-year-old dog who has a huge growth on the side of his left eye and hobbles more than he walks, gets off the couch and comes over and licks my fingers until I let him out. Still spry enough to follow his instincts, he chases a pair of squirrels up a tree then stands there mystified, his nose darting around, wondering where they've gone.

I pour myself some coffee, add lots of cream and sugar, then peel a banana.

There's a pile of mail on the counter, and I hope to find a letter from Juliet, but there's nothing for me. Just the new National Geographic, some junk mail, a postcard from a family friend, and a bill from Mastercard stamped "Final Notice" in bright red ink. In her bathroom, I find my mother putting on make-up, applying something with a brush to the high parts of her cheeks.

"Did I get any mail?"

She shakes her head and rolls her eyes. She's always annoyed at me lately. Everything I say and do is wrong.

"Hi Mom, how are you, how was your run?" she says. "Oh, I'm fine Rainey, run was great, thanks for asking, how are you? Oh, that's good. Lovely day out, isn't it? Yes, it is quite nice out there."

It's as if there's all this new etiquette I keep forgetting about. All kinds of new rules I have to follow no one told me about.

"Sorry. How was your run?"

She dabs a brush into a small jar of powder and lightly brushes it over her puffed-up cheeks. Still not looking over, she says, "No, you didn't get any letters from Juliet."

"You look pretty."

"Thank you."

"Are you going somewhere?"

"Yes. I'm having lunch with Aunt Becky, and then I have a job interview."

"A *job* interview?"

"Uh huh."

"For a job-job?"

"For a job-job."

What? I want to ask more, but she's so distant and focused that instead I make a hasty retreat for my shared bedroom with Walden down the hall. Lately, though, I've been sleeping in my sleeping bag up in the treehouse. The privacy is well worth the discomfort.

Walden agrees to let me borrow his 4-Track, though ever

the entrepreneur, says there's a two-dollar per day usage fee, as well as a five-dollar tutorial surcharge.

"I don't need a tutorial," I say. "It can't be that hard. And I'll use the manual to help me if I get stuck. I'm pretty sure I can figure it out."

"No go," Walden says. He's in the corner of our bedroom practicing on his drum pad. He sets down his drumsticks and wipes his brow with his T-shirt. "I'll need some insurance."

"Insurance against what?"

"Your stupidity," Walden says. "I can't risk you breaking it."

"I'm not going to break it."

"You say that, but how do I know? I saved up for six months to buy it."

"Fine. Can you show me now?"

"Without payment? Surely you jest."

I give Walden a five and four singles, which leaves fourteen dollars left from my tour earnings. Maybe I should get a job too.

"Two days of recording, plus your stupid tutorial."

"Pleasure doing business with you," Walden says. "What are you recording, by the way?"

"Just some stuff. Nothing important."

"Wow, sounds amazing."

I sit down on my bed. In some ways, I'm still mad at Walden for getting my mixtape confiscated, but the sad truth is that Walden is my only ally and confidante in this bizarre and secluded life, and I can't stay mad at him forever.

"Is Mom okay?" I ask.

"What do you mean?"

"I don't know, she seems kind of weird and edgy. She just told me she has a job interview today."

"At T.J. Maxx," Walden says. "That clothing store."

Of course, he already knows. He's always been closer with

Mom. More in sync with her moods. I've always been closer with Dad. It's not The Civil War or anything, but there's always been this quiet division in our family. A sense that if things got really bad and we had to split up, the sides have already been chosen.
"She's under a lot of pressure. I think she got a notice from the bank. Something about the mortgage payment being way late. She holds all of this together with pretty much no help from Dad. It's really hard on her."

"I know. I live here too."

"And all your stuff about wanting to go to school doesn't help much."

I shrug.

"Do you still want to go?"

"Yeah."

"I can't believe you want to go sit in some room and be part of a system designed to homogenize your thinking and steer you toward an average life."

"I just want to see what it's like."

"I'll tell you what it's going to be like. The classes are going to be too slow. The kids are all going to be assholes who think homeschooled kids are aliens. There's going to be bullying and backstabbing galore. And now that you have a nose ring and wear purple lipstick, believe me, you'll have a lunch table all to yourself."

I'm not even totally sure what this means, but it's definitely time to change the subject.

"Are you going to show me how to use the 4-Track, or what?"

Walden stands up. "I'm a man of my word. But I swear to God, if you break it."

"I won't! Jesus, I'm not an idiot."

"That's debatable."

Track Three
A Partnership is Born

This just in from the front—recording is way harder than it looks. Not so much the playing music part of it. That's the easy part. Microphones don't really scare me. But I've always recorded after my dad and Walden have set everything up and my only job is to do take after take until they say it's right. The hard part, I'm learning, is getting the stupid microphones positioned properly and the levels right.

The Tascam 4-Track isn't complicated to use. In theory. Plug in. Hit record. Play. Listen. If you don't like what you record, do it again. Easy enough. But no matter how much I toy with the angle and position of the microphone, the volume of the amplifier, the treble and bass knobs on the control panel, or my singing dynamics, my demos come out sounding imbalanced, fuzzy, and pretty much terrible.

And my songs are not complicated. That's what's killing me. They're the opposite of complicated. And it's driving me crazy that I can play Beethoven's Moonlight Sonata, but I can't get a two-minute rock song with only six chords to sound right.

It's not that I want perfection or polish, either. Hardly. Some of my favorite songs from *Blowin' My Mind Like a Summer Breeze,* like "Joyride" and "Deeper Than Beauty," have a just hit record and let's see what happens kind of feel about them, which is what I'm after. But my demos just sound sloppy.

Which means I have no choice but to ask Walden for help. Again. Which he loves.

He follows me into the back yard, then, one at a time, we climb the rope ladder and step into the stiflingly hot and cramped confines of the tree house.

"I'll help you if I can hear what you're recording," he says, plopping down on the loveseat, which is covered by my sleeping bag.

"Why does everything have to be a transaction? Can't you do something nice for your sister without anything in return? You're such a capitalist."

He doesn't respond, but his face relaxes a bit, and as he scratches at the thin layer of stubble on his chin, I can tell I'm getting through to him.

"I'm not sure you should be spending so much time up here," Walden says, fanning the air, "you're going to fry your brain." Slapping at a mosquito on his neck, he adds, "Unless you die of malaria first."

"It's not that bad," I say, "the heat doesn't really bother me."

This is a lie. It totally bothers me. I'm slowly being roasted like a chicken on a spit, and I barely slept last night it was so hot.

I tune my guitar, watching as Walden surveys my recording set up. A small Fender amp with a microphone lying on the floor in front of it. A vocal microphone on a stand pointed off to nowhere. My cherry red Telecaster.

He chuckles to himself. "You are aware that there's a real recording studio right over there, right?"

"Are you going to help me or not? For once in my life, I want to do something that doesn't involve Mom and Dad, okay?"

"What are you recording, anyway?"

"Just some songs I wrote."

"I didn't know you were writing songs."

"Well, now you know."

Cracking his knuckles loudly, pop-pop-pop, he ponders the auditory possibilities. He's always been a gear head, my brother, at ease among tangles of wires and adjustable knobs. Like my dad, there's something about the recording process that thrills and excites him.

Pointing to the floor, he says, "Well, for one thing, you're never going to get a good sound with the mic in that position. It needs to be on a stand. Plus, you don't want to put it dead center. Off to the side is a little better. And I'll get a pop screen for the vocal mic." I don't understand all the details of what he's saying, but I can feel his excitement. "And maybe a compression pedal so you can control the volume better on the guitar and it won't come through as hot. That amp is pretty bright." He adjusts the amp's tone knobs. "And let's get some more midrange too. Play me a little sample of what you have so far."

Reluctantly, I play him around thirty seconds of my latest attempt, the nineteenth, if my math is correct, at bringing "Ordinary Girl" to life. I hit the stop button halfway through the chorus.

"Did you record the vocals and the guitar at the same time?"

"Yes."

Walden slaps his forehead.

"You don't have to?"

"Rainey. No. That's the whole point of having multiple tracks. You can put the guitar track on one, and then sing over it on another. Doing them separately, you can get a way better sound, and then you can focus on singing without having to nail the guitar part at the same time. You're not making a live album. Were you paying any attention to my tutorial?"

"Yes," I say. But, if I'm being honest, most of it sailed right over my head.

"Believe it or not," Walden says, tapping the Tascam, "this isn't too far off from what the Beatles used to record *Sergeant Pepper's*."

"Really?" I look at the Tascam, which is about a foot by a foot-and-a-half and about as thick as a tray of brownies.

"I mean, this is way smaller and simpler than what they were using, of course. But it's just four tracks like they had." He sounds excited. He's hooked. "Play me the rest of the song."

"If you make fun of it, I swear," I say, but he holds up his hands in surrender.

"I will withhold all judgment. I am merely a humble engineer."

Standing there while my high standards brother listens to my song makes me want to vomit. It feels like being looked at naked. When the song is over, he smiles and nods his head.

"I remember this," he says.

"What?"

"The lyrics. When Mom said that to you at school that day. When you said you didn't want to be homeschooled anymore, and you guys had that fight about being ordinary. I guess art borrows from life."

I shrug. I guess it does.

"Did you play to a click?"

"No."

"Would you?"

I wonder for a moment if Nirvana recorded *Nevermind* using a metronome.

"I guess."

"What else do you want on here? Bass?"

"Yeah."

"Drums?"

"Eventually. And backing vocals. I have the arrangement in my head."

"Okay," he says, standing up, "let me run over to the studio and grab a few more things if it's okay with Dad. You're sure I can't talk you into doing this over there? Or in the house? Even if we record in the bedroom, it's going to sound ten times better."

I shake my head and point toward the floor. Walden is halfway out the door when he stops. "That's a really cool song, Rainey."

I think this might be the best compliment I've ever gotten, and I can't stop a huge smile from taking over my whole face.

A partnership is born.

Track Four
The Treehouse Tapes

Within a week, we've recorded three full songs. Walden insists I record my guitar parts using a click track, which I object to at first because I'm nervous my guitar playing isn't steady enough. But Walden promises it will make it easier to add drums and bass later—which it really does. When you play to a metronome, all the parts fit together more neatly because everything is locked into the same tempo. What surprises me the most is how much Walden seems to want to make it sound like I want it to sound—not how he wants it to sound. I was afraid his taste and musical preferences would sabotage the sound I'm chasing in my head, but they don't.

Going on and on, he talks constantly about classic recording sessions, especially *The Basement Tapes*, which are these legendary recordings made by Bob Dylan and The Band in a basement somewhere in upstate New York. He plays them for me, and though I've never been able to stand the sound of Bob Dylan's voice for some reason, it's exactly the sound I'm going for. A little rough, but in a good way. Loose, but tight.

"The thrown together feel is what's so cool about it," he says. "But it's kind of an illusion. And it's harder to get that sound than it might seem. Especially in a damn treehouse."

One of the first tools he adds to the mix is a distortion pedal, a bright green Ibanez Tube Screamer he got from my dad's guitar pedal stash.

"What's that do?"

"You said you wanted the guitar to have more edge, right?"

"Yeah."

"Check this out. Play something."

I strum a G power chord.

"Okay, now stomp on the pedal and hit that chord again."

When I drop my black Chuck Taylor on the silver stomp pad and hit a fresh G, I'm greeted by a blast of crunchy distortion that sends a thrill raging through my belly and out my fingertips. I can't stop smiling. I think I'm officially in love with distortion.

"Whoa."

"Told you."

"That was awesome."

Contrary to my assumptions, Walden isn't actually president of the Anti-Distortion Society. "It just has to be used right."

We listen to Led Zeppelin and T-Rex. We listen to The Who and "Helter Skelter" off the Beatles' *White Album*. I even play him some songs by Nirvana and Soundgarden and The Breeders that I like.

"I guess they don't suck too bad," Walden concedes.

Over the next two weeks, we swim in the lake, eat hot dogs, record my songs, and not much else. It's the best I've felt since I met Juliet. And it's nice to feel closer to my brother again. I hate when we're mad at each other because we're all we have.

Over the past year or so, I've occasionally worried that Walden and I don't like each other as much as we used to. Not that we can't get along. That we wouldn't be friends if we met randomly instead of being brother and sister.

But watching him turn knobs and position microphones, watching him put the perfect touches on my songs—he becomes my brother again. My lifelong roommate. The boy who used to read me *Matilda* and *James and the Giant Peach* when I had insomnia when I was a little girl. Walden has always been a talented drummer, and he's become a really good guitar player, but I think he might be a recording genius. I can hardly believe the sounds he's able to achieve on such basic equipment. A console you could fit in your backpack. Even more so, there's a tenderness and care he gives to the process. He wants to get it right almost more than I do.

"I think we can do better," becomes the running joke. Let's try it one more time.

Aside from that first compliment about "Ordinary Girl," though, he rarely comments on the quality of the songs themselves. I want to ask him all the time whether he likes them or not, but I'm too afraid of what he'll say, that he'll say they aren't very good. Just teenage crap.

With Walden's prodding, I agree to add keyboards to half the songs, and acoustic piano to a couple of tracks, "Secret Star" and "A Quiet Place."

"Rainey, you're the best piano player I know. You only started playing guitar five minutes ago. It would be truly idiotic not to put any piano on some of these."

So, we stage clandestine recording sessions at the living room piano while Mom is at work and Dad's in the studio.

Oh yeah, Mom got a job at T.J. Maxx. She wasn't kidding. She works four days a week and it makes her even more miserable.

It's not until we're recording the last of my nine songs that Walden asks, "What are you going to do with these demos, anyway? Hell, you just made an album, Rainey."

We're celebrating in the treehouse with Cokes and a box of

Little Debbie Oatmeal Cream Pies. We're both barefoot in shorts and T-shirts, glossed with sweat from the heat.

"I don't know," I confess. And I don't. The Rolling Stones make albums. And my parents. Bonnie Raitt makes albums. I don't make albums. Do I?

Walden reaches out his Coke can, and I lightly knock mine against his.

"To The Treehouse Tapes," he says.

"The Treehouse Tapes?"

"Like *The Basement Tapes*. Only in a treehouse."

"I get it. Clever."

"Until you think of something better."

The Treehouse Tapes. I say the name a few times in my head. *The Treehouse Tapes.*

I unwrap another Oatmeal Cream Pie and take a big bite, the marshmallow sweet and chewy between my teeth. I feel utterly content. And yet, I wish Juliet was here. She'd say the perfect thing. Something funny and wise and cool.

Adding the album to my list of first things feels good.

Things I Did for the First Time When I was Fifteen.

1. Kissed someone.
2. Pierced my nose.
3. Wrote my first song.
4. Got my first tattoo.
5. Made my first album.

Five things already. Not too bad. Look at me go.

That night, during family meeting, Mom announces that she and Dad talked about it and...drum roll please.

"You can go to school," Dad says.

"If you still want to go," Mom says.

"I do."

"But you know it starts next week, right?"

"Yes," I say, swallowing. Next week feels really soon. I'd been counting on them saying yes, but it's not until right now that I allow the reality of it to hit me.

"Then go. I hope it's everything you want it to be," Mom says. I try to read her tone and her facial expression, but there's too many different emotions to sort through. Anger, sadness, fatigue, acceptance.

"What does this mean for the band?" Walden asks.

"What band?" Mom says, then gets up and goes into the kitchen. I hear her start crying softly.

That night as I'm trying to sleep in the stifling heat of the treehouse, beneath the sound of crickets chirping, beneath the steady pulse of my own breath, I hear Dad playing acoustic guitar softly, out there serenading the night. He starts singing and it makes me feel incredibly sad, but I don't know why. I'm getting what I want, but I feel sad all the same. Me going to school and Dad's stage fright means that, for the moment anyway, The Cobb Family Band is no more. The storied duo of Luce and Tracy Cobb, who graced the cover of *Rolling Stone* and had a hit single once upon a time, are no more. Just like that. Somehow it doesn't feel right that something that took so long to build should be so easy to destroy.

I feel like Dad and I ran for the lifeboats and left my mom and Walden stranded on a sinking ship. Or maybe Dad and I are on the sinking ship and Mom and Walden got the lifeboats. It's hard to tell who's on the sinking ship. Is there a sinking ship? Never mind. Maybe it's a bad analogy.

Who cares what anyone thinks? That's what Juliet would say. In a letter the other day, she said *you can't let anyone get in the way of what you really want. Your dreams are too important.* I wonder if she knows how dumb that really sounds. As if life is just a fortune cookie. And yet, isn't that exactly what I'm doing? When you hurt other people, even if you don't want to, does it make you a bad person?

I have the urge to go out there so I can hear Dad better. To be closer to the sadness. To sit at his feet and bathe in it.

I want to ask him, *are you okay, Dad? Are you ever going to be okay again? How can we fix you?*

Just don't stop playing. Never stop playing.

Track Five
Are You Joining a Biker Gang?

"Oh my God, what is that noise!"

I can't see Mom yet, but I can hear her disgruntled, disapproving shout just fine. I click off my stereo, which was blasting Rage Against the Machine, a band Juliet told me about in her last letter. Their music is pretty intense at first, but I kind of love it. Cursing under her breath, I can hear Mom struggling on the rope ladder, the old oak tree creaking as she climbs it, cursing right back.

It's Sunday. School starts tomorrow. As in, the day after today. As in tomorrow I have to wake up early and go to a real school for the very first time. My euphoria has given way to steadily increasing terror and part of me wants to say I was only kidding, let's keep things the way they are instead. Ha!

I'm looking at a copy of the new *Rolling Stone*. Hootie and the Blowfish are on the cover with the headline, "Sex, Golf, and Rock and Roll." The guys in Hootie look like computer programmers.

"What was that music?" Mom says, stepping in the treehouse, fanning herself from the heat.

"Just some band."

"You used to have such good taste in music."

I shrug. Everything with Mom and me lately turns into a fight and I'm not in the mood.

"I have a present for you."

"A present?"

Reaching into her back pocket, Mom pulls out *Blowin' my Mind Like a Summer Breeze*. I feel my eyes open all the way.

"I think you should have this back," she says and hands me the tape.

"Really?"

"Really."

I look at Juliet's handwriting. I think about her pen moving across the paper. The way she cut the palm tree picture just so. How carefully she chose the songs. The love she put into it. All for me and only me.

"Did you listen to it?"

"I did. All of it. A couple of times."

"And?"

"Well. There's some songs on there that I'm not thrilled about my fifteen-year-old daughter listening to..."

"But?"

"But I can also admit that I might have overreacted a little bit."

"A little bit?"

She shakes her head in annoyance. "I'm not trying to fight, Rainey. I'm trying to do something nice. Can't you see the difference?"

"Sorry. Thanks, Mom."

Even in the dimly lit treehouse, Mom's long red hair seems shiny. I can smell her green apple shampoo and a hint of her flowery perfume.

"Growing up happens by degrees, Rainey, not all at once. I

know that's hard, but it's supposed to be that way. It will get easier."

No, it won't.

"Anyway, c'mon, we're going shopping."

"Shopping? For what?"

"For school clothes. And supplies. I thought you could use some stuff before your new adventure."

We drive to the mall. At J.C. Penny, I pick out some black jeans, a black sweatshirt, and black tank tops.

"Are you joining a biker gang that I don't know about?" Mom says.

We get cups of frozen yogurt, then I pick out some band T-shirts from Spencer Gifts. A new pair of black Chuck Taylors.

"Are you going to get anything that isn't black?"

"You're the one that said I could pick out what I wanted."

"I know, I know. But you should get at least a *couple* of nice things." She steers us into the Gap and makes me try on a pair of light brown khakis, a white button-down, and a lime green V-neck sweater that I wouldn't wear under pain of torture. "For days when you want to look nice."

Another mother-daughter combo saunters into the Gap. The complete opposite of me and my mom, they both have shining blonde coifs and wear preppy outfits with lots of stripes and interesting colors that are probably named flamingo and avocado.

"Jesus, look at these two," Mom says, and we share a moment of laughter.

"They look like experimental twins who escaped from a government lab," I say.

Still, it's hard not to feel a little jealous as I watch them go around the store together, best friends who laugh at inside jokes and hold clothes up to each other's bodies.

"Can we afford all this?" I ask at the checkout, watching Mom count out bills from a stack. "I've never gotten this many new clothes before."

"Let me worry about that."

In addition to working at T.J. Maxx, Mom has also started teaching piano lessons to a string of little kids who come and go from my house as Mom teaches them finger positioning, ear training, treble and bass clef. And my dad has started selling his homemade woodworks on consignment at local stores and from a display at the end of our driveway advertising *Luce Cobb Woodworks: Carved Birds, Birdhouses, Bookcases, Commissions.*

I know it makes my mom miserable to have to work a regular job, and I want to ask her about it, but I'm afraid it won't help. That it will just lead to another fight and make her feel bad. So, I don't. I feel guilty that I'm a big part of why her career is on hold, but I don't know what to do about that either. I keep thinking about something Juliet said to me one day.

"Rainey, you're fifteen," she said.

"I know."

"No. Listen to me. You're *fifteen*. Just, try to remember that. You only get to be a kid once, no matter what your parents say."

I wasn't totally sure what she meant, but I think I'm starting to figure it out.

Mom and I drive to an office supply store, and I wander the brightly lit aisles, not knowing what to do. Eventually, I pick out brand new binders, folders, spiral bound notebooks, pencils, pens, erasers, and even a small calculator. For homeschooling, all I've ever had is a huge notebook and a plastic folder. Having so many *new* things feels strange, but I can't deny I love the smell of them, the newness of them, smooth and unmarked. I picture myself sitting in a line of desks surround by other kids, then reaching into my backpack and pulling out my supplies when I need them. How they'll look just like the ones the other kids have. How good that will feel.

"Thanks for letting me get all this stuff," I say, nodding down at my full basket.

"Well, you're going to need it. And I know how important it is to you to fit in."

"Not really," I say, but that's a total lie.

"I don't mean it in a bad way," Mom says. "Fitting in isn't always a bad thing."

"You said being ordinary and fitting in was for everybody else, not for us."

"I know. But people say a lot of things, don't they? Parenting is a messy business. And so is adolescence, if you hadn't noticed."

In the furniture section, we sit down in comfy leather recliners and put our feet up. "Not everything I say is an accusation," she says. "I just meant it's going to be a new experience."

"I know."

"And it might take a little while to get your feet under you."

"I know."

"And make friends."

"I know."

"Well, then I guess I'll stop talking since you already know everything."

At that moment, the same mother-daughter combo from the Gap walks past us. They must be working the same circuit. They haven't lost any steam. Still smiling, still pointing. Still best friends. I want to run over and scream in their faces. Or ask them the secret to how they get along so well.

I'm not sure which one.

That night I sit in the treehouse listening to Juliet's mix, the flow of the songs as familiar as if I'd heard them yesterday. I keep the Polaroid Juliet took of the wall after she traced our hands in my backpack and take it out while I write her a letter. The color is already starting to fade a little. Looking at it always makes me feel better, those two outlined hands, reaching, nearly touching.

Dear Juliet,

It's officially my last night as a homeschooled kid.

In the morning, I'm going to school. Those are words I never thought I'd say. Part of me feels excited, but a stronger part of me feels scared. I keep imagining all these moments where I won't know what to do or say. I know that probably sounds stupid but it's true. My dad says that when the moments come, I'll know what to do and what to say. That the right words and instincts are inside of me, ready and waiting. I hope he's right. My dad and I have gotten closer lately, but my mom and I keep getting further apart.

I don't know if you know this, but I like to make lists. It's what I do when I can't get my

mind to shut up. Here's one I made earlier today.

Things I Hate About my Mom (lately)

1. *She hates the music I listen to.*
2. *She hates that I have a nose ring.*
3. *She hates the way I dress.*
4. *She hates everything I say.*
5. *She hates that I broke up the band.*

You know what? I think I have the title wrong. It should actually be Things My Mom

Hates About Me.

We always think about hating our parents. I mean, not hating them forever, but just for a little bit while they adjust to seeing us as real people. But it never occurred to me that they might hate us right back. Do you think they ever do? That would be an interesting plot twist.

Sorry, this is turning into a depressing letter.

I'll write again soon to let you know how school goes.

Rainey

P.S. My mom gave me your mix back!

P.P.S. You said in your last letter that you were trying to quit smoking for swimming. How's that going? I'm rooting for you.

Track Six
Lying is Easier

Introducing Rainey Cobb, the newest member of the sophomore class at Green Valley High School.

The crowd goes wild.

Actually, nobody goes wild.

As I walk the hallways, thin blue lockers on all sides and gleaming tile beneath my feet, looking down at the pink paper schedule my guidance counselor gave me, I'm both glad but also kicking myself that I turned down her offer to walk me to my first class. I'd feel like a loser being escorted, but then at least I'd know where I was going.

My backpack sags with the weight of all my new supplies, and I suddenly feel self-conscious of their newness. My stomach is in knots, and I wish I'd taken my dad up on his offer to make me breakfast instead of settling for a banana while mom drove me to school.

Though of course they aren't, everyone seems to be looking at me, and I definitely hear the words "new kid" and "nose ring" muttered more than once as I pass. But, all the same, no one trips me or puts a "kick me" sign on my back or slaps my books out of my hands and runs away laughing.

The school is nicer than I expected. Well-used, but bright,

clean, and spacious. The bathrooms gleam and smell reassuringly of chemicals.

In almost every class, we sit in circles and play awkward, get-to-know-you games designed to ease everyone into the new school year. The most common version of this game involves introducing yourself, then saying what you did over the summer. I soon realize, though, that these games are designed to ease all the *normal* kids into the new school year. Weirdos and homeschooled kids who grew up on the road be warned—this game is not for you!

In homeroom, when I say, "I was on tour most of the summer," all I get is blank, confused stares from everyone.

"Oh, that sounds so interesting, on a tour of what?" my homeroom teacher asks, sounding genuinely enthusiastic. He's an upbeat, clean-shaven guy named Mr. Larson who has shoulder length brown hair and leans way forward like what you're saying is the most important thing he's ever heard.

"Just lie," a girl with short hair and a white Adidas hat says to me in the hallway after homeroom.

"What?"

"During those stupid games, if you don't know what to say? Just lie. Remember how I said I went snorkeling in Mexico this summer?"

"Yeah."

"Total bullshit. I haven't been to Mexico since I was two. First rule of high school, lying's easier."

This is something Juliet would say, and it makes me like this girl immediately.

"I'm Rachael Pena," she says. "My parents always insist that I introduce myself using my first and last name. That's why I did that."

"Oh. Hi. I'm Rainey. Cobb."

And presto, a friend.

Starting that day, I begin having lunch with Rachel and her twin sister, Clara. The cafeteria food is as greasy and delicious as I dreamed it would be, including French fries with every meal. Chicken patties and fries. Pizza and fries. Salisbury steak and fries. Beef burritos and fries. Health tip: it's probably not wise to eat fries with *every* meal. And when my pants start feeling tight, I start mixing in regular visits to the salad bar.

Rachel and Clara are both pretty and athletic, with long, straight black hair, tiny waists, and muscular arms and legs full of shadows and slopes. They finish each other's sentences and often seem to share a single brain between them. They also consume an alarming amount of ketchup. Each day, they get a separate plate just for the ketchup for their fries that they douse with salt before dipping. For some reason, they're not the sort of kids I thought I would be friends with, but they don't know anybody here either and we bond over being the new kids. Me new to school, them new to *this* school. The twins moved to Vermont from Brooklyn over the summer because their mom got a job teaching economics at the University of Vermont. They say they've never seen so many trees or so much tie-dye in their lives.

"We heard everybody here is high all the time," Rachel says.

"All the time," Clara says.

"Is that true?"

"Yeah, is it true?"

"I don't know," I say.

Since I imagined myself a mostly friendless pariah, I feel lucky to have friends already, but after a few days, I notice that all Rachel and Clara talk about is soccer, a game I've never played in my life, which, it turns out, sounds pretty ridiculous when you say it out loud to girls who live and die for the sport.

"Like, ever?" Clara asks.

"Not even for fun?" Rachel asks.

"My family isn't really into sports," I say.

"What is your family into, then?"

"Yeah, what are they into?"

"I don't know. Music, I guess. And books."

That's when it hits me. They don't know who Luce and Tracy Cobb are, do they? That means they don't know who I am. Don't get me wrong, my parents aren't Bill and Hillary Clinton, and even I know my parents' fame is waning compared to what it used to be. But still. I think it's the first time in my entire life where someone meets me without knowing who my mom and dad are and doesn't look at me like I'm their well-trained side kick.

Confession #6: Public school is way different than I thought it would be.

First off, it's full of utterly bizarre routines that might make sense if we were six, but given that half the school can drive and some of the kids are old enough to fight in wars, seem asinine and more than a little embarrassing.

Daily attendance? *Why wouldn't you be here when you were supposed to be?*

The pledge of allegiance? *Don't you know the country is run by corporations and fascists?*

Bathroom pass? *You need to prove you're going to the bathroom? Where else are you going to go?*

Homework detention? *Why wouldn't you do your homework?*

Are public school kids irresponsible by nature so no one trusts them, and they need draconian policies to keep everyone from going crazy and burning the place down?

Some routines feel designed just to make me happy. The daily journal prompt in English, for one, writing ideas in my brand-new notebook. Getting things out of my locker, for another. Call me crazy, but I love stopping by my locker and trading books and supplies for one another throughout the day. Sometimes I stop to open the padlock for fun. And for some reason, I love that from the first moment on the first day, when she says, "Bonjour, class," my French teacher speaks to us only in French. Literally not a word of English. While it seems to freak everyone else out, I love the feel of exotic new words as I discover and memorize them. We're encouraged to choose a special French name for class, and I quickly choose Colette, after the writer. I write Colette at the top of my papers, answer to Colette when I'm called on in class. Even the simplest French words sound so much more interesting than their English equivalents, as if they must mean more than just one thing. Au revoir. L'amour. A bientot. Bonjour. Fromage.

Who wouldn't rather eat *fromage* than cheese? Or rather ride in a *voiture* than a car?

Walden was right, though. Most of the classes feel pretty easy compared to what I'm used to. Sort of watered down, thinned out, as if the teachers would go deeper into the topics and subject matter, but they know the students can only handle so much and they don't want to overwhelm them.

Still, the teachers are earnest and kind. Kind of saints, actually. And they're almost aggressively invested in our success. When people in class are being disrespectful or someone doesn't understand something, many of them seem to take it personally. It makes me feel bad for them. I never thought about what it would be like to be a teacher before, but it seems like the hardest job in the world to me.

And though my memory is a huge help when I'm memorizing French vocabulary or important events from the American Revolution, it occasionally gets me in trouble too.

Here's what I mean. One day, we're reading aloud from

Macbeth in Honors English, which is the only class that feels really challenging. My teacher, Ms. Ofalko, whose biting sarcasm and obvious brilliance scared me at first but is starting to grow on me, actually challenges our thinking. Makes us defend our positions. Inspires us to read closely. Constantly sends us back to the text to find proof to back up our ideas. Anyway, she picked people to stand in front of the class and read from *Macbeth* Act II, which we read for homework.

"We'll start with Scene 1. Short, but with one of the most important and brilliant speeches Shakespeare, or anybody to ever pick up a pen I might add, ever wrote," Ms. Ofalko says.

Because Ms. Ofalko says she likes to subvert gender norms, which I think is code for she likes to make us uncomfortable, I'm assigned the role of Macbeth and find myself in front of the class sandwiched between two linebacker-sized males who I might as well call Fleance and Banquo because I don't know their real names.

I'm two-thirds through an utterly monotone and uninspired performance of the "Is this a dagger I see before me?" speech when Ms. Ofalko shouts "STOP!" so suddenly that I expect to find one of my classmates on the floor having a seizure.

"Stop. Right. There," Ms. Ofalko says, only now I can clearly see she's looking right. At. Me.

What did I do? Was I reading the wrong part? More importantly, can I run out the door without anyone noticing? My heart pounds as Ms. Ofalko slowly walks up the aisle toward the front of the room, stalking me like prey.

"How did you do that?" she asks, stopping right in front of me.

"Do...what?"

"You said most of the speech without looking at your text.

You were looking off to the side or up at the ceiling almost the whole time. I was watching you."

Was I? I honestly don't know.

"Did you have to memorize this speech at your old school?"

"She was homeschooled, Ms. Ofalko," a boy says.

"Then at home?"

I shake my head no.

"Have you performed this speech before?"

I shake my head no again.

"But certainly, you've read *Macbeth* before?"

What's the right answer? Yes? No? I have no idea. Somebody help.

"No."

"How many times did you read this scene last night?"

"Um, twice? I think."

Ms. Ofalko puts one of the arms of her glasses into her mouth and studies me like a curious specimen she can't quite identify. She has curly brown hair and bright hazel eyes that are full of wonder and big questions.

"You're telling me that you read this for the first time last night, only read it twice, and casually committed it to memory?"

I want to vanish into smoke. Since that's not an option, I shrug.

Tucking her book under her arm, Ms. Ofalko grips my shoulders forcefully, then grins widely and gushes, "That is one of the *coolest* things I've ever seen!" She turns to the class and says, "Ladies and gentlemen, we have been gifted a genius from the homeschool gods!!"

One boy says, "That was insane, I totally saw her not looking at her book too, and I was like…what?"

"Continue!" Ms. Ofalko shouts.

Aside from the *Macbeth* situation, the near-constant nose

ring stares, annoying questions about being homeschooled, and occasionally getting lost on my way to places I've already been, a month passes without major incident. I gradually learn my way around. I learn the names of the kids in my classes so I can say hi back when they say hi in the hallway, which they never do. I have lunch every day with the Pena twins and listen to them talk about their soccer matches and how unfair the referees are.

"This league is so freaking rigged!"

"So freaking rigged!"

I do my homework at night and tell my parents my day was good when they ask.

I describe my first weeks of school in long, overly detailed letters to Juliet. She writes back somewhat shorter letters and says that I should consider myself lucky. That she can't seem to avoid drama no matter how hard she tries. She tells a story about how a boy in her math class was copying off her paper during a quiz but when she told him to stop, they both got in trouble. And then she got mad and called the teacher an asshole, which led to predictable consequences.

Sometimes nothing in this world feels fair, she writes.

Walden asks if I've written any more songs that we can record, but I haven't. School sucks up pretty much all my energy. Most nights I'm so tired that I start nodding off after dinner and go to bed early.

"Be honest," Walden says. "It sucks, right?"

"It doesn't suck."

"But it's not that great?"

"It's good. I like it. It's only September, Walden. I'm still settling in."

His curiosity is obvious, and though he would never admit it, it makes me wonder if he's actually a little jealous. If part of him wishes he could come too. Walden is technically a senior this year, and an image flashes in my mind of him walking across a stage and accepting a diploma.

He and Mom have been rehearsing with some new musicians and are planning a tour of the Northeast in late October into early November. They have a new band name and everything (Richmond, for the Vermont town where my parents grew up), but we don't talk much about it.

Dad and I go fishing on the weekends. Most of the time we catch one or two perch, and every time I touch one, they feel a little less disgusting in my hands.

"How's school *really* going?" he asks me, as if I'm holding back.

But I'm not.

"It's good, Dad," I tell him. "I swear."

All my worst fears involved being at the center of bullying schemes designed to ruin what little self-esteem I have. But I've probably watched too many John Hughes movies because the truth is that people mostly ignore me.

I do feel lonely sometimes, as if I'm caught between two worlds, and I don't really fit into either.

With Mom's prodding, Dad has started going to therapy, but he doesn't talk about the sessions. The most he'll say is that they're "interesting." He's still working on his Christmas album, and I sing on some of the tracks, adding vocals to "White Christmas" and "The Christmas Song." We laugh and I know Mom is going to love it.

I dread gym class and keep my arms folded over my chest during torturous games of basketball and volleyball and dodge ball, aggressive boys laughing like crazed lunatics as they pelt me as hard as they can, screaming, "You're out!!"

The sight of a six-foot tall boy with dodge ball glory in his eyes is truly a frightening thing to behold.

I am many things, but athletic is not one of them. And you know what? I don't really care. Sports are stupid. There, I said it. I hate gym so badly that I even ask my guidance counselor, Mrs. Putty, if I can get my gym credit in some kind of independent study. "Can I write a paper or do a project or something?" But Mrs. Putty informs me that all students need two full PE credits to graduate. "My advice, sweetie, is just get through it and try to have some fun. It won't last forever."

Track Seven
We're Looking for a Keyboard Player

Along with my English teacher, Ms. Ofalko, my homeroom teacher, Mr. Larson, is my favorite teacher at Green Valley. Mr. Larson sometimes plays CDs of meditation music or Gregorian chant to help us de-stress, and he has about a million plants in his room. He's constantly babying his jades and ferns and peace lilies with a beautiful pair of leather handled clippers or watering them from an elephant watering can where the water comes out the elephant's trunk.

In homeroom, we do these one-on-one check-ins every week to see how we're doing. Mr. Larson, who drinks green tea all day and wears an endless string of khaki pants and patterned button-down shirts, asks me question after question and listens to me talk about my life, as if he really wants to know. He's like a professional listener, bent forward with his elbows on his knees and his chin balanced on his nested fists. During the check-ins, we sit way over in the corner, far from the group, and turn away to create some semblance of privacy.

I don't mean to, but under the spell of Mr. Larson's bottomless patience and meditation music, I find myself slowly opening up, sharing a little more every time we talk. I talk about my life. I talk about what a big deal it is for me to be coming to school. I talk about my guilt.

"I feel so selfish," I say, telling him about the band, and Mom's job at T.J. Maxx.

"I think you're brave," he says. "You should give yourself permission to be happy and feel proud." I've never thought of it like that.

When he admits that he's known the whole time who my parents are, but that he didn't think it was fair for me to have to carry that burden, I like him even more. During our fourth check-in, something interesting happens. I ask Mr. Larson how his weekend was, and that's when he mentions Matthew for the first time. As if it's no big deal, he says "This weekend, Matthew trained our new puppy, Roxy, to roll over and it was the cutest thing."

I wonder who Matthew is, and if it means what I think it means that they have a puppy together.

"Our dog Django is so old he can't do tricks anymore," I say. "He just sleeps all day."

Mr. Larson keeps a massive bag of lollipops in the bottom left drawer of his desk, and as he's handing me one, a root beer flavored Dum Dum, he lowers his voice to a whisper and says, "By the way, that sort of slipped out. I don't really talk about Matthew to my students, if you catch my drift, and that's the way I'd prefer to keep it. I blame you, you're easy to talk to."

I know this is supposed to make me feel good, and it does. It feels nice to be worthy of someone's trust. But I also can't help but wonder how I'm different than his other students. If Mr. Larson senses something in me that he recognizes. Is that why he told me about Matthew?

During our fifth check-in, a sunny Monday morning in late September, Mr. Larson, sipping his green tea, asks me if I'm thinking about trying out for the fall musical, *Oklahoma!*

"Try outs are next week," he says. "Rumor has it you're quite a talented singer."

I shrug. "How's Matthew?" I ask, eager to change the subject. "And Roxy?"

"They're fine," he says, "but let's keep this about you, Rainey."

"I've seen the posters in the hallway," I say. "But I've been trying to keep sort of a low profile so far."

"And?"

"Being in the musical is kind of the opposite of keeping a low profile."

"Well, I'm sure you know best," he says, then adds, "but would it hurt to go check it out? You love music so much. You must be curious. And you're the one who said you wished you'd made more friends by now, right? That you were feeling a little lonely?"

"Yeah."

"Well, I have a hunch being involved in the musical might be a chance to make more friends and meet some kids with common interests."

Why did I ever tell him that? Adults remember everything.

"I'll think about it," I say.

A week later, as I'm sitting there in the auditorium on audition day listening to girls sing "Surrey with a Fringe on Top" and boys sing "Oh What a Beautiful Mornin'," most of them way off pitch and with only a wobbly grasp of melody, it occurs to me for the first time what being there really means. It means that if I get up there and sing in front of all these people, really sing, I mean, I will likely end up in a role. Maybe (ok, probably) a lead role. I came to high school to get away from the lead role.

So, in a fit of panic when they call my name, I fake a sudden case of laryngitis and join stage crew.

Musical rehearsals keep me at school later, which means less time at home. And since I'm on crew, there's lots of sitting around, which means lots of hours to get my homework done. I also discovered a secret dejected piano in a back hallway where all the old set pieces and unused props are kept. There are these big metal shelves packed with masks and dragon parts and random doors to nowhere. Everything is blanketed in dust. Sometimes, while we're on break, I play the piano with the mute pedal down and hum melodies and sing little scraps of song. I miss playing piano. And singing. More than I thought I would.

But, if I'm being honest, the best thing about musical rehearsals is they give me countless hours to study every last square inch of Mary Hanson, the statuesque senior girl who's playing the lead role in *Oklahoma!* and is perhaps the most stunning female specimen I've ever seen. No offense to Juliet, of course, but Mary looks like she just stepped off the cover of a magazine. And she can actually sing. Just being near her sends me into an uncontrollable panic, as if I'm being forced to stare at the sun. I can't help it. It's an alarmingly disorienting experience.

One day, before rehearsal starts, I'm in the bathroom washing my hands when Mary breezes in. As usual, my breath catches, and the room pushes in on me. In the mirror, I watch her turn around and begin undoing the buttons on her white Oxford. For a split second, I catch a glimpse of her bare torso and a flicker of her pink lace bra before the T-shirt she's changing into comes down. It's at that moment that she looks up and our eyes meet in the mirror. I'm so flustered that I turn the wrong way and literally walk into a wall.

"Oh my God, are you okay?" she asks.

"Fine!" I announce with way too much gusto, holding my nose and pretty much sprinting out of there.

Talking to daydream-worthy girls is going to take some getting used to.

One afternoon during rehearsal break, I'm sitting at my secret piano singing "The Weight" as softly as I can when a figure flickers in my peripheral vision and I realize I'm being watched. Panicked, I shoot up from the piano bench and begin speeding past the watcher—tallish, male—head down, feet moving. Flight mode, activate!

"Wait! I'm sorry. I didn't mean to scare you. Stop. Please!"

I turn and brace for a scolding from a teacher, but instead see a boy I recognize from the *Oklahoma!* chorus. Evan something, I think. Tall and a little pudgy, he's got broad shoulders, tightly curled blonde hair, big ears, and glasses. A lost member of Hootie and the Blowfish.

"That was amazing," he says.

"Oh, thanks," I say, slightly relieved not to be in trouble. "I wasn't sure if people were allowed to play this piano or not. I just do sometimes during breaks and stuff."

The boy shrugs, as if he's not sure either and doesn't much care.

"It's kind of out of tune," I say.

"Mrs. Deeter sent me back here to find a box of cowboy hats nobody can find, and I got turned around," he says, looking over his shoulder. "I didn't even know this hallway existed. Hey, where'd you learn to play and sing like that? You're really good."

I shrug, which is the same way I've responded to this question since I was five.

"By the way, I'm Evan. Becker."

"I'm Rainey," I say.

"Rai-ney? Whoa, that's a really cool name."

I don't respond, but he's only the second person ever to say that about my name.

"Wait!" he says, raising his hands in triumph. "I know who you are. You're new this year, aren't you? Weren't you home schooled before you came here?"

"Yeah."

"Someone told me you're famous. Or that your parents are famous?"

"They did?"

Guess my secret is out.

"Yeah! They're a band or something. What are their names?"

I hate this part so much. I'll say my parents' names and wait for the gushing response that always comes with being linked to fame, reminding me, once again, that who my parents are is, and will always be, the most interesting thing about me.

On my tombstone, it's going to read: *Here lies Rainey Cobb, no one noticed when or how she died, but her parents were Luce and Tracy Cobb.*

"Mmm, sorry," Evan says, shaking his head when I say my parents' names. He actually seems kind of embarrassed. "I never know who anybody is, though. When people are talking about actors and stuff, I'm always like—*who*?"

That's the moment I know that Evan Becker and I are going to be friends.

"Anyway," he says, "so, I'm in this band. We don't have a name yet or anything. And we're kind of looking for a keyboard player. Do you maybe want to play with us?"

Track Eight
Chicken in Heaven

On a Saturday in early October, I go to Lakeview Cemetery in Burlington with my mom to say hi to my grandmother's grave. It's a weird tradition. Not the paying our respects to Grandma part. The chicken part. I have a bucket of Kentucky Fried Chicken warming my lap as we cruise up 89 North. That's the weird part.

We walk through the grass, past headstones and over grave markers, some of them dating as far back as the early 19th Century, to where my Aunt Becky, my mom's younger sister, is already standing. Way shorter and more petite than my mom, Aunt Becky has short, styled brown hair and wears big sunglasses. My mom has the chicken now and even outside I can still smell its greasy fingerprint on my clothes.

"Hi, Aunt Becky," I say.

"Hi sweetie," she says and wraps me up in a big hug, then holds me by the shoulders and looks me all over. Why do adults reserve the right to appraise us like we're cars or cattle? Is there an age when that stops happening? And can it be soon, please?

I'm wearing black jeans, a black T-shirt, my black Chuck Taylors, and some purple lipstick that I bought at the mall. It's almost the same shade that Juliet wears. Someone at school called me a "Goth" the other day, whatever that means.

"God, look at you, you're a woman, aren't you? Your boobs are already bigger than mine."

"Becky, leave her alone," Mom says.

"And look at that," Becky says. She reaches out and nearly touches my nose ring. "That's new. When did you get that? I like it."

"Over the summer."

"Yeah?" Aunt Becky looks at Mom. "I'm surprised your mom gave you the green light. My sister is hardly the free-loving hippie she used to be."

"Oh, I wasn't consulted on the matter," Mom says, prying the lid off the chicken bucket. "You want a leg or a thigh?"

"Leg, please," I say, accepting my piece of chicken.

"I'll take a leg too," Aunt Becky says and reaches into the bucket. Mom takes a thigh and sets the bucket down.

"Okay, Mom," my mom says, waving at the air with her chicken and taking a bite, "we're here." We all look down at Grandma's grave and eat our chicken in silence. *Rebecca L. Martin, 1919-1983. Beloved mother, wife, and friend.*

The chicken story goes something like this.

My grandmother had breast cancer and toward the end, my mom and Aunt Becky moved in with her and took care of her. I was only three and don't remember any of this. Apparently, though, it was really bad. Grandma didn't know where she was a lot of the time and would mix up her memories and get confused.

Then one day, for a few stolen hours, she was her old self, and the three of them talked like normal. Stepping through thick fog, Grandma could suddenly remember everything. She talked about growing up in rural Pennsylvania and how her father came home from work with coal soot under his fingernails after long days in the mines. About meeting my grandpa one day when she was working as a waitress. About how they wrote letters to each other every single day while he was in the South Pacific during World War II. About how it poured rain and they ate soggy cake on their wedding day and laughed like absolute loons.

And somewhere in all that remembering, she found her appetite. Apparently, all she'd consumed for weeks was juice and vegetable broth, but she told Mom and Aunt Becky how hungry she was. She was less than a hundred pounds by then, her nightgown baggy like a girl wearing her mother's clothes. "Do you think you could get me some chicken?" she asked. "And a Coke?"

My mom and Aunt Becky ran out to KFC and bought a bucket of Original Recipe. As the three of them ate greasy, crispy chicken and slurped down giant sodas, Grandma, with juicy tears sliding down her pale cheeks said, "I sure hope you can get Colonel chicken in heaven."

And so, a tradition was born. Every year, on the anniversary of her death, Mom and Aunt Becky go and eat chicken at their mother's grave in a deep-fried tribute. This is the first year I've been invited into the chicken inner sanctum. It feels good. Grown up, and important somehow.

"Twelve years," Becky says, then hurls her chicken bone into the trees, whose green leaves have turned all manner of orange, red, and purple, so vibrant and explosively colorful they're like a child's imagining of the word "fall."

I watch the chicken leg go, mildly stunned.

"Twelve years," Mom says, throwing her bone after Becky's.

I've finished my piece and stand there holding the pale bone awkwardly by my side.

"Chuck it," Aunt Becky says. "It's okay, we always do it. It's not trash. The animals eat it."

I smile and launch my chicken bone into the woods.

"Good throw," Aunt Becky says, then winks at me. "Welcome to the club, kid."

We each select another piece and stand there eating our chicken. Nobody says much, which feels a little awkward at first, but the longer we stand there, the more I like it. Mom lays the final piece in the bucket, a juicy thigh, on the yellowing grass in front of Grandma's grave.

"Won't a fox get it or something?" I ask.

"Probably," Aunt Becky says.

We walk back to the cars and stand there catching up. Aunt Becky quizzes me about all things public school. I talk about my classes, about the Pena twins, about *Oklahoma!*

"But I'm just on the crew. I'm not the lead or anything."

"You could have been," Mom says. "I still don't know why you didn't try out. You could sing circles around those girls."

I shrug.

"And end up with a huge target on her back," Aunt Becky says, immediately understanding what my mom doesn't. "She's trying to fit in, Tracy."

"Fitting in is overrated," Mom says.

"You said fitting in was good," I say.

"Will you stop quoting me all the time? I meant there are certain situations."

"Easy for you to say," Becky says.

"Moving on," Mom says.

"What else, sweetie?" Aunt Becky asks.

"I might start playing music with some friends from school," I say, telling her about Evan and how he heard me play and sing, then invited me to join his nameless band.

"Oh, that will be so fun," Aunt Becky says. "Playing with people your own age for once."

"Hello," Mom says, "I'm standing right here."

I've hung out with Evan Becker a few times since the day we first met. We agree pretty quickly that we're cut from the same geeky cloth. We both love tunneling unapologetically into the nether regions of music, books, and math. We have spirited arguments about utterly insignificant topics. We argue about the best season (I say fall, Evan says spring), the best pizza toppings (I say sausage and black olive, Evan says extra cheese and pepperoni), the best jelly for PB&J (I say strawberry, Evan says grape), the funniest Monty Python movie (I say *Life of Brian*, Evan says *Holy Grail*).

We never agree, but the never agreeing kind of becomes our thing.

When he finds out I've never played Nintendo, he invites me to his house after school, and we play Mario Kart and laugh for hours. Before long, I'm kicking his ass no matter what character I play with, even Peach and Bowser. It's fun. And, even better, I get to cross more things off my list of things I've never done and add them to my growing list of year-fifteen firsts.

Things I Did for the First Time When I was Fifteen.

6. Went to school.
7. Made friends.
8. Played Nintendo.

One day I'm at lunch with the Pena twins when Evan comes up and asks if he can have lunch with us. He sounds nervous in a way I've never heard before.

"It's a free country," Rachel Pena says.

"Yeah, it's a free country," Clara echoes.

I scoot over and make space for Evan, who sits down so close beside me that our shoulders are touching. I wiggle slightly away, trying not to make it obvious.

"I'm Evan," he says.

"Oh, we know," Rachael and Clara say at the same time.

"Girl, he totally has the hots for you," Clara says after Evan leaves for class.

"Totally."

"We're just friends," I insist.

"Uh, you might want to tell him that," Clara says. "Did you see the way he was looking at you?"

"What way?"

"Girl, please."

"Yeah, girl, please."

"He looks at you like you're an ice cream sundae," Clara says.

"With extra hot fudge and cherries," Rachel adds.

"Gross, you guys," I say, and we all crack up.

Track Nine
Songs About Being a Girl

Band practice happens on Friday nights in Evan's massive basement to the colorful glow of Christmas lights that never come down. There's five of us. I'm the only girl.

For the first few rehearsals, I hang back, watching, waiting. Trying to figure it out. How to be. What to say. Wondering what they think of me. I feel kind of giddy playing music with people my own age, though, like I've wandered onto the set of a movie about a high school band. I play minimal accompaniment on my keyboard to whatever grunge or classic rock song we're covering. Basic voicings. Simple structures. Just trying to fit in and not draw too much attention to myself. It's easy. And fun. Kind of. I think. Actually, I'm not sure.

The boys look at me a lot, but rarely talk to me.

Evan's mom orders us pizza, and I sit quietly while the boys in the band dip their crust in small tubs of ranch dressing and energetically debate what their unwritten music should sound like. They sound pretty ridiculous, but I don't think they know that.

We're splayed out across the biggest sectional sofa on planet Earth. Freddie, who plays rhythm guitar and sings lead vocals, says we should be a cross between The Pixies and Pearl Jam. Max, who also plays rhythm guitar, argues for edgier Soundgarden and

Dinosaur Jr influences. Chris, who plays bass, pushes for less Pearl Jam, more Pavement. Evan, who is the drummer, says, through a mouthful of crust, "I don't really care what other bands we sound like, but I think maybe, um, Rainey should be our lead singer."

I stare at him in disbelief. He warned me he might do this, but I thought he was kidding.

"Yeah right," Freddie says, clearly thinking it's a joke. He has a buzz cut and lots of pimples and looks a little bit like Sid Vicious. When he realizes it's not a joke, he says, "But I'm the lead singer."

"Yeah," Evan says, nudging up his glasses, coughing into his fist, "but only because nobody else can really sing. You're the singer, but you're not *a* singer. There's a difference?"

"No there's not."

"Yeah there is."

I sit up a bit. Set my pizza plate down.

"I thought you liked my voice," Freddie says, sounding hurt now.

"I do," Evan says, though not very convincingly. "But even you said that your voice wasn't that great. That it was kind of whiny. And you have trouble singing on key."

"Yeah, but, I mean," Freddie says, seeming unsure what else to say, adding, "I'm the most natural front man." He looks from one silent face to another in disbelief. What is it with boys and not talking? "Do you want her to be the singer?" he says to Max.

"He says she's really good," Max says.

"You want to have a girl singer?"

Max shrugs. "Is there any more ranch?"

"What about you?" he asks Chris.

"I gotta piss," Chris says, bringing his slice of pepperoni along. I hope he washes his hands, but I'm not overly confident.

Freddie is aghast. "Is this a mutiny or something?"

"It's not a mutiny," Evan says, "we're barely even a band yet."

"Can you even sing?" Freddie asks, turning to me.

"Trust me, she can sing," Evan says.

"I want to hear it from her."

"I can sing," I say.

"Well, let's hear it then."

Evan retrieves his acoustic guitar from its stand and hands it to me.

"Show him," he says. "Play that one you played me."

"Which one?"

I know exactly which one, thinking back to the other day when, between Mario Kart sessions, Evan asked me if I played guitar, but I'm trying to buy myself some time.

"The one from the last time you were over? I forget the name."

"Sunday Kind of Love?"

"That's it. By what's her name."

"Etta James."

"Etta *who*?" Max says, sounding disgusted.

Evan is looking at me in a way no boy has ever looked at me before, as if my face is the answer to a riddle he's been trying to solve for a really long time. I notice the way his ringlet curls are lighter at the tips and darker at the roots.

With a fresh layer of tension added to an already tense room, the boys fan out further so they can listen. Collectively, their odor is musky deodorant meets gym bag. It's a little funny, having all these boys watch me, their eyes ranging from accusatory to curious to adoring. I feel hyper-aware of my surroundings, of the way my bra is scratching against my side and the way my feet feel in my shoes. My adrenaline is pumping, but I'm not nervous. Reading *Macbeth* in front of the class, I'm nervous. In the lunch line, I'm nervous. Around Mary Hanson, I'm NERVOUS. But old habits are hard to break, and when music is involved, I don't get nervous. I tune the guitar, then pluck a G7 chord. I close my eyes. I sing.

"Holy fuck," Max says when I finish.

"Sorry Freddie," Chris says. "You're cooked, bro."

Evan's smile is so wide it swallows his whole face.

"Told you," Evan says to Freddie, but still looking at me.

Freddie quits the band shortly after, declaring he's "going solo" and that he wishes us luck "being led by a girl with a nose ring."

I try to fit into the dynamic of this unnamed band, whose name is endlessly debated but never settled on, but I can never quite make myself the right shape. And except for Evan, who isn't half bad behind the drums, not as good as my brother but capable enough, the fact is that these guys can't really play their instruments for crap. Don't they practice?

One night we're playing "Black Hole Sun" by Soundgarden, Christmas lights aglow, when Chris, the bass player, who plays whatever notes he feels like at random with his brown hair dramatically down over his eyes as if there's a photographer hidden behind the sofa ready to capture his moody essence, pushes me to the breaking point.

"Hold on you guys," I say, waving my arms.

"What?" Chris says, clearly annoyed I stopped the song.

How do I give this guy feedback without making him an ant I'm about to crush? Maybe if I show him.

"Evan," I say, "can you play the verse drum part, but kind of quiet?"

"Um, okay."

I turn up my keyboard and start vamping a simple bass part

with my left hand that's synced up with Evan's bass drum, then lightly comp the verse chords with my right hand.

"Listen to my left hand. Do you hear how I'm following what Evan's doing, especially the bass drum? Making sure they match? Playing steady on the beat. Nothing fancy. Just a steady pulse."

"Yeah. That's what I'm doing."

"Oh, okay," I say. That's so not what he was doing. "Also, do you, like, know what notes you're playing?"

"Yeah," Chris scoffs.

"No, you don't," Max says, leaning against the wall and excavating a pimple on his chin, as if he's been wanting to point this out for a while now.

"I mean, mostly," Chris says. "For me it's more about feel than obsessing about the notes."

I ignore this idiotic comment. "So, this song is in a minor key," I say. "E minor. That's why it has kind of a sad feel." I play the notes of the E minor scale on the keyboard one at a time. "So, like with any song, there's only so many notes that will sound good with the chords in this song."

Chris looks confused and I'm starting to feel like the teacher ruining the fun the boys are having in the back of class. I think when my mom says I'm mature for my age, this is what she's talking about.

In study hall the next day, I make a chart that shows the notes on the first two bass strings up to the twelfth fret, and then one for each song we play, highlighting the notes that will sound good. I may as well have handed him hieroglyphics.

"What is this, homework?"

But it makes him sound a *little* better.

Another Friday night rehearsal. Another endless pizza-crust-dipped-in-ranch digression where the boys debate whether our first international tour should be in Europe or Asia. Apparently, Asians really dig rock and roll, but the chicks are hotter in Europe.

When you're in a band that isn't very good at making music, I'm learning, you end up sitting around and talking a lot instead. I sometimes imagine trying to explain to these boys what my life has been like up to now and how impossible it would be for them to understand.

"What we need are some originals," Chris says.

"Yeah, but does anybody know how to write songs?" Max asks.

Silence.

"Has anybody ever even written a song?" Evan asks.

As if on cue, they all turn to me. I reluctantly admit I wrote a couple songs over the summer.

"But they aren't very good," I say.

"Yeah, right," Evan says. "I'll bet they're amazing."

Before I know it, I'm holding Evan's guitar again, playing "Ordinary Girl" for these boys I hardly know.

"It's about being a girl," Chris scoffs when I'm done as if he has me cornered at last.

"So?" Evan says.

Chris circles his finger. "Uh, look around, dude, we're not girls."

"Rainey's a girl."

"Yeah, but there's more of us. And if our songs are about girls, they should be about dumping girls, or getting over being dumped by girls, not, like, *being* a girl."

"Don't be so immature," Evan says.

"Name me five rock songs about being a girl."

"No," Evan says. "That's stupid."

Chris stuffs a huge bite of crust into his mouth. "It's only stupid because you can't do it," he says, his words garbled as he chews. "Seriously, can anybody do it?"

"I don't see what point you're trying to make."

"The point I'm trying to make is that her song is a unicorn and I don't know if we want a unicorn running our band, that's all."

"She's not running our band. It's one song. A really good song, I might add."

"I'm still waiting for somebody to prove me wrong."

"Stop it."

"Still waiting."

"Oh my God."

"Waiting, waiting, waiting."

"These Boots are Made for Walkin' by Leslie Gore," I begin. "Seether by Veruca Salt. Jolene by Dolly Parton. Dreams by the Cranberries. Silent all These Years by Tori Amos. Fuck and Run by Liz Phair. My Man is a Mean Man by Etta James."

I can see Evan's smile out of the corner of my eye.

"Oh my God, you're even weirder than you look," Chris says, swiping the back of his hand across his mouth.

I keep going just to spite his stupid face. "I'm Every Woman by Chaka Kahn. The Pill by Loretta Lynn. Just a Girl by No Doubt. You Outta Know by Alanis Morrissette. Army of Me by Bjork. Dreams, but by Fleetwood Mac this time." I pause. "Should I keep going? Girls write more rock songs than you think."

"I get it, I get it, I get it," Chris says, waving his arms for me to stop as if I'm a thunderstorm and he forgot an umbrella. I think about how much Juliet would love this moment.

"Oh my God, this band sucks so bad," he says.

"Do you want out?" Evan asks.

"Do you want me out?"

"I'm not saying that."

"It sounds like you're saying that."

"Well, I'm not."

"Are you sure, because it sure sounds like that."

"I said I'm not."

"Look, dude, if you want me out, just say so."

"I'm not saying I want you out, dude, but if you want out, just say it."

"I'm not saying I want out. I'm just saying this band used to be fun before the fucking Queen of Darkness took over, and now it sucks balls."

"Don't talk about her like that," Evan says, sounding angry. Chris nods.

"I get it now," he says. "This is all because you want to bone her. Then you can be the King of Darkness."

"Fuck you!" Evan says.

"Whatever. I quit."

"Me too," Max says.

They both storm right up the basement stairs in synchronized protest, leaving me and Evan alone.

After they leave, Evan and I sit on the couch watching MTV and eating the rest of the pizza. I feel horrible and don't know what to say. I'm pretty sure me joining the band wasn't supposed to end with the band exploding.

The Smashing Pumpkins' video for "Today" is playing and kids are splashing paint across the side of an ice cream truck and laughing like idiots.

"Sorry I scared everybody out of your band," I say. "And you didn't need to stand up for me, you know. I can fight my own battles."

What's strange, though, is that I kind of liked how he stood up for me. Not at first. At first, I felt a little insulted, but now I'm realizing how much of a risk he took in standing up to his friends, and I kind of love him for it. I want to tell him what a nice guy he is, but I remember something Walden told me once about how no guy ever wants to be labeled *nice*. "Nice is a death sentence," he said. "Nice means I wouldn't kiss you with a gun to my head. Nice means there's no way you're ever getting to second base."

Evan shrugs. "I've known those guys since we were little. We have a big fight over something every couple of years."

"Are you sure?"

"Totally sure," Evan says.

I finish my slice and take a sip of my Coke. I need to eat more salads. I think I've packed on fifteen pounds since school started.

"So," I say. "What now?"

"Now we go fishing for new band mates."

"Maybe since we're starting fresh, we should find some people who actually know how to play their instruments?"

Evan laughs. "Now there's a thought. Any ideas?"

"There's this guy in the jazz band I hear is pretty good," I say. "River McRae? I could ask him. He's in my English class."

"Jazz is granny music. I'll ask this kid, James, in my science class. I heard he got a guitar for his birthday."

"Jazz is *not* granny music," I say, feeling annoyed. "And if he just got a guitar, he's not going to be able to play it." Evan is so sweet, but sometimes I feel like I'm his mother. His musical knowledge goes back about as far as Radiohead's first album. "Have you ever heard of John Coltrane? Ornette Coleman? Billie Holiday?"

Evan counts the names off on his fingers, "Um, let me think here for a second, nope, nope, and...nope."

I laugh.

"But I have a hunch they're totally amazing jazz players who you're going to tell me all about."

"The only point I was going to make is that, if you can play jazz, all it really means is that you've practiced a lot. You think Pat Metheny rolled out of bed one day and could just play like that? I'll bet if you gave him the charts to most of the songs we play, he'd laugh at how easy they were."

Don't say it. Don't say it. Don't. Say. It.

"Who's Pat Metheny?"

Track Ten
Something Liberating About Going Too Far

Since I'm really bad at talking to new people, it takes me a few days to find an excuse to exchange actual words with River McRae in English class. But one day, Ms. Ofalko pairs us up for discussion on *The Stranger* by Camus, which we both agree is a seriously weird but very interesting book. I keep trying to find a suitable pause in the conversation that's both long enough to bring up the band, but also has Ms. Ofalko conveniently out of ear shot. I eventually find it two minutes before we're supposed to report our findings of figurative language in part one, chapter six.

"So, you play guitar in the jazz band, right?" I ask.

"Guilty," he says.

"Cool," I say. "Do you know Evan Becker?"

River shrugs. "A little. Not really. I don't think we've talked since fifth grade. Why?"

"We're in a band together," I say, strangling my pencil so hard it hurts, feeling horribly nervous, like I'm trying to ask him out on a date, which I kind of am, "or we're kind of starting a new band. Anyway, we're looking for a guitar player and I wondered if you might want to maybe play with us sometime or something. Or not. It's okay if you don't want to."

"Sure," River says, looking up from his list of similes and

metaphors, "that sounds pretty cool. I can't right away because I have a butt load of rehearsals for jazz band the next couple weeks, but after that I can. Is that okay?"

"Yeah, that's cool."

"Cool," he says.

"Cool."

So, stuck in a holding pattern, Evan and I wait.

I keep doing my homework. Keep writing essays. Keep solving proofs. Keep translating paragraphs from French into English and from English into French and hating gym class with a red-hot passion. Keep talking to Mr. Larson, who mentions Matthew almost every time we talk, describing movies they've recently seen or the totally adorable trick they taught to Roxy. One day, I bravely ask him a question that's been on my mind.

"When did you know that you were…you know?"

Mr. Larson is making us cups of green tea. He keeps a whole little tea kit on his desk, all the supplies neatly tucked in a metal basket: assorted tea bags, honey, sugar packets, hot water kettle. "Honestly, I think I always knew," he says, squirting a thick stream of honey into each of our mugs, and then handing one to me. He glances around to make sure none of the other kids in homeroom are paying attention. "It took me a little while to realize it, but I think deep down I always felt it, even when I was a little kid. Before I knew what it was I was feeling."

I wish I felt so sure.

I keep having lunch with the Pena twins, whose soccer team lost in the first round of the playoffs, leaving both girls despondent and insufferable at lunch. When Evan starts eating with us full time, the Pena twins occasionally abscond to another group of kids instead. It hurts my feelings a little, but I also understand.

Evan talks a lot. Sometimes too much. But he's funny and

kind. And really smart. He's the first boy I've ever been friends with besides my brother. We lie on his bedroom floor and listen to music, our bodies angled in opposite directions, our faces side by side. I play him Bessie Smith. He plays me Dream Theater. I play him Erik Satie. He plays me Tool.

"I wish I could play drums like Danny Carey," he says.

"I wish I could sing like Bessie Smith," I say.

We play lots of Mario Kart. I help him with English. He helps me with chemistry. I have dinner with his family. He has dinner with mine, which Walden teases me about.

"Your boyfriend looks like Lindsay Buckingham circa 1978," he says.

"He's not my boyfriend."

"Maybe you should tell him that."

Why do people keep saying that? Evan and I are just friends. Why is that so hard to comprehend? Can't a boy and girl be friends without it getting weird and the whole world falling apart?

But Evan keeps giving me that look, as if my face is the answer to a riddle.

I keep going to *Oklahoma!* rehearsals every day after school. Keep staring at Mary Hanson, who has an ocean of lush brown hair the color of melted chocolate and huge eyes the exact same color. I think about running my fingers through her hair. Putting my hands on her body. Sometimes the thoughts keep me up at night.

I keep playing the out of tune piano during breaks, and somehow (ahem, Evan), the word gets out. What starts off as an audience of Evan, turns into an audience of Evan and Evan's friend Ryan, which turns into Evan, Ryan, and Ryan's girlfriend Bianca, which turns into anywhere from 5 to 15 cast members who gather around the piano and listen to me play.

"I can't believe you didn't try out for *Oklahoma!*" Bianca says.

"You *totally* would have gotten the lead. No offense to Mary." Others agree.

I wonder what Mary Hanson, who walks around like she was born to be the lead in high school musicals—and I guess she was—would think of this assessment.

Sometimes, Mary comes and listens to me play, though when she does, she sits away from everyone else, perched on top of a pile of old gym mats eating carrot sticks from a plastic bag with her nose in a book. What she doesn't know, though, is that I've been looking at crowds all my life, and I can tell she's only pretending not to listen.

How do I get close to Mary Hanson? There are so many questions. So many obstacles. I'm two years younger. We don't know each other. I'm a girl, etc. I think about all the things that would have to happen for me to be in a position to kiss Mary Hanson, and I might as well be planning a trip to Mars.

Daydreaming about Mary is nice, but in the end, it always brings me back to the one girl—the one person—I have kissed. The one person who, even months after the last time I saw her, is still sewn into the fabric of my mind and crushes my heart with a deep aching something. Juliet.

Things I Did for the First Time When I was Fifteen.

9. Fell in Love

The nights have gotten cool, and one night I'm in the treehouse in my sweatpants thinking about me and Juliet and what we are. Are we anything? I know Juliet's not my girlfriend. Is she? Does kissing someone a few times mean you're a couple? We only spent a week together, and yet, in my heart, that week feels the size of entire years. I know that I want us to be a couple, that I want us to keep kissing, but I don't know how to make that happen. It's impossible in so many ways. There's the problem of geography, of course, but it feels so much bigger than that. I sometimes imagine us making a pact that we're going to tell our families on the same day that we want to be together, and though they'll struggle to understand at first, they'll support us in the end. Easy.

The line between reality and fantasy is getting blurry. But I can't help it.

I put on some music, light a candle, and with my journal in my lap start writing Juliet a long letter as a way to figure out all my feelings. I don't plan on sending it, but I feel the intense need to be honest and I sort of pour my heart out on the page. I tell her how much I miss her. How beautiful she is. How much I wish I could kiss her again and smell her lotion in my hair afterward. How no one I've met even comes close to her. The feelings keep coming, getting bigger and bigger. I fill two pages, a third, a fourth.

At the end, I tell her what I've already realized. That I love her. It slips out of my pen.

I love you.

I read back what I wrote, and though something inside of me knows I've gone too far and said too much, there's also something liberating about going too far. About saying too much. I've held back my feelings my entire life, and I'm tired of holding back.

Riding a wave of courage, I make Juliet a copy of *The Treehouse Tapes*, which she keeps asking to hear, but I've been nervous to share because of how many of the songs are either about her or inspired by her. The next day, though, I ride my bike to the post office, bundle the tape and letter into a small, padded envelope, take a deep breath. And send it.

Track Eleven
A Little Delay

"So, what kind of music do you guys play?" River McRae asks, hefting a Peavey amp up onto a chair and arranging distortion pedals on the carpet floor of Evan's basement.

"We're still sort of trying to figure that out," Evan says. "We had been playing covers. Nirvana. Soundgarden. Dinosaur Jr. The Pixies. Stuff like that."

"So, *a lot* of distortion," River says. He stomps on a white Boss tuning pedal and begins turning knobs. He's wearing jeans with big holes in the knees, a white V-neck T-shirt, a flannel tied around his waist, and red Chuck Taylors.

"We're also trying some original stuff," I say.

"Cool," River says. Clicking off the tuner, his guitar springs to sound. He rattles off a flourish of notes on his Gibson semi-hollow body, his fingers a blur, and something flutters inside me. It reminds me of the first time I heard Simon, Damon, and Chad from the St. Regis Horns. This guy can play.

"Whoa," Evan says.

"Sorry," River says. "Bad habit. Jazz players like notes."

"Anyway, Rainey's an amazing songwriter. And singer. And keyboard player."

Sometimes I hate it when Evan fawns over me.

"And amazing at poetry," River says. "Thanks for your help

in English the other day. That poem made absolutely *no* sense to me. I'm like, what the hell is an urn? After she read my response, Ms. Ofalko was like, 'well said, River, that's very insightful and some of the best thinking you've done all semester.' If only she knew I just wrote down everything you said."

I'll bet River knows who Pat Metheny is. Not to mention, he's sort of amazing looking. Long, silky brown hair that hangs past his shoulders, a slender face, moody French lips. Almost more beautiful than handsome. For the briefest moment, I think about kissing him. Why do I want to kiss everybody lately?

"How did you know that poem so well?"

"My mom."

"You talk to your mom about poetry?"

"Sometimes."

"The only thing I talk to my mom about is what time she's picking me up."

"Okay," Evan says, smacking his hands together, "and we're back to music. What I was about to say is that Rainey has some amazing original songs."

"Well, let's play one."

I walk River through the chord changes to "Ordinary Girl."

"That diminished chord you threw in there is cool," he says.

"Yeah, it gives it some nice tension."

"Totally. Okay, I think I got it. Wanna try it?"

The first time through is pretty rough. Evan's time is all over the place.

"How long have you been playing drums?" River asks.

"Two years," Evan says, nudging his glasses up. He's sweating like a pig and clearly intimated by River. "Sorry, I know I kept speeding up."

We try it again. And again. After the fifth time, River apologizes, saying, "Sorry, that was me that time, I totally overplayed." He nods to himself, plays with his distortion pedals. "Do either of you mind if I try something a little weird? I have this delay pedal that's pretty cool and I kind of want to try it on this song. I think if over the verse section I don't play straight chords but play arpeggios with a little delay it could sound really cool and give it more space."

"I don't know what any of that meant," Evan says, "but give it a try. Rainey, what do you think?"

"Sure," I say, feeling excited by River's curiosity, by the way he's exploring the possibilities in my song. It's an impulse that reminds me of Walden.

The delay instantly opens things up, and suddenly "Ordinary Girl" is what it was always meant to be.

As the volume is fading, we all look at each other and smile without saying anything. There's this long beat where I can tell we're all thinking the same thing. I had almost forgotten how good it feels to make beautiful music with other people.

"Now I guess we just need a cool band name," River says.

After practice, Evan and I sit on his front porch steps and wait for my mom. Above us there's a dark sky blanketed with shimmering points of light. An invisible chorus of crickets chirps in the grass all around. Sometimes when Evan and I are alone together, there's this sort of dramatic silence when I can tell he's thinking really hard about me, about the words he wants to say. And maybe other things. He fidgets. Breathes heavily. Looks at me, then looks quickly away. At first, I sort of liked it. It feels good when someone pays a lot of attention to you, but lately, that silence makes me nervous.

"You going to the Fall Formal?" Evan asks. He picks up a small rock and throws it into the road where it does a few skips and then flies into the tall grass at the edge of the road.

"Probably not," I say, hugging my arms around my knees against the evening chill.

I don't know a thing about high school dances, except that only losers go alone.

"Why? I'm sure tons of people must have asked you by now."

"Yeah, right. Try no one. You're one of the few people at this school who even knows I exist."

Evan laughs softly.

"You really think that, don't you? Rainey, *everyone* at this school knows you exist."

"Anyway, it's just a dance," I say.

"Well. Maybe we could go together. I mean, if you want. We don't have to. I just thought. Never mind."

"Oh," I say, not sure how to respond to this. I want to go with Evan. I know we'll have fun. But I also have a bad feeling it's going to get more complicated than that. "Yeah, sure, I guess."

"Cool," Evan says.

Headlights crawl through the trees and up the road as my mom pulls into view.

I stand up and so does Evan.

"Can I hug you?" he asks.

"Uh…sure," I say, and Evan wraps his big arms all the way around me.

As we pull away, he quickly kisses me on the cheek. That's never happened before.

"See you tomorrow."

This is not going to end well.

"What was that about?" my mom asks as we pull out of Evan's neighborhood.

I shrug. "Nothing."

"You better spill it. That was a kiss. Are you and Evan a couple?"

"What? No! Mom, we're just friends. Evan's like my brother."

"That's not what it looks like to me."

Somebody shoot me, please.

Track Twelve
I Was Here, and Now I'm Not

With Mom and Walden on tour, Dad comes to *Oklahoma!* alone on opening night. When the stage lights go down during the first set change, I catch a glimpse of him shuffling into the auditorium late after taking the bus, his trucker's cap pulled low over his eyes. For some reason, Dad won't drive at night anymore. I know it's related to his stage fright, but I don't see the connection. Not to mention, now that there are no stages in sight, what Dad is going through has become way bigger, and way harder to understand. He stashes himself up in the very back row where the shadows swallow him up.

Wearing all black, silently moving through the darkness as I place fake fences and cardboard cutouts of horses into position, the anonymity of stage crew is oddly thrilling. And I enjoy doing my part to make the show work.

"Nice job, Rain Man," he says afterward, giving me a hug. "But next time," he whispers, "you should be *in* the show. They could have used you. Except for that female lead, she was pretty damn good."

With just me and Dad at home, it's harder to ignore how much worse he's gotten, how much he's withdrawn into himself. He talks less. He stops shaving. He barely leaves the house, even to go to the grocery store. We live on Kraft Macaroni and Cheese and canned peaches and pears. The milk and eggs run out. The last two slices of bread grow fuzzy beards. The cupboards turn bare.

The thing I notice the most, though, is that he stops laughing. Dad and I joke a lot. It's our thing. We're not Abbot and Costello, but making jokes is part of how we communicate. But even that's mostly gone. He buries himself in massive tomes about The Civil War and The American Revolution and The History of Bebop. He carves and builds and sands endless creations out of wood, his jeans always covered in a burly layer of pale sawdust. He keeps recording his Christmas album. I can tell how much he misses Mom. I think he hates himself for letting her go on the road without him.

One night, we're eating peanut butter and jelly sandwiches for dinner with supplies I picked up from the corner store when the phone rings. It's Mom, calling from a pay phone in Baltimore to say a quick hi before she heads to the gig. Mom and I chat for a minute before I pass the phone off to Dad. I slip into my bedroom and strum Walden's guitar to give them some privacy, and when I hear Dad stop talking, I come back to the table and take a bite of my sandwich, wishing we had some milk. That's when Dad starts crying. Suddenly, there's tears running down his cheeks, but otherwise he's almost perfectly still and staring off at nothing.

"Dad? Are you okay?"

"I don't know where the hell I went, Rain Man. I was here, and now I'm not."

The next day, I get out the number of Dad's therapist, Dr. Powers, and call her. Mom wrote down the number before she left and told me to keep an eye out for "anything really weird." I'm pretty sure this qualifies.

Dr. Powers, a stiff but nice woman with her hair up in a tight bun and huge glasses, comes over and talks to my dad in the living room for a long time. I'm not allowed to hear, so I listen to my Walkman to distract myself.

Before she leaves, Dr. Powers asks if she can talk to me. I say sure.

She tries to explain to me what's going on with my dad.

"You mean with his stage fright?" I ask.

She nods. "I know that's what you guys have been calling it in your family, but what your dad is dealing with is closer to anxiety and clinical depression. Do you know what that means?"

"Kind of," I say.

She explains how depression and anxiety can be caused by a lot of things, but how it's never as simple as one reason. And how it's never going to only show itself in one way, like being afraid to perform in front of an audience. Stage fright is an effect, but it's not the cause. She explains how a lot of what Dad experiences and feels is out of his control, but that doesn't mean he's powerless.

"So, he can get better?"

"Absolutely," she says. "He can. And he will. But he has to work at it every day. It's never going be as simple as flipping a switch. Your father is an awfully stubborn man, Rainey."

"Tell me about it."

"Millions of people deal with depression and anxiety. Far more than we might think. Most of them don't do anything about it because they're afraid it makes them look weak. Especially men. And unfortunately, we live in a society that's obsessed with projecting outward composure and always having it all figured out. But it's not about being strong or weak. It's about being honest about what you experience, and then doing the work so you can keep living your life."

She gives me a plastic bottle of pills and tells me to make sure Dad takes one every day.

"You're a very brave and strong young woman, Rainey," she says. "Your Dad is lucky to have you."

"If he's so lucky to have me," I say, trying but unable to stop my own tears from coming, "then why can't I help him?"

"Sweetie, you are helping him. You are. Right now. This is what help looks like."

When Mom and Walden get home, I've hardly ever been so glad to see two people in my life. Unfortunately, the first Richmond tour didn't go so well.

"The crowds sucked," Walden confesses to me that night. He looks miserable. "Duh. Nobody's ever heard of us. People have heard of Tracy Cobb. They haven't heard of Richmond. And Mom only wanted to play mostly newer songs. We didn't play 'Tell the Truth' once. Or any of the hits really."

"What?"

"It was a disaster. I think I'd rather go to school with you than do that again."

The next week Mom is back to work at T.J. Maxx and giving piano lessons. She seems depressed now, too. My family is officially falling apart.

Evan books our band our first official gig for the second Friday in November at Club 182, an all-ages club in downtown Burlington, about a half hour from Fairview. We've played in Evan's basement for friends a few times at this point, and they didn't run out of the room screaming. But this is a real gig. What happened is that, after I finally broke down and gave Evan a copy of *The Treehouse Tapes*, he gave it to his older brother, Jacob, who's a sophomore in college and works at the club, and also helps with booking. But then Evan did something that really made me mad. He booked our gig under the name Rainey Cobb. As if that was the name of our band.

"I thought we finally agreed on The Ripped Pages," I say.

"We forgot to tell you, we decided we hate that name now," River says.

"It was your idea! We voted on it."

"True," River says, "but now I'm vetoing it. We voted on veto power, too, remember? I thought I liked it, but it's too fancy. Or something. Anyway, we agreed that all three of us had to like the name."

"But Rainey Cobb isn't a band name," I argue. "It's a person's name. My name. And I don't like it."

"But that's the thing. It *sounds* like a band name. That's what's so cool about it."

"Like Veruca Salt," Evan says.

"That's a name from a book, not one of the band members' names. It's different."

"Really? What book?"

"*Charlie and the Chocolate Factory,*" I say.

"Oh my God," River says, "that's why that sounded so familiar!" He teases out the Oompa-Loompa song on his guitar. "What was the fat kid's name? We could call ourselves that."

"Augustus Gloop," I say. "And, no."

"It's already on the flyers," Evan said.

"There's flyers? What's on them?"

"That picture my mom took of us. The one where we're sitting on the couch."

I *hate* the way I look in that picture, but don't mention it.

"Jacob thinks they can get a good crowd when we play."

"But no one's ever heard us," I say.

"Hence the flyers," River says. "And people are already talking."

"What people?"

This is all happening really fast.

Then I get Juliet's letter.

When I see the envelope with her writing on it, my hands nearly start shaking I'm so nervous and excited. Almost two endless weeks have gone by since I wrote my confession and sent *The Treehouse Tapes* to Cascade Family Resort, and I've been in agony wondering what she thought and why she hasn't written back. I run with the letter out to the tree house, scamper up the rope ladder as fast as I can, then break the seal on the letter.

Dear Rainey,

I'm really sorry for taking so long to write you back. My coach has been having us practice twice a day, and with swim meets on the weekend and so much homework at night my eyes are about to start bleeding. I haven't had much extra energy.

I've read your letter about a hundred times by now, trying to decide what I want to say to you about it.

I've decided that I care about you way too much not to be honest with you. Here goes.

Nathaniel and I got back together. It just sort of happened at school. I know how hard that must be to hear. I don't know if you've figured out yet whether you only like girls or whether you like boys and girls, but I'm pretty sure I like both.

I care so much about you, and our week together was one of the best weeks of my entire life. But it's the fall now, and I'm trying not to live in the past. Plus, I live in Michigan and you live in Vermont and we can't ever see each other!

I wish I could, but I don't think I can love you back, Rainey. Anyway, you'll find somebody else soon and forget all about me. I know it. I think you've just never had these kinds of feelings before. Believe me, I know how overwhelming they can feel.

But please don't hate me. I mean, you can at first, but I hope you don't always. I can't stand the thought of you hating me.

I listened to your tape, and your songs are so beautiful, Rainey. You're the most talented person I've ever met, and I know you're going to get everything you want out of life.

You will always be my friend, but maybe it's better for both of us if we take a break from writing for a while. What do you think?

Keep playing music, Rainey. You've got a gift. Keep giving.

Your friend,

Juliet

What's almost worse than Juliet's letter is the fact that there's no one I can talk to about it. No one. Not my brother. Not Evan. Not my parents. I'm marooned on Heartbreak Island, population one. All I can do is add it to my list of firsts, which is turning out to be a more complicated experiment than I meant it to be.

Things I Did for the First Time When I was Fifteen.

10. Got my heart broken.

I'm learning the hard way that not all firsts are ones you can feel good about. Some are ones you wish you could tear up and throw away.

Track Thirteen
You're Not Pretty Enough

The *Oklahoma!* cast party is in Chris Zimmerman's basement. He's the handsome senior with the square jaw and broad shoulders but very average voice who played the male lead, Curley, opposite Mary Hanson as Laurey.

"Make yourselves at home," he says to me and Evan, then, leaning in, adds, "and make sure you try the Mountain Dew."

"What does that mean?" Evan whispers to me.

"I have no idea."

Confession #7: I hate parties.

And why? Let's start with the fact that I'm the world's worst mingler. All my life I've had to mingle, but what are you supposed to say to people you don't know that well? What do you talk about? It all feels so forced and fake. What's strange, too, is that I've spent the last two months around all these people, but somehow, everyone seems different in this massive basement that goes on and on and is bigger than my whole house.

There's a table cluttered with bags of chips, chocolate chip cookies, carrots and dip, and two-liter bottles of five different kinds of soda. I try Fresca for the first time. I eat some Ruffles. The Stone Temple Pilots song "Plush" blares from a boom box. There's a massive, big-screen television, and some kids are playing Mario Kart. Skinny, hysterical theater boys are lifting weights on Chris's Gold's Gym weight set with their shirts off, then flexing in front of a wall-sized mirror, not an ounce of body fat between them, like it's the funniest thing in the world.

After a half-hour, I'm ready to go.

"What time did you tell your mom to pick us up?"

"Eleven," Evan says.

I check my watch. Eight-thirty. How am I going to survive two-and-a-half more hours of this?

"Relax," Evan says.

"I am relaxed."

"You seem weird lately."

That's because my heart got blown up. Sue me.

"I'm fine," I say.

"If you would tell me what's wrong, maybe I could help."

"I'm fine."

Evan's friends, Ryan and Bianca, arrive. Bianca is rail thin, half-Chinese, and has a shelf of silky black hair.

"I love your nose ring so much," she whispers to me in a strangely confessional tone. "I kind of want one, but Ryan thinks they're really ugly."

"Oh."

"Did it hurt?"

"Yeah."

"A lot?"

"Yeah."

"Oh my God, I could never. I'm such a chicken."

Try letting someone stab you in the foot with a needle hundreds of times, I think.

Bathing-suited bodies occasionally run through the basement cooing with excitement toward a hot-tub outside.

"Mary!" someone shouts, and I catch a glimpse of the one and only Mary Hanson rounding a corner in a red bikini, her long legs sturdy and gliding, her body something out of a swimsuit catalog. The sight of her makes my breath catch in my chest.

We play some Mario Kart and some ping-pong. I relax a little. But only a little.

Evan never strays far from my side and, as usual, I wonder if people think we're a couple, hoping they don't, but feeling bad for feeling that. I've tried. I really have. But I can't see Evan as more than a friend. Can't make my heart feel what isn't there. What I can tell so clearly he feels for me.

The four of us wander into a side room where a boy named Luke is playing Pearl Jam's "Black" on an out-of-tune acoustic guitar to a small crowd by the light of assorted lava lamps. We sit down on the floor.

"You should play something," Evan whispers into my ear.

"No *way*," I say, more forcefully than I mean to.

"Okay, okay."

A reaching hand passes Evan a 2-liter bottle of Mountain Dew. He takes a sip, smiling as he winces slightly, then passes it to me. I take a small swig and nearly spit out the fruit-flavored alcohol that fills my mouth.

"Oh my God," I whisper. "What is it?"

"Peach Schnapps," Ryan says, taking the bottle out of my hands and drinking, then passing it to Bianca, who does the same.

Try the Mountain Dew.

We clap when Luke finishes "Black," then starts strumming the chords to "Wonderwall," which always sounds to me like a fake Beatles song. The Mountain Dew bottle comes back and we all drink and pass it on.

Out of the corner of my eye, Ryan and Bianca start kissing. Right in front of us as if they don't even care. It's gross and mesmerizing at the same time, their lips all smashed together.

My eyes have adjusted, but the room is still dark-ish by the glow of the red and purple lava lamps.

Evan puts his gigantic hand on top of mine, moist and humid as if it's been dipped in something. The room grows tight and hot. Evan slowly works his fingers between mine.

I've been waiting for this moment to come, for Evan to act on the look he's always giving me. Now that it's happening, I don't know what to do. I should have decided what I was going to do. Why didn't I decide? What should I do? I'm so stupid. My heart tightens into a fist. I can feel Evan's face close beside me. Smell the fake ocean breeze of his deodorant, the hot sweetness of the schnapps as he breathes hotly into my ear. He tilts my face toward his and kisses me on the mouth. I taste fake peaches and ranch dip.

I pull my face back and shake my head.

"Don't," I say.

"What?" he says.

The room slowly transforms. The guitar vanishes. A strangely large closet on the far side of the room is revealed and opened. Chris Zimmerman, the host, takes over, announcing that only people "who want to have fun" should stay, and bodies slip into the room, including Mary Hanson, who's changed into dark jeans and a white V-neck T-shirt. Chris closes the door.

"I want to go," I say.

"This is going to be fun," Evan says.

I want to get up and run out of this room, but I don't. I'm frozen to the floor.

"Girls on this side," Chris instructs, parting the room with his hands, "boys on this side."

We separate as instructed.

Chris writes all of our names on little strips of paper and drops them into his Yankees hat. The Mountain Dew bottle goes around, and I take a small swig of something watermelon flavored. My head is swimming.

"The game," Chris says, "is simple. Two names. Seven Minutes in Heaven. What happens in there is up to you. Nobody ever has to know."

Chris unfolds a piece of paper from the hat and says my name, pronouncing it "Rhi-nee," then reaches back into the bowl, "aaaaaannnnnndddd," he says, drawing out the word like a game show host, digging around as if the pile of names is bottomless. "Mary! Wait a second."

"That's not fair!" someone says.

"It's supposed to be a boy and a girl, you dumb ass."

"Yeah, draw another name."

"Crap, I think we were supposed to split up the names," Chris says. "Let me get another hat. Hang on, you guys."

But Mary pops up, grabs me by the hand, loudly declaring that rules are rules, and pulls me into the closet after her. I can just make out the rosy bloom on Mary's cheeks before someone shuts the door, plunging us into absolute darkness.

Rap music starts up from the other side and Chris shouts, "Your seven minutes in heaven starts…NOW!"

For a few seconds, I'm hyperventilating, unable to breathe, in shock and disbelief at what just happened. At where I am, and who I'm with.

The darkness swallows us. I fan my hand in front of my face. Mary must be doing the same thing because our fingers lightly collide out in space, and I yank my hand back nervously. Along with the smell of old clothes and ancient dust, I can smell chlorine from the hot tub in Mary's hair.

"Oh my God, it's *really* dark in here," Mary says, laughing.

"I know. I can't see anything."

I wonder if Mary is as nervous as I am. Every breath I take is filling up a balloon that's about to pop.

"I used to be so scared of the dark when I was little," Mary says. "I still sleep with a nightlight."

"Really?"

"But it's a mood light for meditation that changes colors. Not like for babies."

I wait for my eyes to adjust, for Mary's elegant form to emerge, an island in the fog, but there's nothing. Not even the faintest outline of her broad shoulders or her pointy chin or the rest of her perfectly formed body. She might be a foot away or ten and I wouldn't be able to tell. When Mary speaks, her voice is everywhere and nowhere at the same time.

"How long do you think we've been in here?" Mary asks.

"I don't know. Maybe a minute. It's so hard to tell."

"I'm just glad I didn't have to come in here with some gross freshman," Mary says. "I'll bet Evan is pretty disappointed, though. I'm sure he was hoping to be in here with you. How long have you guys been going out?"

"We're not going out. We're just friends."

Mary laughs. "Does Evan know that?"

"Yeah," I say, but then I remember Evan kissing me a little while ago, and I realize how much he does not know that. How that is the farthest thing from his mind. "He's my friend. I don't want to hurt his feelings."

"I think that's inevitable at this point," Mary says, as if Evan's feelings aren't worth worrying about. "I heard you guys are in a band with River McRae."

"Oh. Yeah, we are."

Where did she hear that?

"Now *he* is cute."

"I guess."

Mary asks what kind of music we play. I do my best to explain.

"Jesus, you write your own songs, too?"

"Sometimes."

"Well, aren't you just the little prodigy."

Her tone has become edged with bitterness. I realize that even though I've been staring at Mary for months, this is already the longest conversation we've ever had.

"When I told my parents you went to my school, they freaked. They worship your mom and dad."

"Oh."

I've thought this whole time that Mary didn't even know my name. I hear Evan's words in my head. *Everyone at this school knows who you are, Rainey.*

"I really don't get you," she says.

"What do you mean?"

"You hardly ever talk to anyone. You look like you're afraid of your own shadow half the time. But then you put on your little concerts like it's no big deal and when you sing, you turn into Tori Amos."

I shrug, but a shrug is invisible in the dark. "I've always been like that."

"Like what? More comfortable singing than talking?"

"I guess."

"That's really weird, you know."

"I know. Sorry."

"Oh, c'mon," Mary says, her voice a little wobbly. She must have tried the Mountain Dew too. "I don't mean it in a bad way. And everybody thinks you have a nice voice."

I can't think of an adequate response, so I don't say anything.

"Why didn't you try out for *Oklahoma*!? I'm not the only one who wonders that, by the way."

"I didn't want to," I say. "I like doing crew."

"Sure," Mary says, sounding utterly unconvinced. "You just *love* being where nobody can see you." I'm thrown off by the hard edge of Mary's personality.

"I have my own theory," she says, but stops there, choosing not to share it. "So, who *do* you like, since it's not poor Evan Becker?"

"Nobody."

"Yeah, right! C'mon, tell me. I won't tell anyone. I promise."

"Honestly."

Caught in some kind of web, I'm anxious to change the subject.

"Do you? Like anyone?" I ask. "Or have a boyfriend or something?"

"High school boys are way too scared of me," Mary says. "They can't stop staring at me, but then they're too afraid to ask me out. Apparently, I'm a little intimidating. I get more attention from my dad's creepy friends than the boys in my own grade."

"Gross."

"You have no idea. My parents had this big party last summer. They were all totally hammered, as usual, and I woke up and my dad's boss was sitting on the edge of my bed."

"What? What did he want?"

"What do you think? He was fifty and really fat and he was sweating. He smelled so bad. He started telling me how beautiful I was. How I was right out of an old Hollywood movie and that I was going to be a star. He said he would take care of me and I could live like a princess. It was so weird."

"I think I would freak out."

"I lock my door now when they have parties."

Chris calls out, "One more minute, better get those clothes back on!"

I hear hysterical laughter.

"That's why you wouldn't have gotten the lead, you know," Mary says, her voice tightening.

"What?"

"Even if you would have tried out for a speaking part, I mean. You still wouldn't have gotten it. You're not pretty enough."

"Oh," I say. "Okay." Her voice is like a parent who's decided it's time to teach me a hard lesson.

"It's not your fault," Mary says. "Red hair and freckles, you know. What are you going to do? So, don't feel too bad. People are born how they are. But I thought you should know that."

The door opens. The light floods my eyes.

Track Fourteen
I Have Something to Say

At band practice two nights later, I drive the band hard, like my mom does when she's mad, as if we're being forced to atone for all the world's evils.

I've been unsettled and agitated since the party, and I take most of it out on Evan, who seems flustered and keeps speeding up during songs. Even River can barely keep up with my corrections and suggestions, but Evan gets the worst of it.

"Make it a little more, you know?" I say.

"No, I don't know," Evan says. "A little more what?"

"It just doesn't sound right. We've got our first gig soon and we're going to sound like crap."

"Then tell me how to make it sound right."

"Stop speeding up and slowing down all the time. It's messing everything up."

"I'm trying."

"You have to find the center," I say. It's something my dad sometimes says when a song isn't quite there.

"The center of what?"

When practice is over, nobody is smiling. River says, "Well, that was really fun," and slips off the way he does.

Evan and I watch MTV and eat microwave popcorn. On the screen, Axl Rose is struggling to adapt to city life.

"What's wrong with you?" Evan asks. "You've been acting weird ever since the party the other night. Before that even."

"Nothing. I just want us to sound good for the show."

"You don't think we sound good?"

"Sometimes I do."

"But…?"

"Well, it's hard when one of the *three* people in your band doesn't really know what they're doing half the time."

I regret the words even as I'm still saying them. Even as the syllables are being formed, even as my breath is being drawn. But they slip out all the same. Finally, the tears come.

I cry for what feels like a long time. Though I've just mercilessly insulted him, Evan still puts his arms around me. My tears leave wet spots all over his gray T-shirt.

"Oh no, I'm sorry."

"Forget it. Are you okay?"

I shrug.

"What's wrong, Rainey?"

"I don't know," I say, "I'm just going through something I guess."

"Do you want to talk about it? You can tell me."

"There's nothing to talk about," I lie.

Evan mutes the TV and stands up. His pale cheeks are flushed with red splotches. He takes off his glasses, then immediately puts them back on. He looks like he's about to give a class presentation.

"I have something to say."

Oh no.

"You probably know how much I like you," he says. "Do you know that?"

"Yes. I know."

"So, what I'm asking is, do you like me back?"

"Of course, I like you. We're together all the time."

"Stop it. You know what I mean, Rainey. As more than just friends?"

All night I've been barking orders at Evan and River, but now, when I need them the most, my words dry up and shrivel. How can you be honest with someone without hurting them? Can you be? If I could tell Evan about Juliet, it would be so much easier. Somehow, I think Evan might even understand because he's such a compassionate person. But I can't make myself say the words. They're right there, but they won't let me touch them. So instead of telling the truth, I mumble some clichéd bullshit about how I like him, but only as a friend.

Drooping like a flag on a windless day, Evan sits down on the couch and stares at the TV where Axl Rose is being electrocuted and silently screaming.

"But is that so bad?" I ask. "If we're just good friends? Really good friends."

"I don't know," Evan says.

Track Fifteen
How to Be Happy Anyway

That night, into the wee small hours, I make Evan a mix. It's all I can think to do. I scour my small CD collection and our family records and fill the mix with songs that I think he'll like. Songs like "Over the Hills and Far Away" by Led Zeppelin and "Bang a Gong" by T. Rex and "Northern Sky" by Nick Drake.

I think about how Evan likes to listen to music lying down on the floor and I want to make sure he won't have the urge to get up and fast forward because he always complains about that. "Why don't bands just leave the bad songs *off* the album? Don't they know it will be better that way?"

For the cover, I use a picture of me that Evan took. The sun is in my eyes, and so I'm wincing and looking away, my mouth open in a laugh. I think it's an awful picture, but Evan went on and on about how much he loved it. He said it captured something essential about my nature, but I'm not sure what. All I was thinking about was that I didn't want my picture taken because the sun was in my eyes. As usual, Evan saw something beautiful in me I don't see in myself.

Since every good mix should have a title, I think about what to call this one for a long time. In the end, I settle on one of my favorite Ma Rainey lyrics. *Sun Gonna Shine Through*, I write for side A, *Someday in my Backyard* I finish on side B.

Because I know the combination, I leave it in his locker the next day with a note.

"Thanks for the tape," he says at lunch. But he doesn't say much else.

A few days later, the day of our first show, I'm talking to Mr. Larson over green tea during one of our check-ins.

"How's your dad doing?"

I've told him all about Dad's stage fright, about the breakdown while my mom was on tour. Mr. Larson is a really good listener.

"A little better."

"But not great?"

I shrug. I don't even know what great would be anymore when it comes to my dad.

"And your mom?"

I shrug again.

"I think she blames me more than Dad at this point for the way things have turned out."

"I doubt that, Rainey."

"She barely talks to me."

He gives me a Dum Dum and takes one for himself. Mr. Larson seems so relaxed all the time, as if he has no doubts about who he is. He talks and moves through life's moments with confidence and ease. Like he never worries about how to act or what to say. I wonder if I'll ever feel like that.

"What about your social life?"

"What social life?"

"I see you with Evan Becker a lot."

"God, not you too. We're just friends. We may not even be that anymore."

"Sorry, sorry," he says, holding up his hands. "Forget I said anything."

Mr. Larson has this little rock garden on his desk, and he lets me re-arrange the rocks while we talk.

"What if you hadn't known?" I ask, stacking three small, smooth stones atop one another, taking care to make them perfectly balanced.

"Known what?"

I look around, inch my chair a tad closer to Mr. Larson, and lower my voice.

"You said you always knew, but what if you hadn't known? What if you were confused about it? What if some days it felt like you were and other days it didn't?"

"I think that would have been okay, too. It's complicated and very personal. There's no blueprint for what any of us is going to feel. And the truth is that we don't have much control over how our hearts work." He bites into his Dum Dum, and I can smell green apple on his breath. "Do you feel confused about stuff like that?"

I shrug. "Sometimes."

He waits. "Do you want to talk about it?"

"Not really."

He nods. Mr. Larson is good like that. He doesn't push things.

"You know, Rainey, life is pretty confusing a lot of the time. And I'm sorry to have to say it, but the confusion never really goes away. In fact, in a lot of ways, life gets more complicated as you get older, not less. The challenge is to figure out how to be happy anyway."

"That seems really hard."

"It gets easier."

"Are you sure?"

"I'm pretty sure."

"*Pretty* sure? That's not very reassuring."

"Hey, don't blame me, that's life."
I laugh. I feel a little better.

Track Sixteen
This is a Song I Wrote

We're playing fourth, and last, at Club 182. I'm dressed for battle. Black jeans, black T-shirt, black boots, flannel tied around my waist, hair down, bright purple lipstick.

"That's what you're wearing?" my mom asks.

Before we play, we have to listen to Brontosaurus, then Petty Thieves, then Eraser Cap, followed by Rainey Cobb. I look at my name on the sandwich board on the sidewalk for a long time. I want to hate the sight of it, but I don't. Maybe Rainey is kind of a cool name.

"What's going on with you and Evan?" River asks as we're standing off to the side of the stage, listening to Petty Thieves play a cover of "Blister in the Sun." Evan is in the bathroom again. He's really nervous, I think. And he's avoiding me.

"Nothing."

"Yeah right."

"We had a fight."

"Can I guess?"

"Guess what?"

"He confessed his undying love, and you broke his heart into a million little pieces?"

"Shut up."

"I thought so."

Club 182 isn't packed, but the crowd is bigger than I expected. I've gotten good at estimating crowds over the years, and I'm guessing there's close to a hundred people here. The room is humid and smells like sweat and ginger ale, which they sell in paper cups for fifty cents at the bar, along with candy bars and popcorn. I recognize lots of faces from school, kids from the musical. The Pena twins. I scan the crowd, looking for my family, who I couldn't convince not to come.

"You'd sooner stop the hands of time then keep your mother away," my dad said.

I finally see my parents and Walden way in the back, tucked into a corner. Not far from them, I see Mary Hanson talking to an older looking guy with a beard and glasses.

Great.

Feeling rattled, I go to the bathroom and push open one of the stalls. I sit down, not to pee or anything. Just for a moment alone. It hits me that a lot of these people are here to listen to me, and suddenly this moment feels really important in a way I hadn't thought about. I want to remember it. I want to get it right. For some reason, I wonder how many gigs I've played over the years. After some quick math, I guess it's close to six or seven hundred.

You're fifteen, Juliet said to me. *You're fifteen*, I say to me.

On the stall door someone has carved *my heart is a thousand years old, I am not like other people.*

When Eraser Cap is almost done with their set, I pull Evan aside. He still isn't really talking to me and I'm worried.

"Look," I say. "I know you hate me right now, but can we just play our best anyway? We worked really hard."

"Whatever you say, boss," he says.

Good talk.

Our turn. I stand behind my keyboard, adjust the microphone. The crowd presses forward.

“Hi,” I say. “We’re, uh…I’m Rainey. That’s Evan and River. Thanks for coming. This is a song I wrote.”

I start playing the opening chords of “Ordinary Girl.”

And we’re off to the races.

Track Seventeen
What Did I Do Wrong?

"Chamomile," Mom says, putting a steaming mug in front of me, "with milk and honey."

"Thanks."

She sets down a plate of shortbread, and a box of Kleenex. I wipe my eyes, then dunk a shortbread into my tea, the cookie turning to sugary cereal in my mouth.

We've been home from Club 182 for almost an hour. Walden went to bed, and Dad wandered off to the studio, but Mom said she wanted to stay up with me, if it was okay.

"It's okay."

Her eyes are full of concern. They're a little puffy, too, and wrinkled at the corners. I know she hasn't been sleeping very well.

I used to idolize my mom. People always tell me I'm such a natural at playing music. That I was born with a gift. Like even if I'd been born on a desert island, I'd have eventually started banging two coconuts together. I hear them say "gifted" and "special" and "talented," which, by the way, are about the worst things you can call a kid because they actually make them feel shitty and they don't account for hard work and passion. But people don't know that the real reason I wanted to play music in the first place was because, like everybody else, I wanted to be Tracy Cobb.

When I was still too young to play in the band, I'd sit on the side of the stage with huge protective earphones on and watch her play. She was so beautiful and perfect, and when she opened her mouth pure magic came out. A voice so full of good feeling and soul it would send shivers down your spine and make you feel like everything was going to be okay. I'd think to myself, *that's what I'm going to do*. People love my mom because of the way she makes them feel, and I got to feel that way all the time.

I felt that from the crowd tonight while I played. Next to kissing Juliet, it was the best feeling I've ever had. In some ways, it was even better because for the first time ever, it was my music making them feel that way. My songs. I never knew that feeling until tonight.

And then Evan blew up at me after the show. We got in a huge fight, and I came crashing back down to Earth.

Usually, Mom has to fill every second, but right now she waits for me.

"Evan quit the band," I say and take a careful slurp of chamomile.

"Oh honey, I'm so sorry," Mom says. "What happened?"

"He wants us to be more than friends, but I don't, and apparently that's some kind of a crime that makes me the worst person in the world." I eat another shortbread, replaying Evan's words in my mind. I didn't think he was capable of being so mad.

Mom taps her fingers on the tabletop.

"He said that I've known forever how much he liked me, that I've known since we first met, but that I didn't tell him because I wanted to hurt him more. He called me a tease. That's not true! I mean, I did sort of know that he liked me, but I kind of hoped he would change his mind. I didn't want to hurt him at all. I didn't want this to happen. I really do like him as a friend. He's one of the best friends I've ever had. Maybe the best."

I look up at Mom.

"What did I do wrong?"

"Nothing," she says, reaching out and taking my hand. Hers is warm from holding her mug. "You didn't do anything wrong. Nothing at all."

"I just wish things could go back to how they were," I say.

After Mom goes to bed, I put on my boots and slip into the back yard. My breath blooms in the near-freezing air like puffs of smoke. A bright half-moon smiles down, lightly obscuring a billion stars.

I go up to the tree house and switch on the lantern, shielding my eyes from its harsh yellow glow. I wish I could talk to Juliet, or at least write her a letter. She broke my heart, but she's still the person I want to be around the most. And now Evan's gone too.

I guess I'm doomed to have to figure everything out on my own.

I put *Blowin' My Mind Like a Summer Breeze* into the boom box, rewind to the beginning of side A and turn the volume way down, so that Bjork's voice comes out as only a whisper. I click off the lantern and lie back on the loveseat, listening in the dark, wondering what the hell I'm going to do.

Track Eighteen
They're Worse Than Girls

I wait a few days before trying to make up with Evan, who, instead of accepting my apology, begins a rigorous campaign of ignoring me like his life depends on it. He looks down when we pass in the hallway, flat out ignores me when I try to talk to him. Changes his seat in study hall so that it's the maximum possible distance from mine.

The only good thing about losing Evan is I get the Pena twins back at lunch.

"Boys are so immature," Clara says through a mouthful of turkey sandwich after I finally tell them the gist of what had happened.

"So immature," Rachel agrees, eating her own identical sandwich on heavy-looking whole grain bread.

"They don't know how to separate love and friendship, but it's not that hard if you ask me," says Clara. "People can talk and chew gum at the same time, you know. And I'm not saying that I'm a lesbo or anything, because that's totally gross and I would never, but I'll bet that if I liked a girl who didn't like me back, I'd still be able to be friends with her anyway. That's what I mean. You know?"

I'm a little bit offended by this, and given my experience

with Juliet, totally disagree, but sometimes when the twins are on a roll, it's better just to let them go.

"What you should be more worried about than stupid Evan Becker," Rachel continues, opening and swigging from a carton of chocolate milk, "is all the boys who are drooling every time you walk down the hallway and want to get some of your sweet bootie since your show."

"Whatever, they do not!"

"Girl, you need to open your eyes and take your pick," Clara says. "This is your moment."

"Your moment," Rachel echoes.

"That's what I'd do."

"That's what I'd do."

They cheers with their milk cartons.

As much as my instinct tells me to reject this notion, I have noticed there's some strange affliction that seems to have infected the members of the male species since I played at Club 182, marked by awkwardness, staring, and fumbling for words. Only River McRae, who seems not to care about much of anything, treats me with the same cool detachment he reserves for the entire world. Even better, he says he likes playing together and doesn't mind waiting while we figure out what's next for the band.

Boys ask me out, and because it seems stupid not to, and that's what normal kids seem to do, I go on some dates. I go ice skating with Mitch Harris. Bowling on a strange sort of mass date with the Pena twins and three boys. To a movie with Carson Crawford. I'm not really attracted to these boys, but I'm not *not* attracted either. It's complicated. I still find myself stealing glances at the pretty girls in my classes, but since acting on my feelings is totally impossible, I try to look at boys in a new way.

It would be easier if they weren't so big and smelly.

Carson Crawford is quite handsome, though, with deep

brown eyes and perfect Ken doll hair, and when he kisses me in his car after the movie, I kiss him back. It's the first time I've kissed a boy, and it's kind of nice. Not quite as magical as kissing Juliet, but maybe kissing people happens on a continuum, and it's best to take the experiences one at a time.

When I sit down at lunch with the Pena twins on Monday, though, I'm shocked to find out they know all about me kissing Carson Crawford only two nights earlier.

"How do you know? Who told you?"

I feel flushed and embarrassed. I look around the lunchroom. Clara says she heard it from her friend Pamela. Rachel heard it from her friend Tyson.

Who?

Rachel says that Tyson and Carson are on the soccer team together.

"Be careful," Clara warns me, wagging her French fry before dipping it in a lake of salty ketchup, "they tell their friends about everything."

"They do?"

"They're worse than girls," Rachel says.

"They are?"

"*Way* worse."

"So much worse."

I take a break from dating.

Mom returns the dress we picked out at T.J. Maxx, and I skip the Fall Formal and watch Pink Panther movies with my dad and Walden instead.

The calendar trudges forward, the passage of time marked not so much by days as holidays. My Aunt Becky and Murph come over for Thanksgiving, then for Christmas.

Dad gives Mom the Christmas album he made for her, and

when she listens to it, she looks happier than she has in a long time.

"Oh, Luce," she says.

My parents curl up together on the couch in front of the wood stove and listen to Dad's album. Mom puts her head on his shoulder. Looking at them right then, something changes. Like they've both been wandering in the dark but have finally found each other.

Sometimes I peek over my shoulder at the life I've left behind. A life where my world consisted of only three other people. I feel liberated to have broken free, and now that I've started writing and performing my own music, I know I can't go back to singing my parents' songs all the time. But I also miss the patterns I knew so well, the easy camaraderie I felt among my people. Instead of feeling more at home and accepted among my peers, I feel less so.

Is that okay?

I wonder what I want out of life. For a long time, all I knew was that I wanted something different, but now that I have it, other questions have emerged.

Questions I Have About my Future

1. Where does all this lead?
2. What's the purpose of school?
3. Should I go to college?
4. Can I even afford to go to college if I want to?
5. Will I ever feel really close to anyone again?

Everyone at school talks about college all the time. They can't imagine a future without college in it, as if college and the future are one in the same.

Even Mr. Larson is obsessed with college.

"Even if you don't use it right away, you're still better off having a degree," he tells me.

Yeah, yeah, yeah.

The only thing I know for sure that I want is more of what I felt when I was on stage at Club 182. Playing my music. Everything else feels blurry and far away.

January becomes February becomes March.

River and I get together to play music once in a while. I write two new songs. One called "Longest Day of My Life" and another called "Atomic."

Not surprisingly, they're both about Juliet.

"Man," River says when he hears them. "Somebody really did a number on you."

I write and tear up five different letters to Juliet. Some are angry. Some are pathetic. Some are pleading. All are ones I'm glad I don't send. I keep trying to hate Juliet, but I can't for some reason. My heart won't let me. The emptiness that opened up in me when I read her letter is still there but doesn't feel so hollow and rotten anymore. But I haven't gone on any dates since the Carson Crawford debacle.

"That's cool," Rachel Pena says. "Lay low for a while."

"Yeah, lay low for a while," Clara echoes.

One day, on a freezing cold afternoon with wind like a whip, I'm standing out in front of school waiting for my mom to pick me up when Mary Hanson walks right up and stands next to me.

"Hey," she says.

"Hey."

"I was horrible to you at Chris's party."

I nod.

"I'm really not a horrible person."

"It's okay."

Is it? I'm not sure. In fact, I'm pretty sure it isn't okay. But that's what comes out.

"All I've ever wanted to do is be on stage and make it to Broadway, and my whole life everyone's been feeding me this steady diet of, 'you're going to be a star' and 'don't let anyone stand in the way of your dreams.' Does that make sense?"

"You have no idea," I say.

"Anyway," she says, brushing some of her perfect hair out of her perfect face, "I've never met anyone who I thought was more talented than me. Who might steal my dreams. I know how conceited and bitchy and stupid that sounds, but it's the truth. And I feel like maybe you're the one person who can understand that. It made my claws come out."

"People have been telling me stuff like that my whole life too," I say.

She nods.

"It fucks with your head after a while," she says.

"Yep. Big time."

"Anyway," she says, sounding like she's about to say more, but instead just says, "see you around," and walks away.

I'm in the kitchen eating some brown sugar Pop Tarts and reading *Invisible Man* by Ralph Ellison, which my English teacher, Ms. Ofalko, recommend to me after I loved *Their Eyes Were Watching God* in class.

"You're ready for this," Ms. Ofalko said, handing it to me after class. "Buckle up."

Mom is in the living room working on a bluesy chord progression in B-flat. She plays it straight through, then sideways, then backward, looking at all the pieces, working through how she wants to fit them together. Whenever I hear Mom writing music, I always picture a painter who dabs a little paint on the canvas, then stands far away to see the whole canvas better. Then close again, then far. Close, far.

She's been at the piano a lot lately, and I can see her creative gears starting to slowly turn.

"Rainey baby, come help me with this will you," she says.

She scoots over and I sit down next to her on the bench. I learned to play piano sitting next to her, just like this. She snatches the Pop Tart out of my hand, takes a bite, and then gives it back with a grin.

"Hey," I say.

"Gotta be quick," she says.

She plays me what she's working on.

"It's this transition right here that doesn't quite sit right." She plays the chords again, emphasizing two of the chords, playing them over and over. "Don't you think?"

"Yeah," I say. "I see what you mean."

I start playing the progression in the upper register. I try an inversion of the first chord, which frees up some space and makes the dominant chord pop a little brighter. It feels like turning on a light in a dimly lit room. Suddenly you can see a painting on the wall. Books on the shelf. An old woman knitting in a chair.

"What was that?" she asks.

I play it back a few times.

"If you play the second inversion of the d minor," I say, "then add the sixth in the bass, that F7 will sound a little fuller, I think."

She plays it a few times and nods to herself.

"Thanks," she says.

"New song?"

"Mmm hmm."

"Any words yet?"

"Not quite," she says, tapping her head with her finger. "Still cooking. I'll let you know when it's ready."

Track Nineteen
Look Out World

At first it makes me a little sad how much better of a drummer Walden is than Evan. How quickly he gels with River. How easily he elevates my songs. How quickly our band levels up with my brother behind the drum kit.

But making songs sound better is what Walden has been doing his whole life. It's what he was born to do.

"Holy shit, your brother is insane on drums!" River says to me in English class the day after we play together for the first time. "Why did you even start playing with Evan when your brother can play that good?"

I shrug. "My brother has been in my mom's band. Plus, I didn't want him to. He's kind of bossy and moody. And I don't know if he even likes my music."

"Who cares? He's insane. In-sane!"

"Plus, Evan asked me to play with him, not the other way around. Remember?"

"Have you guys made up yet?"

"I tried," I say. "He's really mad."

"Keep trying. He'll come around."

It happened by accident, Walden joining the band. One day River came to our house to jam, and we were playing in my bedroom when Walden came in to get something, listened for a minute, then instead of leaving, he sat down at the stripped-down drum kit he keeps in the corner and slid right into the pocket.

By our fifth rehearsal, we're starting to sound so good it almost scares me.

In late March, we play at Club 182, then again two weeks later. Both times under my name, which I'm getting used to, even if I still don't like it. By our third show in mid-April, there's barely room to stand and there's a buzz in the air, a sense of electric anticipation you can almost touch. Walden complains that we aren't getting paid, but I don't really care. At least not yet.

After the show, the owner, Paul Posen, a local legend who used to be in a band that got signed, and later dropped, by Columbia when their lead singer drowned in Lake Champlain on the Fourth of July, comes up to us. He asks if we want to keep playing throughout the summer as a featured act. Doing a full ninety-minute headlining show instead of the half hour we've been doing on a bill with three other bands.

"I haven't seen an audience this excited about a local band in years," he says. "Maybe ever. I already had a reporter stop by asking if I knew how to get in touch with you."

"Really?" I ask.

"Really. I told them they should leave you alone. I hate reporters. So, what do you think?"

I look at Walden, who says, "For free?" unscrewing his ride cymbal and slipping it into a padded bag. "Thanks but no thanks, man. You saw the crowd. No offense but I don't think they're coming for the ginger ale."

I shift uncomfortably, but I love my brother so much right now. I think this is what he's talking about when he says I need to learn to stand up for myself.

"You're her older brother?"

"That's right."

"I guess the apple doesn't fall far from the tree, huh? I used to go see your parents play when I was younger. They were unreal back in the day. Almost as good as you two."

Walden waits, so I wait. River is putting his guitar pedals into a bag, casually listening.

"I'll tell you what. I occasionally do ticketed shows here for bigger acts that come through. From now on, when you play, I'll charge five bucks a head, and you guys take half. This room holds two hundred. If you fill it, that's five hundred bucks to you, five hundred to me. Sound fair?"

"To start," Walden says.

"What do you think?" Posen says, turning to me.

"Okay," I say, then turn to River, who's standing there casually listening.

"Works for me, man," he says.

"If you guys really want to start making money, though," Posen said. "You should sell copies of your demo. Or have some stickers made or something. I think about every kid here would buy one."

"You think so?" I ask.

"I know so. Just be careful when the A&R reps start showing up and making you offers you can't refuse. Everything they say is a lie."

"And you're different?"

"Yeah," Posen says. "I am." He starts walking away, then turns back to me. "How old are you?"

I turn to Walden, who shrugs, as if to say, why not?

"Almost sixteen," I say. For some reason, sixteen sounds way older than fifteen.

Posen whistles through his teeth. "Look out world," he says.

Track Twenty
This Probably Sounds Really Stupid

Gradually, and without really trying, River and I become better friends than I ever thought we would be when we first met. The high school rumor mill immediately brands us a couple, of course. High school really is a ridiculous place. Nobody believes anything. Everybody's always looking over their shoulder and hunting for secret meanings and cracks in the sidewalk that aren't even there.

The Pena twins pepper me constantly with questions and accusations, certain I'm hiding something.

"He is totally hot, and you better tell us everything right now!" Rachel says, dipping fries in salty ketchup as usual.

"We're just friends, you guys. Seriously."

"Whatever!" Clara says.

"Yeah, whatever," Rachel says. "I saw you two lying on the grass in the courtyard the other day like an old married couple."

I shrug.

"That doesn't mean we're together."

"Um, yes it does! That's exactly what it means."

"Yeah, that's exactly what it means."

I become a regular fixture around River's dinner table and get to know his mom, Pam, who's always alone with River's little sister, Myra, because River's dad left the family five years ago.

"He took off with this other woman one day and never came back," River tells me. "He sends me a birthday present every year and I throw it right in the trash without even opening it."

"That's crazy," I say, "there could be money in there."

"I don't want anything from him. As far as I'm concerned, I don't have a father."

I think that's part of the reason River is sort of aloof and casual. He doesn't want to get too close to people. It's a way of protecting himself.

With River, somehow, things never get weird, the way things did with Evan. He never gives me that long look like he wants to kiss me. I occasionally catch him staring at my chest, but whatever, all boys do that.

River treats me more like a sister. He teases me about all the black I wear. "Are you allergic to bright colors?" He casually makes fun of my love of country music and is completely unmoved when I play him my favorite Hank Williams and Dolly Parton songs.

"Yeah, still nothing," he says. "Sorry, doc, but we don't have a pulse."

It's easy, that's what it is. And easy is nice for a change. I deserve easy.

One night, we watch *The Shining* at River's house, and I'm a little freaked out when the credits start rolling. I keep seeing those horrible little girls in the blue dresses in my head, asking me to come and play with them.

"Why did we watch that?" I ask. "I'm going to have nightmares for a month."

"Here's Johnny!" River says and lunges at me with a fake axe.

We go out on his back porch to get some air. River brings out a joint to smoke, which he does sometimes. I take a little puff once in a while, but tonight I take a big one and hold the smoke in for a long time, then cough it out in a dense, swirling cloud of blue. River laughs. I don't count an occasional hit on a joint as breaking my pact not to smoke, by the way. I mean, of course you're putting smoke in your lungs. But there's no nicotine. It's not addictive.

We lay down on his deck on our backs and look up at the stars. It's a clear April night, and though the weather is getting warmer, it's cool and when I start shivering, River gives me his sweatshirt.

"I want to tell you something," I say.

"Go for it," he says.

"But you can't tell anyone."

"Okay."

"Do you promise?"

"I guess."

"River! You have to swear. I mean it."

He makes an X across his chest. "Cross my heart," he says.

"I like girls," I say. "I mean, I'm attracted to girls. More than boys. I'm not, not attracted to boys, but mostly I'm not. I don't know. It's weird. But mostly I like girls. Sorry, this probably sounds really stupid. Forget it."

River listens patiently as I ramble on, doubling back, contradicting myself, then finally repeating my central theme once again.

"I kind of figured," he says.

"You did?"

"Rainey, half the guys in school want to go out with you, and you barely even notice."

"That's not true!"

"It's true enough. And the stuff with Evan. Maybe nobody else sees it, but it makes sense to me."

He passes me the joint and I inhale another small drag. I feel like I'm hovering slightly off the ground. The wind whispers through my hair.

"My older sister is gay," he says.

Hearing the casual way he says the word *gay*, which I hear used as an insult all day long in the lunch line and between bathroom stalls, as if it has no more significance than the words "blue" or "loafer," fills me with relief. I've fantasized so many times about this moment of confession, about how it would feel to share my deep secret truth.

How does it feel? It feels really good.

"I remember when my sister was in high school," River says, "my mom was always saying that to her, 'Boys call here all the time, and you don't give them the time of day. You never go on dates. Blah blah blah.'" I turn to River. His long blond locks are dancing in the breeze, the tips shiny with silver moonlight. Even in shorts and a tank top, he seems unfazed by the cool temperature.

"I know other people freak out about it, but it's really no big deal to me."

"I've wanted to tell somebody for so long."

"You've never told anyone before?"

"No."

"Not even Walden?"

I shake my head. I start crying. I hate crying, but I can't help it.

"Hey, it's okay," he assures me.

I sit up and so does River. He puts his arms around me.

"You're all right, Rainey," he says. "It's going to be all right."

And you know what? I actually agree for once.

A while later we're in the kitchen eating everything in sight—cookies, chips, candy, giggling like idiots—when he says,

"I think it's cool you could tell me, but have you thought about telling Evan?"

"He wouldn't understand. He's too mad at me."

"I think you might be surprised," he says.

Track Twenty-One
He Has His Moments

Press the fast forward button. Right there. Stop.

An early Saturday morning in May, and I'm helping Mom load the car, which is stuffed with her Gibson Super Jumbo, her white Stratocaster, a Fender tube amp, a keyboard, a big suitcase full of clothes, another full of shoes and boots, and her cosmetic bag.

Mom's going on an adventure.

She's driving to Detroit to stay with her friend Shay, who's a musician and arranger, and given herself two weeks to turn her new batch of song scraps into finished songs for a new album. Then in June, she's taking a new band out on the road, this time under the name Tracy Cobb, and this time without my brother behind the drum kit or my dad on guitar.

After twenty years tethered to Luce Cobb, and another five to the Cobb Family Band, Tracy Cobb is officially going solo.

She keeps looking at a AAA map of The Great Lakes Region, talking aloud to herself about the fastest way to get to Detroit.

"Call me right away if Dad starts acting weird," she tells me. "You know what to look for?"

"It's going to be fine," I tell her. "He's getting better."

"You really think so? Some days I'm sure he is, and some days I'm not so sure."

"I'm sure."

She looks around.

"You believe it was a year ago we were packing up to leave for tour?" she says.

"That feels like way more than a year ago," I say.

"It sure does. I feel like I've lived a lifetime since then."

"Me too."

"I guess we both have," she says.

She wraps me up in a huge hug.

"I love you Rainey," she says.

"I love you too."

"No matter what."

"No matter what."

Dad comes out and we wave as Mom pulls out of the driveway, already blasting Otis Redding from the tape deck. After she's gone, we stand there in silence for half a minute, then grab our rods and the tackle box and walk to the pond.

"So, you're officially retired from music?" I ask him, baiting a worm and casting out into the pond. My lure hits the water and sends out ripples that chase each other across the glassy green surface.

"Just from playing live, Rain Man. I'll never retire from music. I don't know how to do anything else."

Instead of casting out, Dad likes to drop his lure right over the side of the canoe. He brought a couple beers for himself and some Cokes for me. We sit drinking in the early afternoon stillness, the sun beginning to warm the top of my head.

"What are you gonna do?"

"You mean other than sit around and feel sorry for myself?"

"I didn't mean it like that."

"I know," he says. "That's my guilt talking. I can't help it. I haven't been much of a father to you kids lately and it hurts to let down the people you love the most."

I feel a bite on my line, but I reel in too hard and lose it.

"To answer your question, though," Dad says, "I'm going to produce, engineer, that kind of stuff. I've already got a few projects lined up. Some bands that want to rent out the studio and have me help them out behind the board. It's not going to make us rich, but it beats making bird houses. And you know how much I love pushing buttons."

He's not kidding, either. He loves it so much it's freaky.

"And Murph thinks I should release my Christmas album."

"Really?"

"Really."

"You gonna be okay with Mom gone?"

"Sure," he says. Then adds, "I've got you," and winks at me.

"Pretty sure you're supposed to be taking care of me."

"Right, right. I always forget that part."

"Just no weeklong mac and cheese binges this time," I say. "Last time I almost died. That stuff's loaded with sodium."

"Deal." He chuckles. "Sodium. How'd you get so smart anyway?"

"I get it from my dad."

"Sounds like a hell of a guy."

"He has his moments."

"I'll bet."

Track Twenty-Two
That Song Could Be About Me

Friday, June 14th, 1996—the last day of school.

I push open the double doors of Green Valley High School and exit the building alone, the same way I entered it eight months prior. On the air, I catch the oily scent of sunscreen and a burst of tangy lilac. I plan on walking back through these same doors for my junior year in a few months, but for the first time in as long as I can remember, the present feels pretty good, and I'm not too worried about the future.

The Pena twins give me a ride home, and when I get there, somehow, River is already there with his guitar, his amp, and his bag of pedals.

"Can I catch a ride to Albany?" he says.

"Very funny."

Like all the gigs I've played in my life, tonight's gig in New York's capital was booked by someone else, in this case, my brother Walden. Apparently, he knows a guy who knows a guy in Temporary Secretary, the band we're opening up for at an all-ages club slash Tex Mex restaurant called The Giddy Up. We've printed some stickers with my name on them in swirly script and plan to sell them for a buck a piece after the show.

Hey, you gotta start somewhere.

With Walden at the wheel, we drive Howard the Duck

down Route 7 through Vergennes toward the New York State Thruway, passing around a bag of Jax and swigging ice-cold Cokes, thick orange dust gathering on our fingers.

"You sure this thing will make it to Albany?" River asks, who looks a little worried about Howard.

"Don't you worry about Howard," Walden says. "He's made it a lot further away than Albany."

"We pretty much grew up in this thing," I say.

"No wonder you're so messed up," River says, and I punch him in the arm, cracking us both up.

As the rule goes, music is driver's choice, and thus a tape of Bob Dylan's *Self Portrait* blares through Howard the Duck's aged speakers. I'm riding shotgun and River and I exchange secret looks of disdain in the light up vanity mirror as River keeps fake vomiting down the front of his T-shirt. He hates Bob Dylan even more than I do.

Over the past two months of rehearsal, Rainey Cobb—the band—has polished our set to a deadly point, pushing deeper into the songs, examining and adjusting arrangements, tweaking song order, adding harmonies, guitar loops, instrumental breaks, walls of sound. We've replaced all but two covers with new original songs, leaving in only Sinead O' Connor's "Nothing Compares to U" and "Where is my Mind?" by the Pixies, with River on lead vocals.

We're a force to be reckoned with.

Before we take the stage in Albany, we huddle up and Walden, looking deadly serious, says, "Let's fucking destroy these people."

River bursts out laughing.

"I can never take you seriously when you say that."

Except the joke is on us because there's only about thirty people in the crowd. Of course, most of them certainly aren't here to see us, but there is a group of college-aged looking girls who come up front and listen intently while we play. I swear I even see one of them singing along at one point, but I'm sure my eyes are playing tricks on me.

After the set, with our meager $100 earnings folded and tucked into my pocket, I'm sipping a Coke in the shadows by the bar, a huge black X on my hand, when a pale girl with a pixie cut and ripped Levi's steps forward.

"Excuse me," the girl says. "Hi. Sorry to bother you."

"Hi," I say, and I instantly recognize her as one of the girls who came up close to the stage while we were playing.

There's a glint of light as an object in the girl's hand is raised and briefly reflects the bar lights. She hands me the object, which turns out to be a Maxell jewel case with a cassette inside.

"I can't stop listening to it," she says, her voice that blend of boldness and shyness I've heard so many times after shows. She looks down at her Chuck Taylors, at the flannel tied around her waist, then back up at me. "It's so awesome."

For a moment, I'm completely baffled. What is she talking about? Then I look more closely at what I've been handed.

Written on the tape case's spine in block print are the words *The Treehouse Tapes—Rainey Cobb.* I rotate the tape and read the handwritten track list off the back.

1. Ordinary Girl
2. Secret Star
3. Peter Pan in Reverse
4. Anger, Part I
5. Everysecondeveryminuteeveryday
6. Anger, Part II
7. Anger, Part III
8. Bye

9. A Quiet Place

I can't believe my eyes.

"Can you sign it to Svetlana?" she asks, handing me a pen, "that's my name. I can spell it if you want. It's Russian, in case you were wondering. My mom's from there. But I was born here."

"Where did you get this?" I say, not meaning to sound so accusatory.

She edges back slightly.

"Um, from my cousin Kendall in Indiana? She sent it to me a couple months ago. She thought I would like it. I'd never even heard of you before. Then yesterday, it was so weird, I was walking home and I saw your name on the board they put out front to say who's playing this week, and I couldn't believe it. Me and my friends go to SUNY Albany."

My mind races, trying to fill in the gaps in Svetlana's story. I'm fighting my way out of a vivid dream. "So, where did your cousin Kendall get it from? Before she sent it to you, I mean?"

"From her sister, I think. Or her sister's friend. I'm not really sure. People pass tapes around, you know? Am I not supposed to have it or something?" She leans in and excitedly whispers, "Did somebody steal it?"

"No," I say, "it's not that. It's just. I don't understand how you could have, or how your cousin could have, or her sister, or wherever it came from. I mean, I never even gave—" but here I break off. A window opens in my mind. Because of course I did send a copy of *The Treehouse Tapes* out into the world, didn't I? To Juliet. I bundled it up in a padded envelope with my confession and sent it off to Michigan over six months ago. So, then, Juliet gave it to someone? Who gave it to someone? Who gave it to someone? Who gave it to someone? Who gave it to Svetlana? It's the only logical explanation.

As for Svetlana, she hasn't budged. In fact, she's just staring awkwardly, waiting for me to speak.

"You really like it?" I ask.

"Oh my God! I love it," she says. "It's one of the best tapes I've ever heard. And Ordinary Girl..."

"What?"

"Nothing. Just. That song could be about me. Sorry." Svetlana wipes at the corners of her eyes, which are now moist with tears. "Sorry. I just feel like that all the time, like everybody else around me is trying so hard to fit in, but that's such bullshit, you know? Especially when you just want to be yourself. It's really nice to hear somebody else say it."

"Thanks," I say.

It's a strange sensation, seeing this piece of myself in the hands of a stranger. In the heart of a stranger.

"Have *you* taped it for anyone else?"

She doesn't seem to want to answer this question.

"It's okay if you have," I say.

"Um, yeah. For my sister. And half the people on my dorm floor." She motions to her friends sitting at a table over by the door. "And I think maybe some of them have taped it too. Maybe you should start selling them," she adds, trying to sound helpful, "then people would buy them instead. I would. Like, if it was a real tape, or a CD, I mean."

After I sign Svetlana's tape on the empty side B, with a little help on the spelling, Walden comes over.

"Who was that?"

I do my best to explain the encounter with Svetlana to Walden, who seems not only unmoved, but unsurprised. He casually swigs from a bottle of Budweiser, and combined with the way his facial hair is finally starting to fill in, he looks just like Dad.

"It's really good, Rainey," he says. "People want to share good music. Where the hell is River, by the way? I want to get going."

"Getting pizza, I think."

"God, is he weird."

"I just think it's strange she never told me she shared it with anybody," I say.

"Juliet? Maybe she forgot. You guys still writing?"

"No."

"She was a crazy girl, man. I still remember that day you showed up to school with your nose pierced. You got balls, Sis, I'll give you that."

He laughs to himself at the memory.

For a split second, the time it takes to flip a fried egg, I remember when Walden walked in and almost caught me and Juliet kissing. I've always wondered what he saw that day. If he saw anything. What he might have thought. But I can tell by the look on his face that he's forgotten all about it.

"Do you really think my album is good?" I ask.

"That's a dumb question. Don't you think I do? I helped you make it, didn't I? I'm playing with you. You think I'm putting time into music I don't like? That I stopped playing with Mom for my health?"

I shrug.

"You actually thought I didn't like it?"

"I wasn't sure."

"God, you're such a freak sometimes." Then, he reaches out and puts his hand on my shoulder. "I love it okay, so stop worrying all the time."

Not able to hide my smile, I pick up a box of matches off the counter. Written in western style script around the body of a wagon wheel, it says *The Giddy Up*. The bar has sort of a pseudo-western theme that's not very convincing: a picture of John Wayne over the bar, faux cowhide bar stools, saloon doors to the bathrooms. As if they started strong with the decorations, then said, "Aw, screw it."

"Who gave you beer, by the way?"

"The bartender is pretty cool," Walden says. "His name's Rick. Like in Casablanca."

I look at the bartender, a ropy, greasy guy in baggy black jeans and a flannel.

"I didn't know you liked beer."

Now Walden shrugs. We're a family of shruggers, I guess. "It's kind of growing on me."

I grab the bottle out of his hand, look around, then take a quick sip and pass it back. Walden laughs.

On stage, the members of Temporary Secretary, four college-aged guys, are still setting up their gear. Tacked to the edge of the stage, there's a bed sheet with the band name written in black magic marker, not very neatly.

"What a weird name for a band."

"It's a Paul McCartney song," Walden says instantly. "From *McCartney II*. 1980. Kind of a deep cut."

"Of course, you would know that. And you say I'm weird."

With the dark road drifting past us as we drive back to Fairview, Walden driving quietly and River sleeping in one of the captain's chairs, I keep replaying my encounter with Svetlana on repeat.

My mind wanders.

I imagine Svetlana opening up her mail one day to find a tape by a singer she's never heard of. Maybe she doesn't put it on right away. After all, who's Rainey Cobb? She does her homework first, theorems, maybe, or research on colonialism, maybe dissecting a poem by Milton. But at some point, there's a moment, maybe over a steaming Cup O' Noodles fresh from the microwave, where she slips it into the tape deck, pushes play, and "Ordinary Girl" comes through the speakers for the first time.

My song.

I imagine the moment when Svetlana's ears perk up. Maybe her roommate is leaving for a date. Maybe the TV is on in the background. Maybe she's just gotten off the phone with her mom. But there had to have been a moment when she realizes she likes what she hears. That she wants to keep hearing it. A moment when she turns up her stereo, stops everything else she's doing, and listens.

Even after the two-hour ride back to Fairview, I'm still too wired to sleep when we get home.

As usual, my mind won't turn itself off all the way and little moments from tonight keep pinballing around. I think of a small mistake River made during "Anger Part III," where in the second chorus he played an A flat 6 instead of an A flat 9. How Walden's brush tempo was a little fast on "A Quiet Place."

I don't mention these mistakes that only I ever notice, but not because people will think I'm weird. Because I've realized that they don't always matter.

I eat a huge bowl of Honey Nut Cheerios, then get out my journal and my lucky pen. Since I turned sixteen a couple weeks ago, I can't add to my list of firsts anymore. Which means it's time for a new list.

Things I Learned When I was Fifteen

1. Mistakes are okay sometimes. Mistakes might even be good.
2. You'll never just wake up one day and be a different person. You're always becoming the person you're going to be.

3. Love is really complicated.
4. I have the best parents in the world.
5. If you spend too much time listening to what other people think, you'll stop listening to what YOU think.
6. If you hurt the people you love, chances are they'll forgive you.
7. Getting your heart broken is really bad for emotional stability, but really good for songwriting.
8. My brother is the most important person in my life.
9. Normal is 100% relative. Maybe nobody ever feels normal.
10. I love music more than anything in the world. I'm going to play it forever.

Track Twenty-Three
A Good Music Manager

Evan and I are lying on his bedroom floor listening to the mix I made him. It's been a week since I finally took River's advice and told Evan the truth. I think we were equally relieved.

"I wish you would have told me sooner," he said.

"I know. I'm sorry."

"I feel like such a jerk for how I treated you."

"What are you talking about? I was the jerk."

"Maybe we were both jerks."

I don't know if my mix is as good as *Blowin' My Mind Like a Summer Breeze*, but it's pretty damn good. Perfect song flow. Good balance of moods. Nothing you want to fast forward through.

It doesn't matter so much what I think, though. It's Evan's mix. I made it for Evan to love it. And he does.

"You know what I've been thinking," Evan says, taking my hand, which doesn't feel weird at all, by the way. It feels nice.

"What?"

"That I might make a good music manager," he says.

I laugh.

"For me?"

"Yeah. To book shows and sell CDs and stuff. You're going to need one eventually."

"Let's get through junior year first, okay."
"Okay."
"Can you turn it up?" I ask.
"Sure."

Hidden Track
Crazy Thoughts

The two boxes arrive a little after noon on a Monday in early August. Walden and I have been waiting impatiently for them for days and run out to the porch to bring them inside. We tear into them like kids on Christmas morning.

Inside of each box is 250 CD copies of *The Treehouse Tapes*. 500 felt like such a huge number, but that was the smallest quantity you could order. Walden thought we should have ordered 1,000, but I told him he was crazy.

"They're not gonna last," he says. "You'll see."

Over the summer, with Dad's help, Walden and I mastered the album and sent it off to a company called Northway Sounds in Springfield, Massachusetts.

I had planned to use Dad's studio to re-record a lot of my vocals and guitar parts from the original treehouse sessions, but he said we were crazy to mess with the spirit of the original, imperfect as it was.

"Dad, you can hear crickets on some of the tracks."

"Look," he told us, sounding really serious. "You might go the rest of your lives and never come close to what's on here. The feel of it, I mean. You can always sing it a little better. Play it a little more perfect. Get rid of all the crickets, both real and metaphorical. But getting it to *feel* just right, that's the real magic. Trust me."

So, we did. When it comes to music, it's usually better to trust my dad.

"What the hell, they're not even shrink wrapped!" Walden says, taking a CD out of the box. "I thought they'd be wrapped like real CDs."

I pick one up and look at it.

Rainey Cobb—*The Treehouse Tapes*

"Maybe you have to ask for that special," I say.

"Well, that's dumb," Walden says. "It should be automatic. Who wouldn't want them shrink wrapped? We want people who buy the album to be able to unwrap it, so it feels more official."

"They look fine," I say. "And shrink wrap is annoying anyway."

I turn the CD over and look at the track listing and credits on the back.

All songs written by Rainey Cobb.

Recorded, mixed, and produced by Walden Cobb.

Walden took the cover photo. I'm leaning out the window of the tree house, looking straight down at Walden, who you can't see but was directly below me, my eyes looking right at the camera. It was a gray day, which Walden insisted on for "dramatic effect," and my red hair is the photo's only bright spot, almost like the rest of the photo is in black and white but my hair is in color.

I open up the CD and pull out the sleeve, which I designed to be a schematic of a brain divided up into nine sections. Inside of each section are the song lyrics, which I handwrote in tiny print. It's weird and wonderful to see my words in front of me, and it almost feels like someone else wrote them.

That night, I have an idea. Since the CDs aren't shrink wrapped, I decide to number them.

"Like artist prints," I tell Walden.

He thinks it's a silly idea, but I don't.

So, I put my hair up in a bun, make a cup of coffee, grab a stack of cookies, throw a record on the turntable, and sit down on the living room floor. In the corner of each CD booklet, I write the number out of five hundred. 1/500. 2/500. 3/500. And so on.

I write the numbers in black ink, forming them as carefully as I can.

I pretend that years from now, people will be able to brag they had one of the originals.

I don't say this out loud.

But it's okay to think crazy thoughts.

Acknowledgements

This little book and I have been on quite a journey. The novel that became *Blowin' My Mind Like a Summer Breeze* began as a collection of linked short stories I wrote for my master's thesis while receiving my MFA in creative writing from Lesley University. At that point, it was a story centered around an aging blues musician named Luce Cobb and his family, which included his daughter, Rainey. But stories change, especially if you give them time, and if you're willing to listen. Thank you to Rainey for helping me see that this was always meant to be your story.

I owe enormous thanks to so many people for helping this book come to life. This is the part when I say sorry in advance for anyone I forget to mention. You're awesome too.

To Craig and John at Deep Hearts YA for believing in this book, and in me. And for being such thoughtful collaborators along the way.

Thank you to my community of friends and teachers at Lesley, especially A.J. Verdelle, whose encouragement, high standards, and passion for craft continue to put wind in my sails.

Early readers gave me valuable feedback to improve this story. You have my whole heart. Thanks to Angela Cruz, Amy Grace Lombardo, Celeste Mohammed, and Laurie Young for so many thoughtful notes and conversations. Thanks also to Karen Dailey, Douglas Dailey, John Roesch, Jacob Roesch, Sonya Klinger, Sean Dailey, and Daniel Dailey. Special recognition to my aunt Margaret Roesch, whose invaluable perspective and enthusiasm for this book found me at a time when I really needed to hear it. And big ups to the members of my wife's book group for reading (and enjoying...phew!) an early draft of this novel.

To my fearless writing group members, Amy Klinger and Suzanne Loring, where would I be without you? You've reminded me to never underestimate the power of community, and held me accountable for trying to be a better writer with every sentence. Retreat for life!

To the hundreds of students who passed through my doors during my twelve years as a high school English teacher. You made me a better person in every possible way. You reminded me of the richness, complexity, and challenge of what it's like to be a teenager and in pursuit of this fickle thing we call a self. I never, ever could have written this book without you.

To my cover designer, Chloe White. I almost have no words for how much I love this cover. Thank you for your collaboration and brilliance. Thanks also to Sam Aprea for a kick ass book trailer, and to Kaitlyn Savage for amazing design help down the stretch.

To my sons, Felix and Leo, for making do without me as I spent many a weeknight, early morning, and weekend toiling away to tell my stories. Let this book serve as a reminder throughout your life that it's always a good time to pursue your dreams. I love you more than the world.

To my parents and the rest of my family for reading my work, always believing in me, and seeing beauty in my persistent quest to write.

And, finally, and forever, to Shannon. You are my everything and this book would not exist without you. You have sacrificed and supported me every step of the way. You have listened to twenty years of keyboard clacking, and somehow, you are still here. I love you.

About Benjamin Roesch

Benjamin Roesch is a writer, musician, and podcaster. A former high school English teacher and graduate of the MFA program at Lesley University, his stories and essays have appeared in *Brilliant Corners, Seven Days, Kids VT, Word Riot*, and other fine purveyors of the written word. He lives with his family in Burlington, Vermont.

More From Deep Hearts YA

Mark of Ravage and Ruin
Jacyn Gormish
Trapped in the Asylum and destined to become an assassin, Barli wants nothing more than to escape and return to the arms of her girlfriend. But when the moment arises for possible freedom, she learns that a friend is to be killed—and only Barli can save him.

Gerald Ribbon and the Bird in His Brain
Maxwell Bauman
Gerald Ribbon has a habit of ruining his love life, and the bird in his brain that gives him terrible advice certainly isn't helping.

The Mixtape to My Life
Jake Martinez
Justin has always been comfortable in his skin, even if the world around him wasn't. A junior simply counting down the days for when he can leave for college, Justin's life is thrown for a loop when the one thing that helps him feel like himself suddenly slips away from him. But an unexpected blast from his past puts summer on a new and exciting path, one as random and unexpected as a mixtape.